THE DUKE I TEMPTED

COPYRIGHT

This book is licensed to you for your personal enjoyment only.

This is a work of fiction. Names, characters, places, and incidents are either products of the writer's imagination or are used fictitiously and are not to be construed as real. Any resemblance to actual events, locales, organizations, or persons, living or dead, is entirely coincidental.

NYLA Publishing
121 W 27th St., Suite 1201, New York, NY 10001
http://www.nyliterary.com

The
DUKE *I*
TEMPTED

SECRETS OF CHARLOTTE STREET
BOOK ONE

SCARLETT PECKHAM

DEDICATION

.

For my mom, my grandmas, and all the other ladies who left their romance novels lying around where I could steal them.

This is all your fault.

(I'm eternally grateful.)

CHAPTER 1

Threadneedle Street, London
May 31, 1753

"*B*loody codding hell," Archer Stonewell, the Duke of Westmead, murmured to the midnight darkness of his deserted counting-house. Beside him a lone wax candle flickered and went out, as if in sympathy. There was no one here to see him slump, a grown man unmoored by a single slip of paper from a girl no more than twenty.

Your days as a bachelor are numbered, my dear brother, Constance had scrawled in a script so curlicued it gloated. *The ball is set for the end of July and it is going to be sensational. No lady who enters Westhaven will wish to leave as anything other than your duchess. Try to enjoy your final month of grim, determined solitude—for I intend to have you married off by autumn. (And do stop glaring, Archer—I can feel it through the page!)*

Rain splashed across his expensive leaded windows, a fitting accompaniment to the dread pooling in his stomach. Normally he took pleasure in the empty counting-house, with its rows of ledgers chronicling the growth of his investments into empires and the maps that slashed the country into markets ripe for exploitation. The building was a temple to the gods of order and control, and there was no match for its soothing effect on his soul.

Except tonight, it wasn't working.

Already, the old fog was descending.

He was not insensible to his absurdity. It was he, after all, who had gritted his teeth and declared the begetting of an heir a matter of urgent moral imperative. It was he who had hired architects to restore the ravaged halls of Westhaven and proclaimed it time to expunge the decaying pile of its ghosts and find a wife to install in it instead.

He'd ordered it. He'd paid for it. Never mind that he preferred his life the way it was: deserted. Pristine. Absent of all reminders of the past.

Never mind that the only thing he wanted less in this world than a wife was a child.

Enough. He picked up his quill and did what was befitting of his responsibility to his tenants, to his family, and to the Crown. He dashed a word of thanks to Constance for her efforts, scrawled his signature, melted a puddle of vermilion wax across the folded paper, and stamped it with the seal of the title that he'd not for one day wanted, and was duty-bound to protect at all costs: *the Duke of Westmead.*

He put on his coat, extinguished the fire, and walked down the dark staircase to Threadneedle Street, where his coachman was waiting.

"Home, Your Grace?"

He hesitated.

He had been so very, very careful for so very, very long.

"A stop first. Twenty-three Charlotte Street."

He closed his eyes and sank back into the rhythm of the carriage as it wound its way west toward Mary-le-Bone. It had been weeks since he'd visited the address. Weeks during which rumors of the establishment's existence had made sneering speculation about the acts that were administered there—and the kinds of men who craved them—a sport in gentlemen's clubs and coffeehouses.

His interests were precarious. Now was not an ideal time to be branded deviant, or worse.

But some nights, there was a limit to one's capacity for caution. Some nights, a man needed to be wicked.

And he'd be damned if he wasn't going to enjoy it.

The town house looked the same. Pale bricks, an unobtrusive terrace. The old black door unmarked, discreet as always. The street blessedly deserted.

At his knock, the maid, a sober girl, took his iron key from the cord he kept around his neck and led him without comment to the proprietress's parlor. Elena sat by the fire in her customary black weeds. Unlike most women of her profession, her attire was chaste and severe—more like the robes of a papist nun than a courtesan's plunging silks. Which was appropriate, given that her métier was closer to punishment than pleasure.

"Mistress Brearley," the maid announced, "a caller."

He said nothing. Elena knew him well enough to surmise that if he was here, he would not be in the mood to exchange pleasantries.

"Choose your instruments, undress, and wait," Elena said.

The maid led him to the spare, windowless room. It was lit by candles and held little beyond a hassock and a rack. The girl left him, and he went through the ritual he had perfected over a decade's attendance in these chambers. From the shelves along the wall, he scanned Elena's wares. Leather straps, cat-o'-nine-tails, all manner of restraints. As always, he gathered the crisp rods of birch, kept pliant and green in a shallow tub of water, and an elegant braided whip with golden tails. He laid them neatly on a velvet cloth left for that purpose on a sideboard, and folded his clothes beside them. Nude but for his linen shirt, he knelt, facing the wall, to wait for her.

She would keep him waiting. Testing one's endurance for suffering was, after all, her gift.

He heard her footsteps down the hall before she entered. "Be silent," she said as she came into the room. "Or I shall gag you."

She placed a rough black cloth over his eyes and tied it tightly, so it bit into his hair. The fabric smelled of lye.

"Did I not instruct you to undress?"

She had. But defiance made the proceedings far more interesting.

She jerked his shirt back by the collar and he felt a prick of metal at his nape—the cold blade of a pair of sewing shears. He heard a snip, and then the ripping of fine fabric. His shirt fell from his shoulders to pool around his thighs. And with it went the rod of tension that he carried in his neck.

He could feel her skirts brush against his skin as she tied a fist of birches into a sturdy switch. He braced, listening for the high-pitched whir as she tested it against the air.

The first stroke shocked him, though he had expected it, invited its bite. He sank his palms into the floor and arched back against the next lacerating hit.

His mind emptied.

For the first time in days, he smiled.

He closed his eyes at the relief and felt himself, at last, begin to stir.

CHAPTER 2

Grove Vale, Wiltshire
July 14, 1753

Opening shipping crates was not a ladylike activity. But Poppy Cavendish had precious little faith in the advantages of being mistaken for a lady.

She thrust her hammer claw around the final nail and bore down with all the considerable force her wiry body could muster. She had waited months for this particular box, stamped with its labels from Mr. Alva Carpenter across the Atlantic. She had no intention of waiting any longer.

The nail gave way with a satisfying pop. The smell of dried leaves and sphagnum moss wafted out around her. She closed her eyes and breathed it in—it smelled like musk, and earth, and opportunity.

Inside the box the trays of roots and bulbs had been packed gingerly, each item tagged with numbers corresponding to a sheet of sketches of the mature plants they would become. She willed her hands to unwrap them steadily, careful not to damage the dry, fragile cuttings that had traveled so long and so far. She held her breath as she reached the bottom of the crate.

Her hands found what they were seeking. *Magnolia virginiana.* At last.

The cuttings had survived the moisture and jostling of the journey across the sea and up the Thames and down the bumped and winding country roads to Wiltshire. There were eight of them here, thick, sturdy branches, their waxen leaves gone dry and dull but still intact.

She only hoped they hadn't arrived too late.

A month ago she would have wasted no time removing the lower leaves from the branches and transplanting them to pots in the greenhouse to take root. Now that work would have to wait. She wrapped the cuttings in damp cloth and placed them in a shaft of sunlight for safekeeping. She had more pressing matters to attend to.

A life needed saving. Her own.

She returned her attention to her desk, where her fat, soil-stained ledger noted in row after odious row the impossible sums she needed to save her nursery and the improbable amount of time she had to find them.

Two weeks: the span of time her fate had been reduced to. All her dreams shrunk down into what she could cart three miles down a country road between now and the first of August.

She rubbed her eyes. No matter how she rearranged the numbers, they didn't add up. The task before her required at least one of two things: labor or capital. But even if she somehow found the latter, the inquiries she'd made to hire temporary laborers had all come back with the same maddening answer: unavailable, due to the renovations at Westhaven. Every able-bodied soul in Grove Vale, if not the entirety of Wiltshire, had been hired away by the Duke of Westmead.

If extra men could not be hired, the nursery could not be moved, and her entire future would be at the mercy of—*Stop,* she commanded herself. If she let her thoughts wander in that direction, her mind would crater down a whirlpool of increasingly disastrous scenarios. She needed to focus on the tasks at hand. Her only possible salvation was in working quickly.

"Poppy."

She whirled around. A broad-shouldered man was leaning against her workshop door, lounging against the frame with such a sense of ownership you'd have thought he had built the place himself.

"Tom!" she yelped, clutching her heart like the old crone she was no doubt fated to become. Tom Raridan's ability to come and go undetected was his greatest talent. That he had been pulling this trick since they were children did little to lessen its ability to startle her.

"Poppy," he said, running his eyes over her in that way that made her feel too visible for comfort. Never a diminutive man, he had grown broader in the two years he'd spent in town. Away from the summer sun of Wiltshire, his hair was darker—less the flaming shade of carrot from his boyhood, tending now toward auburn. But his smile was the same as it had been when she'd last seen him. A touch too familiar.

"I came as soon as I heard about your uncle," he said. "You should have written to me. To think I had to hear it in the post from Mother."

Damnation. He was right. She'd been so plunged into panic by her uncle's sudden passing, and the chaos it had made of her life, that she'd given inadequate due to the niceties of mourning. Letters had not been sent. Customs had not been properly observed. Her uncle had been fond of Tom, and the kindly old man deserved better.

"I'm sorry, Tom. I'm afraid I've been preoccupied. Uncle Charles's heir is arriving in a fortnight to take possession of Bantham Park. I've been in a rush to ... arrange my effects."

"A fortnight?" He whistled at the shelves of plants and cuttings all around them, the walls lined from floor to ceiling with tools and pots and sacks of seed and moss. "What are you going to do with all this?"

"My uncle left me the cottage at Greenwoods—the only part of his holdings that wasn't entailed. I intend to move the nursery there."

"Move an entire nursery? How do you expect to do that?"

She sighed. "With a great deal of effort."

Tom shook his head. "You always did love an impossible task. Never the easy way for our Poppy."

She sighed again. He was not wrong, but she had grown weary of his proclivity for commenting on matters that were none of his affair.

Not that it was only Tom who commented. She had made quite a reputation out of being impossible, though not because she enjoyed it. It was only that the so-called easy way rarely coincided with her getting what she wanted. The world was not built to suit ambitious spinsters. One had to be a rather demanding and unpopular character if one wanted a chance of success.

But even she would not have taken on such a degree of madness by choice. For years, her uncle had made it clear that he would leave her his private fortune. Only at the reading of the will had it been revealed that for over a decade Bantham Park had been unproductive.

There *was* no private fortune. The fate of her dreams and her livelihood would fall upon the whims of a distant cousin she'd never met. And her uncle, the dear old man she had loved and trusted beyond anyone, had somehow not found within himself the will to tell her.

"It's too lovely a day to be in this musty old shed fretting over plants," Tom declared, flicking her ledger distastefully. "Take a turn in the garden with me."

She looked down at her ledger and hesitated. She had no time for leisurely strolls. But Tom could be difficult. It was easier to accede to his will and wait for him to grow bored and leave than to provoke his temper with a fuss.

"Very well. But just to the greenhouse. I must finish pruning while there's still light."

The path from the workshop traversed her small empire, dazzling in the summer sun. The nursery and walled gardens were bright with the blooming vegetation of July. In the field beyond, groves of fruit trees and her prized exotic saplings grew, along with row after row of English trees. Sunbeams danced from the roof of the small greenhouse, where her forced flowers basked in the afternoon light. She could scarcely believe that in two weeks' time all this would be lost to her.

"What have I missed in Grove Vale these past months?" Tom asked, moving closer so that his arm brushed hers.

She edged away. "The renovations at Westhaven are nearly done. You should ride out to see the house. They've made a palace out of it. I've even sold them a few trees."

He looked at her with interest. "I don't suppose you've had any dealings with the duke? I have a venture that might be of interest to his investment concern. I'd give my right hand for an introduction." He winked.

"I'm afraid my dealings were with no one loftier than the head gardener. He is quite an imperious fellow in his own right. I shudder to think what the duke must be like if his gardener has such airs."

She glanced up at the sky. It was growing late. She needed to return to her work. "It was kind of you to come, Tom," she said, hoping he would take the hint. "Unnecessary, but kind."

"Poppy. For you, nothing is unnecessary."

She chose to ignore the catch in his voice and walked more briskly toward the greenhouse, but he stopped her beneath a mature apple tree. Boldly, he took her hand and clapped it in his own.

"Allow me this liberty," he whispered. He placed a kiss at her wrist.

Horror curdled in her gut. Of course. This was why he had taken the time to come all the way from London when a letter of condolence would have suited.

Now that she was alone, he thought he had his chance.

"Tom, please," she objected, twisting her hand away. He moved closer anyway.

"You know why I've come here, don't you? I've made no secret of my fondness for you. My position in London is secure—I have enough to make a life for us in town."

He sank to his knees on the grass, a gentle, knowing smile in his eye. "Poppy. Do me the honor of being my wife."

She keenly wished he would get up.

"You flatter me. But you, above anyone, know that I have no wish to marry."

He grinned up at her, expectant. "You *feign* that you don't wish to marry to save people thinking no one will have you. You don't have to do that anymore. Don't you see? You aren't what most men want, but you are what *I* want. All that rig about you being a mad old spinster—I'll turn it on its head."

She bristled. "*You* will do nothing of the sort. Please—"

"Poppy, don't be foolish. You can't stay here alone. You can leave all these shrubs behind," he said, gesturing at the plants she had so carefully nurtured since girlhood. "I'll buy you new gowns. We'll take private rooms, bring in a cook and a maid. In a few years I'll have enough for a horse. Sooner if I can find a better place. Come to London with me. As my wife."

"No," she said firmly, her sympathy for the disappointment she was causing him having eroded with every sentence of his speech. "And do please get up."

His face fell. The light behind his eyes went dull, then dark. She looked away.

"I'm sorry, Tom. Truly. And I am grateful for your friendship. But my life is here."

He went bright at the cheeks. "Friendship. That's what you'd call it? Because I might call it something else. Or do you spread your favors around to all your friends?"

She closed her eyes. It had been a single moment in the woods. One very brief moment, nearly five years before, when he had come to help her gather moss and she had laughed at something he had said, and he had pushed her against a tree and kissed her. And for about one half second, she had permitted it—if to permit was to freeze—before she pulled away in shock.

They had never spoken of it. But ever since that day, he had looked at her like he knew something about her that she did not.

Like he had some claim on her.

And because he was a favorite of her uncle, because he helped her in the nursery, because he sent her plants from London, she'd gone on smiling and pretending not to see it, pretending it did not seep inside her skin and rankle her from within her very bones.

She was deathly, deathly tired of it.

She inhaled, and met his aggrieved look calmly. "Tom, you have always been a friend. I hope you will remain one. But I have no wish to marry you, or anyone else. If that is why you came here, I must ask you to take your leave."

His mouth fell open. His face clouded over with some mix of bemusement and hurt.

Her anger melted as the man took on the old, pained expression of the boy he'd once been. Poor Tom. He was full of bluster, but he was no worse than other men, and he'd been kind to her, for all his unbearable presumption.

"I know you'll find a lovely wife. No doubt someone far more suitable than me."

His eyes went dark and flat as glass, like those of a dog that might attack. "But you'll not do better, Miss Cavendish. That's a promise." He turned and quickly walked away, his thick neck and arms huddled over his ribs as though to protect a smarting heart. She watched him go until she couldn't bear the sight of it.

How could he so mistake her intentions? He, who had listened to all her grand plans for years? To think she would give up her life's work—the passion into which she had poured all her efforts and every last shilling—for a flat in London and a maid? She'd more likely sail to India, or cut off her own arm and present it to Tom Raridan's London cook to serve for supper.

What she wanted in this life was not a husband. It was freedom, finally, from dependence on men. Her entire life had been dictated by their fortunes: their deaths, plunging her from crisis to crisis; their charity, allowing her to survive, to scrape by, to make her tenuous foothold in business; their half-truths, sabotaging her ambitions. She was tired of needing permission, dispensation, kindness. She intended to be the mistress of her own fate. And there was one thing she knew with absolute certainty from observing the ways of the world: one did not get that kind of power by marrying it.

She sank back against the warm glass wall of the greenhouse and stood there for a moment, letting its heat soothe the goose bumps that had risen on her forearms despite the glare of the sun. Tom was correct about one thing. She was utterly alone now. Breathing in the loamy, balmy hothouse air, she felt it keenly. If she was to have any chance of securing her independence, she would need to find in herself the ferocious iron will that so many had accused her, not fondly, of possessing.

She waited until her hands stopped trembling and set about pruning her rows of potted plumeria—a repetitive, physical task that always helped clear her mind. The perfume of the flowers drifted around her as she worked, and she welcomed it into her lungs. She strained on her tiptoes to reach the branches of the plants on the highest shelf, humming to herself.

"Miss Cavendish, I presume?" a man's voice said, startling her.

She lost her grip, and a plant came careening down toward her head.

The man leapt in its way, just barely blocking the pot's impact with her nose by diverting it to land with a thump against his own shoulder. In so saving her face from the blow, he pinned her body between his larger person and the shelves in front of her. Bits of fragrant foliage stabbed at her cheek and throat. Something brushed across the back of her neck—the starched linen of the man's cravat.

Oh, this blasted day. Had she not enough to face without uninvited gentlemen showing themselves into every last room of her nursery? Unsettling her with unwelcome suits of marriage? Assaulting her with plants?

She craned her neck to get a better look at this latest intruder, who had steadied the pot back on the shelf and was now attempting to unravel the buttons of his waistcoat from the lacings of her sturdy leather work stays.

And then she blushed, overtaken by a sudden rush of mad desire to be wearing anything—anything—other than a straw hat and a faded old gardening dress.

He was not precisely a pretty fellow, whoever he was. His nose was crooked, as though once broken, and his eyes were dark and heavy browed. But his hawkish profile, taken with his immaculate clothing, great height, and slim build, nearly stole her breath away. Had he not barged in on her and wreaked havoc on her last shred of peace on the most upsetting day of her life, she might have even been inclined to like him.

Instead, she narrowed her eyes. "Who are you, sir?"

"Archer!" a woman's throaty, cultivated voice trilled from the doorway. "Please tell me that woman you are accosting is not our Miss Cavendish."

The man freed his final button and stepped away, turning to the young woman with a mordant smile. "I couldn't say. I'm afraid we haven't had a chance for introductions."

"I am indeed Miss Cavendish. And this is my nursery. May I be of some assistance, or have you merely come to overturn my plants?"

The petite woman sailed inside with a gracious chuckle, her hooped skirts flouncing perilously close to the fragile tendrils of Poppy's passiflora as she walked.

"Forgive us, Miss Cavendish. My brother has such a curious approach to making introductions. I am Lady Constance Stonewell and this poorly mannered fellow is the Duke of Westmead."

Poppy bit back a bitter laugh. Westmead. *Of course.* When the universe took it in mind to test what you were made of, the trials came raining down at once.

Westmead inclined his head, causing a white petal to flutter from his fine head of glossy hair. "My profuse apologies for startling you, Miss Cavendish. There was no one outside."

"It's a pleasure to meet you, my lady, Your Grace," she said, making little effort to infuse sincerity into her tone. "To what do I owe the privilege?"

"You won't like it when I tell you," Lady Constance said, leaning in with a sparkle in her eye, as though she and Poppy shared a long history of private jokes. "You see, I understand you have had dealings with my gardener, Mr. Maxwell."

Maxwell. Poppy nearly groaned aloud at the man's name. He'd been after her for weeks to take on a floral design commission for a ball at Westhaven—repeatedly failing to understand that she was not a decorator, and most definitely not available. The confusion had begun when she'd made gifts of floral arrangements to a number of the larger estates in the shire, hoping the striking designs would attract more customers to her exotic cultivated plants. Along with new clients, the scheme had won her an accidental reputation as an artisan of ballroom fancies. One that was flattering, but did little to further her ambition to sell trees.

"A most persistent fellow, your Mr. Maxwell," she said. "I'm afraid, however—"

"Evidently not persistent enough," Lady Constance interrupted. "I've been quite despondent to learn his pursuit of your talents has been fruitless, for much depends on the success of this ball, and I'm told you are a genius. So I've come to beg. Or, failing that, to bribe you with my brother's worldly goods."

Westmead, she noticed, had turned his back on the conversation in order to survey the contents of her greenhouse. She took a small flicker of pride that it was not yet torn apart. Her exotics were radiant, fragrant, a riot of color and green. Nothing like the staid rows of carnations and orange trees he'd find in the middling force houses at Westhaven.

"You are kind," Poppy said, reabsorbing herself in snipping leaves to signal that she did not have time for a long interview, "and I hate to be repetitive. But I already made clear to your Mr. Maxwell my inability to take on the commission. I am otherwise engaged, and as I have tried to explain, this is a nursery, not a floral society."

Westmead glanced at her over his shoulder and caught her eye. "But it is a *business*, is it not, Miss Cavendish?"

She rewarded him with a tight smile. She disliked being condescended to. Especially by a duke.

"That is correct, Your Grace," she said pleasantly, locking her jaw around her words like he did. Her grandfather had been a viscount, and her mother a lady; she could speak like one if she wanted to. "But I find I am unable to fulfill new commissions owing to the fact that every man in the whole of Wiltshire seems to be under your household's employ."

Lady Constance clapped her hands, as though this was delightful news. "But, Miss Cavendish, if labor is the issue, I would be pleased to put my brother's resources at your disposal. I'm sure His Grace can be of assistance in whatever you require."

Poppy gave them both her sweetest smile. "How kind. His

Grace might begin by moving these to that higher shelf," she said, indicating a row of succulents in heavy pots.

She waited, expecting her temerity to earn her a prompt rebuke, followed by the departure of her unwanted guests.

Westmead returned her smile just as agreeably. Then, he removed his gloves one by one, took hold of a tub of houseleek by his bare hands, and placed it where she asked.

His sister looked on blandly as though the sight of a duke doing the bidding of a nurserywoman were wholly unremarkable. "Miss Cavendish, do you read the London papers?" she asked.

"Not frequently," Poppy said, enjoying the sight of the duke brushing soil from his immaculately cut waistcoat.

"Then perhaps you are unaware of my reputation for planning unholy spectacles at ungodly costs," she said brightly, as though this description was a point of great personal pride. "Tell her, Westmead."

"I can attest, at the very least, to the ungodly costs," he said, picking up another plant with a wink.

"No one save for family has set foot at Westhaven for ages, and so it is very important that my guests are dazzled. I wish to transform the entire ballroom into an enchanting indoor garden," Lady Constance continued. "Something so singular, beautiful, and lavish that every fashionable hostess on two continents will be in a frenzy to replicate it—particularly after I have it written about in every paper in town."

She paused, and the sparkle in her eyes had hardened into a rather determined glint. "I am no expert in trade, of course, but I should think a clever woman of business might weigh whether the opportunity to exhibit her talents before the country's wealthiest clients offers adequate incentive to rearrange her previous commitments."

Poppy tried to refrain from glaring at the implication she was dull-witted. "My previous commitment, as you call it, is of greater value to me than the opportunity you describe. In fact, to me, it is priceless."

At this, Westmead turned to her with a delighted grin. "But, Miss Cavendish. Nothing is without a price."

"Your gardener already offered me triple my customary fee."

He smiled. "I wasn't talking about money."

Lady Constance rolled her eyes. "Now you are in for one of his tedious lectures on business."

"I would merely advise Miss Cavendish that a shrewd investor knows that coin is but one of many forms of currency, and often the least valuable."

"Maybe to *a duke*," Poppy could not resist saying.

Westmead chuckled. "Let's test the theory. You mentioned you are in need of able-bodied men. How many do you require?"

Poppy put down her trowel and crossed her arms. For the sake of argument, she doubled the minimum number. "Twelve."

"Done!" Lady Constance cried.

"Well, it really makes no difference how many men you could provide, because if I were away planting drawing room shrub-beries, there would be no one *here* to oversee their work."

"Unless, of course, you had a steward," Lady Constance said. "Westmead has a frightful number of stewards wandering around. I will see you are assigned one."

Poppy sighed. "I don't think you quite understand. The work I am already engaged in must be completed in a fortnight, and it involves moving several acres of plants and goods three miles up an unfinished road."

Westmead raised a brow. "Now you are making excuses, Miss Cavendish, when you should be extracting promises. A skilled negotiator must have an instinct for when to turn the screw."

The cur was *grinning* at her.

She wiped her hands on her apron. She had told herself she must live up to the iron in her character. If the duke wanted to see a fierce negotiation, she would show him one.

"Very well. Here are my demands. Fifteen men, a skilled steward, and as great a sum in expenses as is required to transport my goods by the thirtieth of July. In addition, for my time and services I will require a fee of six hundred pounds to be paid in advance."

The figure was outlandish. It could save her. No sensible person would agree to half so much.

"Very well," Lady Constance said.

Westmead arched a brow. "Well done, Miss Cavendish. I daresay you're learning."

She schooled her face into the expression of a woman who did not need any lessons.

"There is one more thing I will require. A friend of mine is interested in making a proposal to His Grace's investment concern. You'll allow me to make an introduction."

"A friend?" Westmead asked.

"My brother would be delighted to entertain an audience," Lady Constance said quickly, shooting him a pointed look. "Is that not so, Your Grace?"

"Delighted," he drawled.

"Perfect." His sister beamed, once again the picture of sunshine and light now that she had gotten what she wanted. "Miss Cavendish, I will send a carriage to collect you in the morning."

She extended her gloved hand.

Poppy took the only option she had left herself: she shook it.

CHAPTER 3

"What an intriguing woman," Constance said as Archer helped her up onto the seat of his curricle. "Maxwell said to expect a 'mad spinster harridan,' but Miss Cavendish can't be more than five and twenty. And she did not seem even slightly insane."

He nodded, and did not add that Maxwell had also failed to mention that the nurserywoman was rather winsome. And immensely pleased with herself, judging by the smile that had toyed about her lips after he had, for reasons he could not entirely explain, goaded her into extracting a preposterous sum for a few days of work.

"I'm so glad I was able to prevail on her," Constance continued as he climbed beside her. "I told you my arguments would persuade her."

He smiled. "Yes. That and your six hundred pounds."

"Well, what would be the pleasure of having the richest man in England for a brother if one can't spend all his money on a ball he won't enjoy at a house he never visits?"

"Anything to please my ward," he said, urging the horses forward.

She shot him that same wry look she had been leveling at him since he first sent her to live with their aunt in Paris at the age of eight. As if to say, *Yes, let's pretend that's how it goes. Let's indulge in that more pleasant fiction.*

He felt a pang. He had done his best as her guardian, but she was effusive and affectionate by nature, and he was ill-suited to respond in kind. Spending a fortune was a meager penance if it helped her believe he was sorry he could not be better. So was accompanying her on foolish errands, as he had agreed to do today.

He reached out and put an awkward hand to her shoulder. "I'm here, aren't I? Doubters be damned?"

"Oh, indeed. Perfectly against your will, and utterly morose in spirit. But present? You are that."

He shook his head. "You know, small Constance, I believe I have missed you."

"Oh?" she said, in that bone-dry style she had learned at French court. "In spite of my provoking nature?"

"Because of it."

She grinned at him. The air around her gave off the silvery smell of French perfume. It was the scent their mother had worn. He leaned away before she could notice that he shuddered.

They were quiet as he drove over the leafy roads that led back from Bantham Park to his family seat at Westhaven. The estate's vast, rolling parkland was the same luminous green that he remembered from his boyhood, dotted with bales of hay and roaming sheep. As a younger man, he'd felt it unfair that his native southern England did not receive due appreciation for its bucolic glory—a landscape that rivaled the hills of Italy with its cresting downs and golden light.

He had loved this place.

Until, of course, he hadn't.

He gazed out at the horizon, taking satisfaction at the cozy cottages and neatly tended grazing land. It was still a shock how the mud-thatched, squalid dwellings that had once blighted the landscape, and the reputation of the house of Westmead had been replaced by this scene of agrarian well-being. Equally striking was the elegant manor that now rose up from the hilltop where his crumbling family seat had moldered. The sloping eaves gave no trace of the fire that had once buckled and pockmarked the upper stories.

He handed the reins to a groom and helped his sister onto the steps, then ceded his hat and gloves to the small militia of footmen whose presence at the door never failed to startle him. In London, he lived simply, without ceremony. Here, one could not so much as scratch one's chin without six livery-clad servants coming forth to offer up their eager fingers.

Constance perched on a settee in the center of the grand salon, perfectly backlit by sunshine streaming through a wall of windows.

"Well?" she said, gesturing at the massive gilt-spangled room that rose up around them. Light danced in air that smelled like roses. "The footmen finished placing the last of the paintings while we were out. Admit it. It's stunning."

He allowed her a forbearing smile. "It is, at the very least, unrecognizable."

"That, my dear brother, was the point. Don't you like it?"

He took in filigreed gilt work, gray-veined marble, Savonnerie carpets she'd gotten from God knew where, for God knew how many guineas. He did not like it. In point of fact, he found it rather suffocating.

"You certainly spared no expense," he said mildly.

"Indeed I did not. If one must find a wife for a man of your disposition, one needs better tools than homespun and tallow at one's disposal. You certainly will not be winning any woman's hand on charm alone."

"Your renovations are impressive. Now I must return to my study to invent ways of paying for them."

She held up a hand to stop him. "One more thing. I've taken the liberty of having reports compiled on the ladies attending the ball. I think you will find them an accomplished lot."

He sighed. "Accomplished? Constance—we discussed the kind of women you were to invite, did we not? Eager? Mercenary? Easily had?"

She wrinkled her nose in distaste. His desire to find a suitable spouse with the utmost efficiency stood in conflict with her view that matrimony should be the stuff of sentiment and poetry. On this he could not be conciliatory; it was his personal edict to avoid sentiment and poetry with the same care one avoided broken bones and plague.

"Actually," she mused, rifling through papers on a delicate Sèvres-plaqued *bonheur du jour* writing desk that would not have been out of place at Versailles, "I wonder if you could look through the candidates now. If any of them are of special interest, I will assign them the best rooms."

He sighed. "Fine." He reached for the tea pot.

Constance immediately confiscated it from his hands and replaced it with a stack of papers. "First we have the obligatory crop of gently bred ladies. Many with titles, considerable fortune, and faultless manners. I have also included a few more spirited candidates of my own acquaintance. Beauties all, and a few are rather witty."

He made a mental note to avoid the women on both these lists. The last thing he wanted was a wife with a fortune. She would need his own too little. Nor was intelligence an attraction. If his bride was clever, he might be tempted to like her. That would merely complicate his purpose.

What he wanted was a woman who saw him as a title and a bank vault. The kind of wife who would, when afforded certain enviable comforts, bear him an heir and not expect him to take more than a strictly legal interest in the proceedings. The kind of woman who would not require an investment of emotion he was not equipped to give.

Toward the bottom of the stack, an entry caught his eye. Miss Gillian Bastian, of Philadelphia.

"From the colonies?"

"Oh, Miss Bastian? She's gorgeous but has the conversation of a parakeet. Her parents are so mad for her to find herself a title that I asked her out of charity. I was thinking of her for Lord Apthorp."

A man did not come to rule the City of London without knowing an opportunity when he saw one. He closed the book. "There we are. Give Miss Bastian a nice room."

Constance snorted. "Miss Bastian? Did you hear a word I said? I doubt you could stand her for an hour."

"They all sound qualified. Put them in whatever rooms you like."

Constance snatched back the reports. "*Qualified.* How unromantic, Archer—even for you."

"I'm not looking for romance. I'm looking for a wife."

She curled her lip. "You are never more His Grace," she said, referring to their late father, "than when you profess such horrifying statements."

Given she had hardly known their father, Archer knew she said this because she had deduced comparisons to the man were the surest way to rile his temper.

"I am marrying precisely to ensure that our tenants are spared a recurrence of the conditions that plagued them under His Grace's stewardship," he said, in his flattest, most arctic tone. "Never mind what should become of *you* if, God forbid, Wetherby gets his hands on the title."

"Please. You are scarcely four and thirty and he must be at least sixty."

"Smallpox does not discriminate by age." It had taken the life of his previous presumptive heir, a distant cousin whose death at the tender age of twenty had put Wetherby in line for the title and necessitated the farce of this quest for a wife in the first place.

"It's been a year since Paul died and you're still with us. Surely, you can afford yourself another month or two to find a wife who actually suits you."

"Having *no* wife suits me, so I'd bid you to content yourself that I'm marrying at all and find me a proper candidate for duchess. The duller and more willing, the better."

"I'm sure you'll get exactly the duchess you deserve with an attitude such as that. And what an awful waste."

She left the room with a toss of her blond head.

He leaned back in his chair, grateful to be left in peace.

His sister was right. With any luck, he *would* get the duchess he deserved.

One who understood that marriage was a cynical pursuit. That he would invest no more in the arrangement than name, coin, and seed. Attachment—love—would not factor.

He had tried that condition once. The consequences had been such that he'd go to great lengths to never suffer them again.

He reached beneath his neckcloth and ran his fingers along the leather cord he wore around his neck. The jagged iron key it held was cool against the surface of his skin, a reminder of what hung in the balance. His salvation. His sanity. His secret, private self.

His wife would be granted more than most women could hope for: her freedom, his title, and his wealth. In return he asked only for a womb and a lack of curiosity.

For however much he was prepared to sacrifice for duty, this key would not be among his losses. He had responsibilities, after all. He required the strength to meet them.

No one need know the depths from which he drew it.

Least of all, his future wife.

CHAPTER 4

*H*er hem was frayed.

She'd only noticed now, stepping down from the ducal carriage.

Bollocks. Poppy rarely went anywhere in her good gowns, but she had considered them rather lovely. In the shadow cast by the imposing house, she suddenly saw her gray muslin for what it was: a tattered imitation of gentility.

She squared her shoulders and took a deep breath, her neck held high. After holding her own with the duke and Lady Constance, she would rather expire than seem intimidated by the immensity of their house, but it was rather difficult to remain impassive when the doors alone were three times the height of a well-built man. They swung open, revealing a phalanx of footmen and an inner atrium that would rival the royal palace for the sheer expense of its finery. It made the modest comforts of Bantham Park look like a workhouse.

"Lady Constance, Miss Cavendish has arrived," the footman informed her hostess, who was seated at an ornate writing desk, scribbling with an intense degree of focus. Lady Constance turned, revealing that today her blue eyes were framed by a pair of spectacles. She wore a diaphanous summer gown made of a fabric so fine that it floated around her like a corona when she rose to greet Poppy. The delicate fabric was faintly smudged with the same dark ink that covered her fingertips and, here and there, her cheekbones.

"Miss Cavendish," she said, filling the room with a smile of genuine warmth, "welcome to Westhaven. I hope you can forgive me for imposing on your time, for I wish for us to be great friends."

Poppy curtsied, somewhat taken aback by this speech. "A pleasure, my lady."

"Oh, do please call me Constance! We're really quite informal here."

"So it seems," Poppy said, allowing her gaze to fall from the friezes along the ceiling, to the floor-length gilt-inlaid windows, to the India carpet on the floor, as soft and thick as a mattress.

"Join me for a cup of tea before we begin." Constance gestured to a sofa upholstered in silk finer than any dress Poppy had ever owned.

"I had envisioned the garden beginning here, at the reception, such that the guests must follow the trail of greenery to the ballroom," she said as she proffered a bowl of delicate porcelain.

Poppy looked up and felt her stomach drop. The room was the size of a modest cathedral. It would take the contents of six greenhouses to fill it.

"What an inspired idea," she said lightly, hoping she might change the young lady's mind once she had a better understanding of her thinking.

Constance smiled, and the expression in her eyes was not one that suggested a habit of yielding to compromise. "My ambition, Miss Cavendish, is to leave every guest agog with wonder. I hope you will let your imagination run absolutely rampant. No idea is too grand or too whimsical."

Poppy hoped her face did not betray her mounting horror as

Lady Constance led her through a colonnaded corridor to a ball-room that could easily accommodate the entire population of Grove Vale. "I do love carnations and tulips, but I hate to be ordi-nary. Maxwell says you are known for exotics, so I will leave it to you to dazzle us with your most unusual plants from abroad."

Maxwell was clearly out to get her. Poppy's nursery was known for exotics. Namely, trees. She could not very well fill a ballroom with two-year-old saplings.

"The motif will indeed need to be unusual to match the ... singularity of the space," she said, racing through her modest inventory of flowers. Her hydrangeas and roses were blooming, which was fortunate as they were elegant and durable. With more warning, she could have ordered plants from nurseries elsewhere. But with less than a fortnight, there simply wasn't time.

She looked at Constance's expectant face and envisioned six hundred pounds slipping through her fingers. Her throat began to itch.

"And what latitude have we to make use of the parklands?" She gestured out the window at the rolling downs and thick forest that made up the better part of Westhaven's grounds beyond the manicured pleasure gardens.

Lady Constance laughed. "The parklands, Miss Cavendish? Do you mean to dress my ballroom in gorse and meadowsweet?"

Poppy tapped her chin, an idea flickering into focus in her mind.

"I've always thought there is nothing more evocative of the countryside than our beautiful native flora. The wildflowers are at their most gorgeous and romantic this time of year, and they would look remarkable in contrast with the grandeur of the ballroom. After all, without a touch of the wild, all we will have are rooms overfull with dull ... *ordinary* flowers. Don't you agree?"

She held her breath, hoping she had read the girl correctly.

Constance clapped her hands. "Why, it's *brilliant*, Miss

Cavendish! Why stop at a ballroom garden if we can have a ballroom forest?"

Poppy let out a sigh of relief. There would be plants enough to fill the rooms of Westhaven if she had to forage every last bluebell from the forest floor herself.

That left her only the next miracle to perform: finishing such a task in the unthinkable span of a fortnight.

~

ARCHER ONCE AGAIN CHECKED HIS WATCH, UNABLE TO concentrate on the pile of letters from London. He had spent the day riding with his land steward, an activity that reminded him why he had not returned here in thirteen years. He'd thought the estate had been stripped of the worst remnants of his father's madness, but the obscene nymphs his forebear had erected in the grotto beneath the trout pond turned his stomach. If accidents of birth and death meant he must oversee a land he wished only to forget, he preferred to do it by correspondence.

Unfit to be alone with the kind of thoughts that kept overtaking his reports on coal prices, he went in search of Constance. The sound of laughter drew him to the library, where his sister and Miss Cavendish sat side by side in a shaft of late afternoon sunshine, their heads hunched over a sketchbook.

It struck him once again how lovely the gardener was. Like a willow tree, with her slender neck and her tumbling mass of plaited hair escaping from its pins.

"I think a bower of ivy draped over the windows in the colonnade," she was saying. "Arranged so the leaves trail down over the glass and cast shadows in the candlelight."

"I love it," Constance breathed.

He leaned over them. "May I see?"

Both women jumped, too absorbed in their planning to have noticed his entrance. He held up his hands in mute apology. Westhaven made him this way. Awkward. Unable to comport himself properly. It eroded his veneer of control like the sea chipping away at a cliff.

"Good heavens, Archer, do announce yourself next time," his sister said. "We ladies are at *work.*"

She gave him an ironic smile, anticipating his amusement at the notion of her working.

Behind her, his father's ornate pleasure gardens twinkled in the afternoon light, like the old man winking at him from the grave. Unlike the lewd frescoes the duke had painted in the library, the collection of follies were not openly licentious. Nevertheless they had drained the family's coffers while the estate fell into neglect. He should have had them razed.

"Your beloved gardens are at their most beautiful this time of year, don't you think?" Constance chirped sweetly, following his gaze. "We're going to light them with torches for the ball and build a platform right at the edge of the lake for dancing. Mr. Flannery is coming all the way from London to write it up for the *Peculiar.*"

Lord deliver him. It was his sister's fondest wish to make her mark as a legendary hostess in the Parisian style. He'd been unhappy when she'd befriended the editor of London's most notorious gazette in the service of her goal, and begun hand-feeding him her finest morsels of intelligence.

"See, there is no trouble. Now is not the time for scandal."

He had spent half a lifetime repairing the name of Westmead from the shame his father had cast upon it. Securing the succession would finish the work. After that, Constance could do as she pleased.

"I would never dream of making scandal on the eve of your engagement," she said, the picture of blatant insincerity.

"Oh dear, it's growing late," Miss Cavendish said suddenly, drawing to her feet. "I lost track of the time. I should return home before nightfall."

"Oh, do stay for supper, Poppy. Archer is so dull. I am desperate for company."

He ignored his sister's provocation, preoccupied by the sight of Miss Cavendish gravely rolling up a scroll of sketches. So she called herself Poppy. Quite a name for a gardener. Not entirely fitting, given her demeanor. Thorn might be a better name for her. Or Stinging Nettle.

"You are kind, but I must return home before Mr. Grouse departs. Another time."

"I trust Mr. Grouse met with your satisfaction?" Constance inquired. "My brother assures me he is our very best land agent."

"He seems capable. I'd like to visit the nursery before dark to inspect the progress his men made today. Perhaps you could call for the carriage?" She glanced worriedly at a clock.

"It's much faster in the curricle," Constance said. "Archer, would you mind driving Miss Cavendish?"

"If Miss Cavendish does not object." In truth, he welcomed the distraction. He was curious what exactly the gardener was undertaking to require so many men and such a state of haste.

"Thank you, Your Grace."

"You'll want this before you leave," Constance said, drawing a banknote from the drawer of her escritoire. I assume you have some means of drawing from it?"

"Indeed. My solicitor will see to it," Miss Cavendish said, tucking it tidily into her ledger. Her manner was utterly imperious, like bills for a small fortune passed through her fingers several times a day.

Archer waited as Constance embraced Miss Cavendish like an old friend, then led her into the corridor.

As soon as they were alone, she crooked up a corner of her lovely mouth. "You do the work of the coachman as well as the gardener, Your Grace? The papers are right to call you industrious."

Was that a slight twinkle in her eye? Perhaps the six hundred pounds had had an effect on her mood after all.

She exhibited no particular cheer as they made their way toward Bantham Park, however. She seemed distracted, or perturbed.

"I hope my sister was not too plaguing in her demands," Archer said, his fifth attempt at making conversation in as many minutes. "She can be capricious but is susceptible to reason when pressed."

"Not at all. Lady Constance is a pleasure," Miss Cavendish replied in a firm tone that did not welcome further inquiry.

He repressed an inward groan. He was not particularly known for his charm, but he rarely found himself incapable of engaging another person in civil pleasantries. Was she nervous in his company? It had been years since he'd been alone with such a pretty woman. Perhaps he had erred in agreeing to drive her home without some form of chaperone. But then, they were in an open carriage on a sunny afternoon on a well-traveled road, and she was not a newly minted miss, but a seasoned nurserywoman with clients across the countryside. The rules of trade did not adhere to the rules of the drawing room, and a woman of her reputation as a supplier of plants would surely not be unaccustomed to dealing with men on her own authority.

Which likely meant *he* was the problem. She trained her eyes upon his profile pensively, confirming his suspicion that Westhaven had already succeeded in making him visibly insane.

"Forgive me, but I can't shake the sense that we have met before, Your Grace."

He shook his head, mildly relieved that she had at last said words unbidden.

"Not that I recall." He had never seen her face before the moment he had sent a potted plumeria crashing toward it. It was not one he would easily forget.

"Is it not possible we were introduced in the past? Perhaps you knew my late uncle?"

"I'm afraid I did not have that privilege."

He had spent his youth buried in books when he was not away at school. Mingling with the local gentry had been his elder brother's job as heir.

"I must be mistaken." She wrapped her arms tightly around her chest. He saw gooseflesh along the back of her wrist beneath the faded ribbon of her cuff.

"Are you warm enough?"

"Yes," she said through chattering teeth.

"You're shivering," he could not resist observing.

"I forgot my cloak," she admitted darkly, like he had won a concession.

He was tempted to smile. Her stubbornness reminded him not a little of himself.

"Here, hold the reins." He handed her the horses, which she accepted capably, and reached below the seat for the soft, woolen shawl kept there by his sister. "Take this."

After a brief hesitation she accepted it, arranging it gingerly around her plain gray dress. He wondered at her choice of garments. She had the polished speech of a noblewoman, yet dressed like a farmer's daughter. He had been distantly familiar with Bantham Park in his youth and knew her uncle had been a comfortable squire. That she chose to engage in trade and work out of doors surely won her no approbation from the genteel residents of Wiltshire.

He supposed he could forgive her for being rather brittle and unfriendly, the mysterious Miss Cavendish. He was well aware that the satisfactions to be won by flouting the customs of society did not come without a price. He had spent the better part of the last two decades paying it himself.

She pointed at a wooded path so narrow and overgrown it barely qualified as a road. "Turn here."

"Bantham Park is miles off," he corrected her, not bothering to slow the horses.

"I'm going to Greenwoods House. My new nursery. Quick, you'll miss the turn."

He swerved onto a narrow path, ducking to avoid being smacked in the head by passing branches.

"Might I ask why you are moving your nursery into the middle of an inaccessible forest?"

"This is a shortcut."

She was skirting the question.

"Actually, Miss Cavendish, I am curious why you are moving your nursery at all. Your plants seemed to be thriving as they are at Bantham Park."

She glanced at him as though deciding whether she could trust him with her private business. Evidently, she ruled against it. "The reasons are personal, but I assure you they are sound."

"By my reckoning, if you were to add a few more weeks to your schedule, there would be less risk of error."

"I appreciate your concern, Your Grace," she said with a glacial, insincere politeness that would make his sister proud.

He rubbed his temple. He was clumsy. Irritating her had not been his intention. There was a reason he was called the Merchant Duke. Efficiency in business was his particular passion, the way some men were obsessed with horse racing or Egyptology.

The path widened, revealing several acres of farmland in the clearing. A dilapidated wooden cottage sat in the middle, its boards peeling, several windows lacking panes of glass. To the side was a crumbling old stable, and beyond it the foundations of several smaller buildings, freshly laid.

Here was at least part of the explanation for her urgent need for laborers: her new nursery was, as far as he could see, not yet built.

He stopped the horses in front of the shabby old house.

"Miss Cavendish?"

"Yes?"

"How do you plan to move the contents of your greenhouse when this property lacks a greenhouse to move them *to*?"

"Your men are going to build me one, Your Grace. Thank you for driving me." She hopped down from the curricle without waiting for his assistance. "Good evening."

He stared down at her.

"You can't think that I am going to *leave* you here." It was approaching dusk, and the house, as far as he could tell, was deserted.

"I'll be fine. 'Tis a short walk back to Bantham Park from here. Two miles."

He smiled at her with icy patience. "Take your time. I'll wait."

She shrugged and disappeared behind the house. He amused himself by stepping down to the path and peeking inside the front door of the cottage. If the place looked uninhabitable from the outside, it looked worse from within. Cobwebs, collapsed floor-boards, damp stains, mice. He would have a word with Grouse. If she intended to inhabit this firetrap, it would need more than fifteen men to restore it in a fortnight.

He returned to the curricle and arranged himself in front of the reins as though he'd never left, sensing she would not look fondly on him prowling around her grounds uninvited.

She surprised him by returning in a quarter hour sporting a blinding smile. God's nails, the transformation. She was so lovely that he had to prevent himself from staring.

She accepted his hand and swung into her seat. "It's actually astonishing, how much they've accomplished in one day."

"I expected no less than perfection," he said, tightening his jaw to keep from beaming right back at her. It would not do to seem giddy, but after two days of pure peevishness, he felt like a boy who'd finally wrested approval from an exacting governess.

The feeling did not last. Her mouth returned to its down-turned resting place. They made the rest of the drive to Bantham Park in silence.

Miss Cavendish allowed him to help her down. "Thank you for driving me. Good night."

He watched as she made her way inside. The house was dark, with only a servant's lamp burning in the kitchen.

Everything else was sheer chaos.

The orderly scene he'd encountered the day before was now in a state of bedlam. Grouse's men had wasted no time uprooting trees, hauling off crates in carts, making tracks in the soil. It looked like the place had been ransacked by a roving pack of thieves.

The question was, why?

Why risk such haste?

He made a mental note to speak to Grouse. If Miss Cavendish was in some kind of trouble, it would be best to know the nature of her circumstances before the Westmead name was hopelessly entangled.

For looking at these grounds, one thing was clear: it was madness, whatever Miss Cavendish was up to.

Yet she didn't strike him as a woman whose sanity was in question.

She struck him as a woman who had something to hide.

He intended to find out what.

CHAPTER 5

"The atrium ceiling will be strung with seven hundred ribbons of bedstraw and meadowsweet, each sixty feet in length. Which means we need—" Poppy chewed her quill, calculating in her head. "Oh dear. Thirty bushels of foraged blossoms and five hundred skeins of white linen thread."

"Hmm?" Constance asked absently, scribbling away in her journal with fingers specked in their customary splatters of ink. Poppy sighed. It was essential that they complete the inventory for the ball today, but Constance's interest in the task was proving elusive.

"Sorry, darling," she said. "Yes, of course. Oh—but what if we used *gold* thread?"

Poppy's head ached. "The cost of five hundred skeins of gold thread would be—"

Constance waved the thought away. "Nothing to bother ourselves about. Gold it is. Unless you think—silver?"

"Right. Next on the list, the pergolas of roses in the ballroom will need to be built by Maxwell's crew by next Tuesday in order to be wired and strung by—"

"Oh, Poppy." Constance placed her forehead on her ink-spotted hands. "How might I convince you to resume this in the morning? My eyes water from the dullness."

"We're nearly finished," she coaxed.

"What will you wear to the ball?" Constance asked, suddenly perking up. "My mantua-maker is arriving tomorrow to finish my gown. She is terrifying. You will adore her."

Poppy had not for a single moment contemplated *attending* the ball.

"The ballroom is not my native climate, I'm afraid," she said lightly.

"Oh, but you must attend! Once everyone sees your designs, they will want to meet you, and once they meet you, they will want nothing more than to purchase your plants. Desmond will write about you in his gazette—we've already come up with a nickname: *the Beau Monde Botanist.*"

"That's very kind. But as soon as my work here is finished, I need to turn to an urgent matter at home."

"Poppy Cavendish," Constance growled, playful but by no means joking, "you *will* come to my ball. After all, there is no greater pleasure in life than dancing. Don't you agree?"

Poppy tried to summon a breezy response, but with the full, radiant beam of Constance's attention trained on her, her wit failed.

"I'm afraid I couldn't say. Dancing is not part of the curriculum in the greenhouse."

"Do you mean to tell me," Constance said, drawing to her full height, "that you have never *danced*? But surely you had a season? Mrs. Todd told me you are a viscount's granddaughter. Your mother was presented at court. You must have had a season!"

Poppy was growing tired of this line of inquiry. "I am a gardener. Maxwell is also a gardener. Did *he* have a season?"

Constance flicked her with her fan. "Maxwell looks dreadful in satin. Don't be perverse."

"Miss Cavendish, may I have a word in my study," Westmead's

low voice called from across the room. He was walking briskly toward them, carrying a sheaf of papers. He looked positively fierce.

"Miss Cavendish and I are exceedingly busy with our inventory," Constance said with mock seriousness. "Do come back later."

"I need to speak to Miss Cavendish. Alone." He stood and waited, the line of his back tense.

Constance glanced at Poppy with concern. "And he doesn't even know about the gold thread yet," she whispered. "You'd better speak to him."

"Yes, of course, Your Grace," she said, rising.

He led her down the corridor to his private wing. She had not yet seen this part of the house. It was dark, austerely furnished—clearly he had his limits when it came to his sister's fondness for gilt—and smelled of sandalwood.

He held open the door to a study and pointed to a chair before an imposing mahogany desk. "Please, sit."

His words were solicitous, but something seethed beneath his tone. He leaned his long body against the front of his desk, his arms crossed over his chest in a way that, with his height, was almost menacing.

"Miss Cavendish, I have just concluded an interview with your friend Mr. Raridan."

He said the name distastefully, his finger tapping a brisk rhythm on the desk, angry and percussive. "It was a most *unusual* conversation. Perhaps you might help me make sense of it."

She arranged her posture as straight as it would go, hoping not to reveal her unease. Westmead had been almost defiantly affable in their previous conversations. Arrogant, perhaps, but calm as a lake. Where had that man gone? And what could Tom have said to drive him there?

"Certainly, Your Grace. What is it you were discussing?"

The duke stared at her a second too long. "Mr. Raridan thought to warn me that you are removing the plants from your late uncle's land illegally. And using *my* men to do it before it is discovered by his heir."

Exhaustion pooled through her. Tom. Forever overstepping. Forever living in a world with a loose relationship to reality.

"Mr. Raridan asked for my assistance in blocking your scheme, for your protection," the duke said. "He suggested that I should leave the matter with him, given he is your fiancé, and has a duty to protect your best interests. I believe the word he used to describe you was 'confused.'"

His face was unreadable, and his fingers continued to tap, tap, tap on the desk. Her pulse quickened with the time he kept.

"I advised Mr. Raridan that your work here was contracted by my sister, not myself, and sent him on his way," he went on, "but you can understand that this interview leaves me with a great many questions. For you see, Miss Cavendish, if there is one word I would not use to describe your manner, it is *confused*."

"Your Grace," she said evenly, trying to maintain a cool head. "Mr. Raridan is not my fiancé. And there is no scheme. You are mistaken on all counts."

"Ah. I am mistaken," he breathed. He closed his eyes and nodded, as though overcome with relief. "Of course."

She hated him in that moment, for his japery of her. "I simply mean you would be wrong to believe Mr. Raridan."

"I did not say I *believed* him, Miss Cavendish. But since I have spent the better part of an hour attempting to unravel truth from nonsense from a man brought here at *your* behest, perhaps you might indulge me in a clarification. Let's start with what precisely you are undertaking at Bantham Park."

"I am removing goods from my late uncle's property in advance of his heir taking possession. That is correct. However, I do so legally."

"Raridan claims the estate is entailed. Is this true?"

"My nursery is not included in the entailment. I have paid my uncle a tenant's duty for use of his land, with funds from a small inheritance from my mother. We arranged the matter with a solicitor so that there would be no question. The goods I am moving belong to me."

"Yet the fact remains you are removing them from the property covertly."

He stared at her intently. She hated it, this assault on her integrity.

"The business is profitable. After many years, it has developed a steady stream of customers. Whereas my late uncle's estate is not productive and requires independent fortune to maintain."

His eyes softened slightly, but she could tell he was not fully convinced.

"Furthermore," she went on, gaining momentum, "I have no relationship with the family that is to take possession of the estate. Should they challenge my right to the nursery, the legal fees alone would ruin me. Surely, Your Grace, as a man of business, you understand the fragility of an enterprise in the early stages of success."

"As a *man of business*, I understand the impulse. As a *rational person*, I do not understand why you would betroth yourself to a man who believes you are a thief and then send him here to accuse you of the crime in person."

She threw back her head in frustration. "Please do not insult me further by suggesting I am betrothed to him. He did offer for me. I declined. He is not aware of the particulars of my circumstances and clearly is mistaken in whatever he said." She paused, and clasped her hands so he would not see that they were shaking. "And might I add, Your Grace, that my personal circumstances are no more your affair than they are his."

"I assure you I have no interest in your personal circumstances, Miss Cavendish. But I confess I do find it difficult to understand why you would put Raridan forward for an introduction, if you think so little of his character."

She closed her eyes. The actual answer was too vulgar to

disclose to a person who would never be able to understand the endless concessions one must make as a woman living in the world of men. How one must resign oneself to the ever-porous line between friend and foe, weigh expediency against principle.

Principle was a virtue dukes could afford. Gardeners had to be more judicious in their allocations.

"For all his failings, Mr. Raridan has done me a great kindness and I owed him a favor. I am certain that he did not intend to call my integrity into question."

Westmead looked at her for a moment, then ran a frustrated hand through his hair. "If he would say these things to me, you realize there is no telling who else he might say them to."

She had no answer to this. He was right, and the truth of it was chilling. She had considered Tom, for all his faults, to be her friend. And now, as her reward for this misjudgment, she had to mollify yet another male who, for an accident of birth, had the power to destroy her.

Westmead sighed. "Allow me to offer you some advice, Miss Cavendish, one tradesman to another. Commerce is not just contracts and terms. Success requires a keen eye for the character of the people with whom one associates. You would do well to take better care."

Resentment flared in her stomach. The great duke, with his hard-won riches, offering lessons out of lofty condescension. She would like to see him sit in her seat, staring at the desperate columns in her ledger with the horizons of the world closing in, and see what choices *he* might stoop to making, what characters *he* might associate with, to stay afloat.

She rose from the chair and crossed her arms. "I did not come here for advice. I apologize for Mr. Raridan's impertinence, but I would remind you that I would not have made the introduction had your sister not prevailed on *me* to disrupt my activities to come *here*. If you find my practices so irregular, I am happy to suspend them. I will inform Lady Constance that in light of receiving excellent advice, I have decided to take better care in choosing the people with whom I associate. Good day, Your Grace."

He stared at her, no doubt mute with renewed affront at her audacity.

She whirled around and left the room.

ARCHER LISTENED TO MISS CAVENDISH'S FOOTSTEPS RECEDE DOWN the hall. The sound of feminine voices—his sister's dulcet tones beseeching forgiveness, the nurserywoman's terse responses—became fainter.

Fuck.

He had offended her.

He needed to apologize.

He was not a man who lost his temper. Ever. But his blood had begun to rise the moment that pompous young man had saun-tered into his study and implied he had enabled Miss Cavendish to fleece half the countryside.

Not because he had believed him. Because he *hadn't.*

None of it had squared with her reputation. A brief query to his steward the day before had made it clear she was a person of considerable talent. She'd been ahead of the fashion for plants from the colonies that was becoming so popular among the gentlemen gardeners of Britain's great estates. In a few years, if she continued on her trajectory, she would have an enviable busi-ness. Of course, locating it here, in Grove Vale, away from any viable waterways, was not ideal. But with the right land ...

She was not unlike the men in whose enterprises he invested. Prescient, hardworking traders with potential greater than they had capital. If she presented him with an investment proposal, he would sign off without a second thought.

He had not called her into his study to insult her. He had called her in to warn her. But something about the idea of her with that swaggering, bog-witted specimen of manhood had made him lose his temper. At least she wasn't actually marrying the oaf, with his blazing innuendos and squint-eyed understanding of lending covenants. To think of all her ambition and sharp intelligence laid waste to domestic indolence in some dingy apartment in Cheapside. The very notion of it made him depressed.

Constance interrupted his thoughts by throwing open the door. "What have you done, you miserable cod?" she hissed.

He looked up, stricken. "I—yes. Badly done of me."

"Archer," she said with deadly precision. "Four hundred of the most influential people in the country will be at this house in *two weeks* expecting to see a ballroom forest. God help you if there is no ballroom forest when they arrive."

"I will make my apology known to Miss Cavendish—"

"Immediately," his sister interrupted. "You will make it known *immediately*. Before she leaves. *Go.*"

For once, he was grateful to the footmen haunting the halls, who pointed him to the portico, where Miss Cavendish was waiting for a carriage. She stood stiffly, her posture so tightly drawn she looked like she might shatter.

"Miss Cavendish?"

She turned around and pinned him with her eyes. "What could you want with me now, Your Grace? Perhaps you think I am parting with the silver?"

"Miss Cavendish, I have insulted you. It was not my intention to do so. I don't know how to offer you an apology that could be adequate. I hope you will reconsider."

She kept her arms crossed over her chest, clearly unmoved. Anyone observing could be forgiven for wondering who, between them, was the duke.

"You see," he went on, clearing his throat, "I found Mr. Raridan's claims baffling given what Mr. Grouse has said to me about your affairs and reputation."

"Ah. Of course. You've been prying into my affairs," she said, not bothering to hide her anger. "And what did you learn? That I reside in Grove Vale? Subsist on a meager income? Grow plants?"

"I learned that you began gardening as a girl at the knee of your mother and continued to teach yourself the principles of botany after her death. You used a small inheritance to start a nursery and developed a knack for adapting exotic breeds to the English climate. You correctly anticipated the appetite of gardeners here for foreign plants. You are positioned well. Enviably well. And you have done it all yourself."

He paused. "Do you want to know what I think?"

"I'm sure you will tell me."

"That combination of ambition, vision, and industry is something I constantly look for in my investment concern. I pay men small fortunes to roam around the country seeking it out. And so I know better than anyone that it is …" He locked eyes with her in the dim light. "Exceptionally rare."

He cleared his throat once more and went on gruffly. "Given I rebuked you for your lack of transparency, honor obliges I disclose to you that I became rather dismayed when I learned you were betrothed to Raridan. I suppose I thought, *How dare she? How dare she squander such gifts on so middling a creature?* Or, more to the point, on *anyone?*"

SHE DIDN'T SPEAK. SHE COULDN'T, BECAUSE HER BREATH WAS caught. She had never heard herself described in such terms by anyone. How could she, when the local gentry who had known her all her life told a different story about her? One of an eccentric spinster who coarsened herself with commercial enterprise. An arrogant, unlikable woman, unhealthily obsessed with plants.

"Thank you," she said, hoping her voice did not convey how

deeply what he said affected her. It would not do to seem overly moved.

He shrugged, as though his words were unremarkable. As though such assessments of her worth were lobbed at her all day.

The carriage she had been waiting for at long last appeared through the stable gates and rolled up to the bottom of the steps.

"Miss Cavendish, in light of my lapse of judgment, I fully understand if you do not wish to return to Westhaven. But if Constance believes me guilty of ruining her plans, I shall have to live with her mortal disapproval. I don't suppose I could prevail on you to reconsider finishing the work for my sister? I assure you that I will not attempt to intercede in so much as the placement of a vase."

The contours of his face should not have a say in her decision, and yet she could not help but admire them as the fading light danced across the planes that made him sometimes handsome, sometimes fierce.

Or perhaps it was only the way that he looked at her. As if her respect meant something to him. As if *she* did.

"Very well," she said. "I shall return in the morning. For Lady Constance's sake."

He nodded. "I'm glad to hear it. For Lady Constance's sake."

And then he smiled.

Boyishly and quick and warm, like the sun darting out from a bank of clouds. It was so unexpected and disarming that without thinking, she craned her face toward his to get a better view of it. Their eyes met, and a chill ran down her spine. Because for just a moment, she thought he might lean in, close the distance, and kiss her.

No. Not *thought* he might. *Wanted him to.*

She *wanted* him to kiss her.

Instead, he folded his mouth back into its usual grim line, bent in a deep bow, and offered her his hand to help her into the carriage.

But it did not escape her notice that he held her fingers just a beat too long as he said: "Be well, Miss Cavendish."

That he stood at the steps to his house and watched her carriage drive away until it went out the iron gates.

She hugged herself.

Not return to Westhaven? It was unthinkable.

She had spent far too many years of her life insisting she was worthy of the future she imagined to well-intentioned people who dismissed her as intractable at best. But she knew—*knew*—what she was capable of. She knew it the way she knew her own soul, her own breath, her own pulse. What she had not realized was that she had been pining for someone who knew it too.

She was going to prove that it was the Duke of Westmead, not the others, who was right about her.

She was going to leave them stunned by what she would accomplish.

CHAPTER 6

*I*ndomitable, Poppy coached herself as she marched to the door of Westhaven, clad in boots and men's breeches. *You. Are. Indomitable.*

She had lain awake for hours replaying Westmead's speech about her in her head. At dawn she had come to a decision: she had chosen to simply believe him.

She would no longer attempt to pass for a mannerly maiden with her awkward curtsies in her mended dresses. She would simply be Poplar Cavendish, named for a tree. A brilliant nursery-woman who wore breeches and rode astride and did not require society's approval. She would use her inborn gifts to design the most remarkable ballroom in the history of Great Britain and leave this house with a legion of new customers and her independence finally secure.

"Lady Constance has requested the pleasure of your company in the morning room, Miss Cavendish," the butler said, his face frozen in alarm at her appearance.

She smiled, ignoring his discomfiture. "Certainly. Lead the way."

The room she was shown to was a jumble of disorder. The

chairs and sofas had been pushed to the walls to make a large empty space in the middle of the chamber, and every surface was slung with colorful bolts of fabric and boxes of lace and feathers.

Constance stood on a round stool at the center of this chaos in a confection of shimmering pink taffeta, her arms held out to either side as a seamstress stood behind her, sticking the seams with pins.

A woman in a striking scarlet dress observed with regal bearing. "Tighter still around the waist, I think," she said grimly to the needlewoman.

"Valeria, if she fastens it any tighter, I shall be capable of nothing beyond fainting. All of England's oldest families will think I have a wasting illness." Noticing Poppy, Constance smiled. "Ah, Miss Cavendish, you've arrived! I'd like you to meet Madame Valeria Parc, my mantua-maker."

The tiny woman stood, revealing herself to be as striking as her gown, all angles and swirls of long black hair. Her green eyes flashed over Poppy, from her unkempt head to her men's attire.

"*Enchantée,*" she said, looking quite the contrary.

"There's a dressing gown for you behind the screen," Constance called. "Do get changed. It's time for your fitting."

"My what?"

Hopping down from her perch, Constance linked her arm with Poppy's and inched her toward a pair of Chinese screens. "I want you to have a new gown for the ball. Something that is as stunning as your designs. It is the least I can do after the *profound* misunderstanding last night. Now hurry up and disrobe! If Valeria is given any more time to straiten my stays, I will suffocate."

Poppy opened her mouth to object—she was here to work, not accept gifts she had no use for. *Indomitable,* she reminded herself. The ball was an opportunity to win new customers. She couldn't very well do that in her fraying dun-colored muslin.

"How kind of you," she said firmly, and marched behind the screen to remove her clothing.

When she had changed into a shift, Valeria whisked her onto the stool and began measuring her with efficient little flicks of her wrist.

"She'll need a proper set of stays," she sniffed.

Poppy frowned. She favored the leather stays worn by working women, cut to allow movement. One could not tend plants if one could not bend at the waist.

Constance draped her with a selection of fabrics and trimmings. "I think the jade silk for her. It makes a wonder of her eyes."

"Perhaps. With ivory petticoats and a gold sash."

"The cut must be rather dramatic. Nothing maidenish," Constance said.

The women pulled fabric across Poppy's arms and chest and hips, pinning here and there, and then stepped back to inspect their handiwork.

Constance spoke first, allowing her lips to curve in a barely perceptible smile. "Well, well. Perhaps there's a viscount's granddaughter in you after all, Miss Cavendish."

Valeria turned her around to view her image in the looking glass. Where moments ago had been a girl with the dimensions of a weed, now an altogether different kind of woman gazed back at her. A slender sylph with a wasp waist and a snowy expanse of upward-sloping bosom. Poppy immediately covered the exposed tops of her breasts with her hands.

"I couldn't wear this. It's *indecent*."

Constance, Valeria, and the seamstress laughed.

"My dear, in that dress you will have every man in the room developing a sudden strong interest in botany," Constance said.

She felt her cheeks turn bright red. *Indomitable,* she ordered. She squared her shoulders and smiled at her reflection. "Then I will do what I must in the service of horticulture. But now you must get me out of this. I am late to meet Mr. Maxwell."

"Of course," Constance said, unfurling her from yards of fine fabric. "But join me at five in the library. I'm afraid we must go over expenses with my tedious brother."

WHEN CONSTANCE INSISTED THAT ARCHER JOIN HER IN THE LIBRARY to review the expenses for the ball with Miss Cavendish, he had sensed she was plotting some act of mischief; no one was more bored by expenses than Constance. He therefore arrived late and silently, his years as her older brother having taught him the benefits of stealth.

As he peeked through the half-open door, he saw that the account book was forlorn in the corner, its pages undisturbed. Beside it was Miss Cavendish, whose drooping posture and expression of dread indicated Constance had once again taken her hostage. He silently edged into the room. After yesterday he owed it to her to prevent further injury.

Constance rifled through sheet music at the pianoforte. "Ah, here we are, a minuet. Brilliant. *Everything* worth happening at a ball occurs during the first minuet."

She played a few bars. "It's a six-beat count, you see, not so difficult. Do you hear it? *One* two three *four* five six."

The nurserywoman looked both beautiful—he could never stop himself from noticing how pretty she was—and amusingly sullen. "This is preposterous, Constance," she muttered.

He was inclined to agree with her. She was, after all, dressed like a man.

"What is preposterous is yourself not knowing how it is done. What do you expect will happen if a handsome gentleman wants to dance with you?"

"I expect I shall politely decline."

Archer laughed to himself.

"Nonsense," Constance called, continuing to play the tune. "You will say 'The honor would be all mine' and be swept off your feet to fall in love under the stars. That, you see, is the *sole* purpose of dancing."

Leaving the instrument, she took Poppy's hand and pulled her to the center of the room. "The gentleman will bow, and you will curtsy. You will place your heels together, just so, do you see? And then he will place his hand in yours. And it begins." She demonstrated, gliding across the room with an imaginary partner —first forward, then backward, calling out *"one*-two-threes" as she went.

Intent on her demonstration, Constance became more focused and creative in her steps, allowing her ghostly partner to escort her across the room with ever-greater flourish.

Enjoying the dismayed expression that had overtaken Poppy's face, he could not resist coming out of hiding to whisper in her ear. "Has my sister been seduced by a spirit?"

She gave him a pained smile. "A drunken one, by the looks of it."

"Oh, Archer!" Constance said. "Excellent timing. Here, you lead and I will play the accompaniment."

"Not a chance," he said, backing from the room. "I don't dance."

"You do now," Constance said, snatching him by the hand and pulling him back into the room. "I daresay it would serve you well to refresh yourself if you wish to charm the Miss Bastians of the world."

Without waiting for a reply, she placed his left hand in Poppy's right one.

Given he had spent the bulk of the past waking hours reciting to himself the varied and excellent reasons for staying as far away from Miss Cavendish as possible, the only rational response was to let go of her fingers, make his apologies, and dash away to the sanctuary of his rooms.

And yet, now that he had Poppy's fingers in his own, he could not find the strength of will to make himself release them. It was the same queer feeling that had overtaken him when he'd bidden her farewell the night before.

Having adjusted their arms to her satisfaction, his sister scurried back to the pianoforte and began to play. He mouthed an apology at Poppy and then, at her reluctant nod, began to guide her through the first mincing steps, hoping he remembered them himself.

The dainty prances of the minuet were nothing short of absurd for a man of his proportions, and his tall frame had never felt larger or less elegant as he went bounding through the steps and bows, arm held out aloft.

He noticed Poppy's lip twitch at the sight of him. She darted her eyes away, kindly attempting not to laugh. He snickered. She choked back a snort. And then they both lost their composure entirely.

The music clanged to a stop. Constance glared at them over her shoulder. "There is nothing *humorous* about the minuet, children. Do collect yourselves."

Poppy looked guiltily down at her feet, then glanced up at him with a devilish glint in her eye, biting that lower lip of hers in a way that made him want to remake the kinds of mistakes he had sworn off many years ago. He gave her a wink and took her hand as the music resumed.

The awkwardness fell away and he became absorbed in the feel of her hand meeting his, in the sight of her small, inward smile as she became more confident in the steps. All at once it was a pleasure to dance with Poppy Cavendish, Constance's jangled style of musicianship notwithstanding.

They both looked up in surprise when the music came to an end.

"Well done," Constance sang out. "Shall we try a gigue next?"

"I should return home," Poppy said. "It's growing late."

He was shocked to feel a momentary twinge of disappointment. Certainly it was the first time in his life he had ever regretted missing the opportunity to dance a gigue.

"Very well. I will ring for the carriage," Constance said.

"There is no need. I rode my horse," Poppy said.

"Well, you mustn't ride back alone," Constance said, aghast. "Good heavens, the ideas you have in that gorgeous head. And they say *I* am eccentric. Archer, you'll escort Miss Cavendish home?"

His sister's face was a caricature of innocence, all wide-eyed, guileless placidity. The face of a person who had hatched a plot and felt it was proceeding along in a swimming manner. He glanced at Poppy to see if she noticed his sister's obvious chicanery, but instead saw that her face was a careful study of blankness.

How curious.

He was no particular expert in the fairer sex, but in business it behooved one to be perceptive. And if he was not mistaken, Miss Cavendish wore the face of someone who wanted him to escort her, and did not want to *admit* that she wanted it.

Which meant that he absolutely, categorically would be escorting her to her door.

"Of course I will see Miss Cavendish home," he said, waving his sister away.

Constance shot him a smug grin and went off, humming a minuet as she left.

"There's really no need for you to accompany me," Poppy said when Constance was gone. "It's not yet dark and I'm an excellent horsewoman."

"I have no doubt. But given the hour, I would be derelict in my duties as host if I let you ride home unescorted. If you would prefer to take a carriage, I will see that a groom returns your horse to Bantham Park."

Her eyes sparkled with mischief. "I prefer to ride. Alone. The evening air favors my constitution."

Was it possible that Miss Cavendish was *flirting with him?*

"As it does mine," he agreed. "In fact, I am suddenly overtaken by a most pressing desire for an evening's solitary exercise. I believe I shall ride to Bantham Park. Alone."

He strolled off in the direction of the stables.

"Farewell, Miss Cavendish," he said, pausing to look back over his shoulder. "Do give my compliments to any poachers or high-waymen you should encounter along the road."

He chose not to let her see his smile as she fell into step beside him.

CHAPTER 7

*I*t was difficult to seem impressive when one was constantly on the verge of swooning.

All day Poppy had instructed herself to avoid the Duke of Westmead.

There were few benefits to being in his company. First, there was his pedantic and quarrelsome nature. Added to that was his fondness for giving her condescending lectures on business. He was peremptory and demanding, traits she liked to reserve for herself. And he was kind and understood her, which made all his other qualities unnerving.

Dancing with him had been a torture devised by the gods to test her. For there had been a moment, just after they both dissolved in laughter, when their eyes had met and their hands had lingered and she had once again imagined what it would be like if he was to lean in and kiss her.

And worse, wished that he *would*.

How frustrating that she should spend most of her last decade dodging any signs of cordiality from gentlemen, only to find herself drawn to the one man to whom it was essential she maintain a cool distance.

She was here to impress the Duke of Westmead so as to secure a crucial advantage in trade. One did not win a man's respect by becoming breathless at the sight of his shoulders.

And now her punishment for being so weak of will was the challenge of riding beside his handsome form, straining to maintain her composure as he peppered her with questions about her very favorite subject: plants.

"What is that tree up ahead?" he asked.

"A smooth-leaved elm."

"One of my partners recently returned from the British colonies. He was very taken with the tulip trees. Are you familiar with them?"

"Magnolia," she said. "They're my favorite. It is the central frustration of my life that it is so difficult to acquire them in a great enough quantity to cultivate here in England."

"You've tried?"

"I never *stop* trying," she sighed, thinking of poor, long-suffering Mr. Carpenter.

"What is the difficulty?"

"Dependence on the kindness of one's friends. Not to mention the perils of the seas."

"You can't purchase them from abroad?"

"It's not that simple. To get new varieties, you need to charm some poor soul into climbing trees and stumping through forests for just the right cones and branches."

"If you were my partner, Cavendish, I might tell you it is always better to provide incentive than to beg."

All she heard was "Cavendish." He had called her by her surname. As though she were a *man*.

It stung.

It shouldn't, for everyone knew she was improperly domineering and masculine, and she had always considered it a point of pride. Had she not, a quarter hour ago, enjoyed this very man's rather discomposed expression when it had dawned on him she intended to ride astride?

But that was just it. The words came from *him*. Him, whose reactions she found herself minutely attuned to, as though he were a weeping birch branch when she desperately wanted to check the direction of the wind. Him, who had for the first time since her youth made her feel *girlish*.

It was a brisk dose of reality.

She was being very, very foolish.

"Well, *Westmead*," she shot back, hoping to cover her dismay, "it's not just the begging you're at the mercy of. It is complex to get plants across the ocean intact. Cuttings grow moldy in the damp. Rats abscond with the seeds. It has taken me years to find a method that doesn't end in disaster, and even still, my customers' appetite for new exotics far exceeds what I can get from Virginia or Carolina."

"It sounds like a market in need of investment."

"Precisely!" She looked back at him, pleased he had reached the same conclusion she had. "I've been pondering the merits of a subscription-based model between nurseries trading overseas."

"Subscriptions can be risky unless you are sure of adequate custom. Are you?"

"Oh, there's a hefty appetite for exotic plants," she said over her shoulder. "The trouble is convincing quality nurseries it is worth the initial investment without a guaranteed—"

"Stop!" he shouted.

She glanced ahead of her just in time to see the low-hanging branch looming much closer than it ought to be. She furiously tugged at the reins, but her horse had far too much momentum. With a sickening clarity she realized she was going to fall off.

And then—humiliation settling in as her balance receded—she did indeed.

Westmead was off his horse and running before she even hit

the ground. She had landed, thank God, in a shrub, which had partly broken her fall. But her ankle had wrenched unnaturally, leaving her in a heap, her head shrouded in a tangle of leaves and unruly hair.

Westmead knelt over her. "Speak to me," he demanded.

"I'm quite all right." She pushed his hands away and tried to stand. Pain blossomed so quick and hot that sparks shot across her field of vision. She collapsed back into the bush.

"My ankle," she gasped.

"Let me see." He crouched over her boot and gingerly touched the offending foot, provoking another rain of stars as the pain radiated up to her shin.

She gasped and clenched her eyes together, but it was too late.

Hot, angry tears instantly soaked her lashes.

To her utter mortification, Westmead immediately noticed.

"No, no," he said with alarm. He rummaged in his pocket for a handkerchief and held it out. She waved it away.

"Please don't cry."

She would give anything not to, as it no doubt made her appear more ridiculous than falling off her horse had. But the exhaustion and stress of the past weeks were mingling with her acute humiliation and the sharp throbbing in her ankle, and the tears simply wouldn't stop.

The look on his face was so utterly chagrined it made her cry harder.

Hesitantly, he touched her shoulder with his hand.

"I shouldn't have distracted you. Forgive me."

She shook her head wordlessly, her embarrassment amplifying her distress, and continued to fall to pieces in a bush.

Helplessly, he reached out and pulled her from the shrub, picking small sticks and leaves from her waistcoat. He helped her to a seated position and then, with a glance at her face, used a stiff arm to put her head against his shoulder and let her weep there, as if she were a distraught child he didn't quite know what to do with.

She knew she should move away and collect herself. But the solidness of Westmead's body, his smell of sandalwood and clean linen, the awkward gentleness with which he patted her back, were so comforting she couldn't force herself to move. She cried into his shirt. His fine linen shirt, which no doubt cost him more than her entire wardrobe.

He silently stroked her back. She should stop him, but it was a feeling her bones remembered from the earliest days of her childhood, before her parents had died and her nurse had gone missing and her uncle's distant, distracted guardianship had replaced the animal comfort of simple touch. Before she had become so thoroughly, doggedly alone.

"I'm sorry," she said, trying to collect herself.

"Not as sorry as I am." He ran a thumb beneath her cheek, smoothing away the last traces of her tears. She lifted her face toward the warmth of his palm, glancing up at his eyes to assess what scornful sentiment she would no doubt see in them. But there was no trace of judgment in his gaze. Just still, dark pools of quiet kindness. She closed her eyes to keep from drowning in them.

And felt his lips brush her cheek.

It happened in a heartbeat, as faint as a breath. She froze, opened her eyes. She saw heat, and shock, in his.

"Christ," he muttered.

He immediately let go of her and moved away. She was left stunned, her body protesting the abrupt loss of his warmth. It was as distant from the sensation she had once felt in the woods alone with Tom as a feeling could be.

The Duke of Westmead cleared his throat. "It seems that I must beg your forgiveness once more, Miss Cavendish. I am unfit for company."

She shook her head in silence. She didn't want an apology. Her entire body vibrated with what it wanted: *Do it again.*

But he had jolted to his feet, and the moment was broken.

EVER-LOVING HELL.

What had he just done?

And why?

He did not know what he wanted more: to take Miss Cavendish back in his arms and comfort her, or to go barreling through the woods in horror that this woman he had no business laying hands on was turning him into a puddle.

He settled on inspecting her offending ankle.

"It's not broken. But you won't be able to walk on it."

She looked at him darkly. She was no longer crying. "I'm sorry. I was giddy with talking of plants."

He lifted her up. "It was my fault. Here, put your arms around my neck."

He tried not to focus on the fact that she was light and soft, but his body had missed the feeling of a woman in his arms. Being here, in these woods, he felt it keenly.

He lifted her gingerly onto his horse and settled her there with as brotherly a pat as he could muster. "There we are. Try not to fall off while I see to your mount."

He winked.

She snorted. He collected her mare and tied it to his animal, then swung up into his saddle in front of her.

"Hold tightly to my waist and lean on me if you feel dizzy." He waited as she adjusted herself against him, trying not to enjoy the feeling of her straddling his hips with her thighs.

When she was settled, he signaled to the horses to reverse course.

Poppy tapped his shoulder. "Your Grace. You're going the wrong way."

"We're much closer to Westhaven. I'm taking you back. Your ankle needs ice, and rest."

"My household will be alarmed if I'm not back before dark."

He doubted it. The place had been deserted when he'd visited. If she had proper servants, they certainly had not been hovering about awaiting their mistress's return. It occurred to him, not for the first time, how alone she was.

"We will send word from Westhaven."

He rode slowly, conscious of Poppy's sharp intakes of breath at every sudden movement of the horse. He was also conscious of the light pressure of her fingers on his waist. She no doubt held him that way to avoid a more direct grip and would be aghast if she knew she was teasing the sensitive flesh above his hips.

He tried to be more aghast at himself for enjoying it.

He dismounted as soon as they reached the stables and called for the nearest groom, who steadied the horses as Archer lifted Poppy down and carried her inside the kitchen yard.

The buzzing kitchen came grinding to a halt at the sight of their lord with the crumpled form of Poppy Cavendish suspended in his arms.

Mrs. Todd, the housekeeper, came hurrying toward them. "Your Grace. Miss Cavendish! What's happened?"

"Miss Cavendish was thrown from her horse. Have ice and clean linen brought to my study and a room made up for her. And see that necessities are sent over from Bantham Park. She'll need enough for a few days."

"A few *days?*" Poppy objected.

"There's no sense in you spending hours hauling back and forth across forest roads on a ruined ankle. I insist you stay. Lady Constance will not hear otherwise."

Phrasing it that way added a veneer of propriety, though

propriety ranked low among his concerns. He wanted her here, where he could see she was looked after. He didn't like to think of her all alone and injured in a distant house so recently visited by death.

She glanced up at him, then down at her rapidly expanding ankle. It was already swollen majestically compared to the rest of her slim leg, puffed under her stocking like a snake that had swallowed an apple.

"Oh, very well," she sighed, and wrapped her arm around his neck to be carried onward, suddenly as imperious as a queen. "But do get on with it."

A FIRE HAD BEEN LEFT BURNING IN THE DUKE'S STUDY, AND POPPY tried not to shout with pain as Westmead settled her on a velvet sofa in front of it. He disappeared for a moment and returned with a stack of pillows, seemingly from his own bedchamber, which he used to create a small mountain to elevate her leg.

Satisfied, he turned to his imposing desk and poured a generous quantity of amber liquid out of a decanter and into a fat glass tumbler. He swallowed it down in a single gulp, refilled it, and handed it to her.

"Drink this. It will numb the pain."

She took a tentative sip. Pear and smoke and vanilla, followed by a ragged burning in her throat. She sputtered as it went down.

He placed himself at the opposite end of the sofa, where he sat staring unhappily at her protuberant ankle.

"I will go find Constance to help you with your boot and stockings."

Poppy shuddered at the thought. Constance's hysterics at the sight of the puffed ankle would be possibly worse than the pain itself.

"Must you?" she countered. She sipped again at the brandy,

which distracted from the pain in her ankle by producing a new one in her throat.

"It's important to get the swelling down if you hope to walk in the near future."

She knew he was only being polite by summoning his sister, but she was not one to observe the tedious proprieties of feminine comportment if it came at the expense of the use of her limb.

"It will be much faster if you do it," she suggested, taking another fortifying sip of the brandy.

He gave her a strangled look, and suddenly she felt very bold.

"Go ahead," she commanded. *"Carefully."*

Something inside her knew that given how much she had enjoyed his embrace on the forest floor, and the feeling of his waist below her hands as they rode back to Westhaven, it was a mistake to demand that the Duke of Westmead undress her.

Even just her ankle.

Even for her health.

Nevertheless she waved him airily toward her foot.

"Right, then. Shout if I hurt you."

"It's not my ankle I worry for—it's my pride," she heard herself say. This remark was intended to be made silently, in her head, but evidently it had been allowed out of her mouth by Westmead's brandy.

"Why is it that every time I am near you," her mouth continued to say, never mind it hadn't consulted her, "it ends in my utter humiliation?"

He paused. "Humiliation? I'm just removing your *shoe*, Cavendish. Is your foot so unsightly?"

She closed her eyes and decided to continue to talk to distract herself from the pain.

"Cavendish. You would call a lady by her surname—like a man?"

"Only if she were domineering and obstinate, like a man," he said, not without a distinct note of appreciation.

"Then I shall call you Westmead."

"My name," he said affably, "is Archer."

"Do you know, *Archer*, that in the four days I have known you, I have been injured and embarrassed more times than in the previous year of my life?"

"Is that so?" he asked, all innocence, removing the lace from her boot.

"Indeed. First you falsely accused me of committing fraud. And being betrothed. To an oaf."

He very gently pulled the shoe from her foot. "A *lying* oaf," he clarified. "But I was wrong. Surely that was my embarrassment, not yours."

She scoffed. His fingers edged beneath the hem of her breeches for her garter and flicked efficiently at the tie.

He lifted the thin fabric of her stocking and carefully began to roll it down her calf. The sensation of him slowly pulling the stocking down her leg made her eyes shoot open. Not with pain— he was being delicate with her ankle—but with awareness of his fingers on her bare leg.

"Then Constance forced you into giving me a dancing lesson."

"You weren't bad at all for a beginner. At any rate you certainly proved better at dancing than you did *riding*."

"Exactly! And now I have managed to be thrown from my horse." She laughed in dismay. She rather liked saying what was on her mind. It was highly relaxing. Perhaps she should always drink brandy and invite men with kind eyes to undress her.

"Well, yes, that was rather badly done of you," he allowed. "Hold still." He propped her ankle back on the mountain of pillows and began to fashion little squares of ice wrapped in muslin.

"And then of course you *kissed* me," she heard herself say.

She could actually feel herself turning red—the heat pricking first at her hairline, descending to her face, then flooding down her neck. The relaxing qualities of honesty had their limits, it seemed.

Westmead froze. For a second he paused in his ministrations to look at her. His eyes were dark. "And that was ... *humiliating?*" he asked slowly.

There was a touch of something in his voice she couldn't read —not anger, but far from the light, teasing tone he had used before.

She squeezed her eyes shut. She had gotten herself this far with the truth, so she might as well blunder ahead. "It was not *exactly* humiliating," she admitted. "That is, until you *stopped.*"

It was madness, to speak to him this way. Anathema. She had not spent two decades learning how to outmatch every man in spitting distance only to shamelessly flirt with the Duke of Westmead as she reclined on his sofa with his hands on her bare leg.

He was silent as he arranged the packets of ice around her ankle and gently wrapped them in another layer of muslin to keep them in place.

Then he stood and removed the tumbler from her hand. He neatly downed the liquid that remained in the glass.

"Did you think," he finally asked, "that I stopped because I *wanted* to?"

A MAN WITH MORE TALENT FOR SELF-PRESERVATION WOULD HAVE removed himself from the vicinity of Poppy Cavendish immediately. He would have noted the sight of her on his sofa in front of his fire and the effect it was having on him and discovered a sudden urgent need to balance the estate accounts or rekindle his boyhood love for conjugating Latin.

He would not have moved a pile of books so he could look directly into her eyes as he said: "Cavendish, what I *wanted* was a very different type of kiss."

He would not have leaned into her ear and whispered: "And if you don't want to be embarrassed, I'll spare you what I *wanted* when your thighs were wrapped around me on my horse."

A man who did not want to drown would have gotten up the second she had whispered back: "And what do you *want* right now?"

He would not have answered: "This." And put his mouth on hers with the force of all the hunger he had been fighting since the moment he first saved her from the blasted plumeria in her bloody greenhouse.

If there was any doubt she wanted him back, it was lost in her lips, those soft, pink, pliable lips, which trembled, then opened for him. And in her hair, that long, dark mass that was forever tempting him with its wildness, exactly as soft and fragrant as he had imagined. In her mouth, sultry with brandy, allowing his tongue to dart inside, turning up at the corners as he took her lower lip in his and ever so gently pulled, teasing her with his teeth.

When she *bit him back*, and he was lost to sensation entirely, his jawbone chafing against her slender neck, his ear catching her sigh as his hands traced, unbelieving, the contours of her shoulders, her beautiful, delicate collarbone, the hollows of her throat.

He pulled her close to him, wanting to envelop her, to inhale her. Her hands reached out to run her fingers through his hair, to caress his face. Only when she yelped and reeled back was he able to find the strength of mind to break his lips from hers.

Ever so belatedly, he recalled her ankle.

"Codding hell. I hurt you."

Her eyes were filled with lightness. "I didn't mean to stop you. It's only that I knocked my ankle against the sofa. Add that to my list of humiliations."

She was relaxed, recumbent, and glowing in the firelight, her lips swollen from his kisses. He wanted to pick her up and carry her directly to his bedchamber and unwind her from her clever breeches. He wanted more of her skin on his. It had been so long since he'd allowed himself to be touched in such a way that he now perceived he was starved for it.

And that was dangerous for her.

But unacceptable for him.

He let out a ragged sigh and stood.

"Oh no," she whispered. "There you go, again."

To his tremendous relief, a knock sounded on the door.

"Archer," his sister cried. "What has happened to Miss Cavendish?"

CHAPTER 8

*I*t was like a fairy tale: with a knock at the door, the spell was broken.

Westmead was on his feet, the vulnerable expression wiped clean from his face.

Poppy felt the change in herself as well. As if by some act of sorcery, the sensuous, curious woman in the firelight straightened and stiffened until once again she shrank into the contours of the tightly coiled nurserywoman with the rigid timetables and the ever-present ledger.

The door opened and Constance came rushing in.

"Oh, I was so worried about you," she cried. "Is it thoroughly broken?"

Poppy shook her head quickly. "It's only a sprain. I would have gone home, but His Grace insisted we return here for ice."

Constance shot Westmead a look that Poppy couldn't read. "Of course you should be here," she murmured. "We will take such good care of you that you'll never want to leave us. Todd has prepared a room for you. Archer, you'll carry Poppy? She mustn't walk."

He bowed. "Where am I taking her?"

"The ivory room."

A strange look crossed his face. "The *ivory* room?"

"Yes, of course," she said, with a tone that almost sounded smug to Poppy's ears. "She mustn't climb stairs, and it is the only bedchamber on the ground floor. Besides your own, of course."

She thought she heard Westmead curse under his breath, but before she could parse the meaning of this exchange, he was lifting her once again.

When they crossed the hall, she immediately saw the source of his discomfort. The ivory room, so-called, was clearly the bedchamber meant for the lady of the house. The one meant for his wife.

The walls and floors were of a dark, gleaming wood, but the furnishings were sumptuous and feminine. A thick woven carpet in shades of ivory and gold spanned the greater part of the room. Creamy marble and gilt work crowned the massive fireplace at the room's far end. Before it sat a polished copper bathing tub, nearly big enough to swim in.

Westmead excused himself, and she was left alone with Constance, who fluttered around, helping her undress and insisting she pick at a tray of broth and toast sent from the kitchen.

The effects of the brandy were fading and her ankle throbbed. She hissed at the pain.

"Poor darling," Constance murmured, lending her shoulder and helping Poppy hobble toward the massive bed. "Here, take a few drops of this to help you sleep."

"What is it?"

"Laudanum."

Poppy had read of the tincture, made from a solvent of opium, but had never taken it. The botanist in her wondered if the drug was indeed as effective for pain as people claimed.

She accepted the phial and placed a single drop on her tongue.

"That's better," Constance said. "Here, let's tuck you in." She lifted the counterpane and made a cozy berth for Poppy, piling pillows beneath her swollen ankle.

"This room is very pretty," Poppy murmured, burying herself in the feather mattress. The sheets were scented with rose sachets. She could not remember ever feeling more comfortable.

"Isn't it? I designed it myself. When Archer announced he planned to marry, I became excessively excited. I had so nearly given up on him."

"He is *betrothed?*" Poppy sputtered before she could stop herself.

Constance either did not hear or was kindly pretending not to hear the note of horror in her laudanum-heavy voice.

"No, not yet. That is what the ball is for. They don't know it, but the unmarried ladies I've invited have been handpicked for the role of the Duchess of Westmead."

Oh.

So this was why Constance had been so insistent she be hired. Why the decor for the ball had to be so spectacular. She was building the very scenery beneath which the duke intended to woo his future bride.

Perhaps it was the laudanum, but all at once she felt so leaden with exhaustion she had to close her eyes. When she opened them again, Constance was still there, staring at her intently.

She ran her fingers along Poppy's brow. "I'm glad I found you. I was so worried he was about to make a terrible mistake."

She wanted to ask what that meant, but the thickness of the laudanum made her too drowsy, and the thought drifted away as lazily as it had come.

Constance patted her head. "I will leave you to your rest, my poor invalid. Good night."

As she drifted off to sleep, Poppy found herself piqued at the woman whose future life she was borrowing for the night—the phantom duchess who would someday sleep in this bed and bathe in the shiny copper tub.

No doubt, she would be a fine lady of breeding and accomplishment. The sort of lady who did not engage in trade and whose fingernails were never lined with dirt.

Poppy had never been such a lady and never regretted that she wasn't. She *liked* the feeling of dirt beneath her fingers.

But now she perceived that such a lady might have one advantage over an ill-tempered gardener who fell off her horse.

That lady would be permitted to luxuriate in the Duke of Westmead's arms whenever she bloody well wanted.

ARCHER SAT VERY STILL AS HE LISTENED TO THE FAINT MURMUR OF his sister attending to Miss Cavendish across the hall.

This feeling.

This was the reason why he did not dance.

Why he confined his intimacies to those that could be bought.

Why he had not slept with a woman—*kissed* a woman—since he was last in this house. A man of one and twenty so lost to grief he could not rouse himself from bed or meet his responsibilities. A man who had fallen, for a time, completely and utterly apart.

He stood and poured himself another brandy. To stew in the past was the surest, fleetest path to ruin. A decade's forward, plodding march had taught him that.

There would be no further dallying with Miss Cavendish. No more twilight rides or dancing lessons or intimate conversations.

For her sake, yes. But most especially, for his.

He rose. He needed a distraction. He joined Constance for an informal supper in the library, drawing it out by teaching her five-card loo, allowing her to smoke a cigar, and, as a final act of desperation, looking at her sleeping arrangements for the ball.

When she wandered up to bed, he turned to work. He read his way through two investment proposals, responding with detailed notes and questions even though it was clear that neither venture offered adequate return on capital.

Somehow, there were hours still to fill before dawn. He paced his study, conscious he was stalking like some kind of brooding panther. He recalled that Constance had found a number of old boxes in the renovation and saved them for inspection in case they had pertinence to estate business.

He retrieved them from a cupboard. Nothing like mildewed accounts of historic wool prices to clear a roiling mind.

He took a knife and pried the first crate open, wincing at the mess inside. Ledgers were piled on mismatched stacks of correspondence, stuffed with faded bits of paper and damp-spotted bills of sale. He rolled up his sleeves and plunged in with a grim kind of satisfaction. Sorting papers into tidy stacks: one of his life's finest pleasures.

There was little worth recovering, save for a lumpy, threadbare bag. He pulled the contents from inside: two square frames that felt like—

Miniatures.

Two portraits. A dark-haired woman with golden eyes. A smiling boy with white-blond hair.

Christ.

The old black feeling soared around him, as suffocating as an underwater current.

He shoved the paintings back in the bag and the bag back in the box and staggered backward until his shoulders met the solid door behind him.

He leaned his head against the wood and tried to breathe.

"Fuck," he whispered.

It rose in his throat. It climbed up around his ears, roaring in his blood, making his skin so hot he wanted to rip off his shirt.

It had been a mistake to come back here. He longed for the low gray maze of London. For his empty, sterile house. For Elena. For the searing crack of leather on his spine. The engulfment by numbness that would follow.

He straightened up. There were other ways for a man to forget. Namely, brandy. And he was going to dose himself with it until he could no longer recall his own name.

"No!" someone cried out, faintly.

"Yes," he muttered back, reaching for the decanter.

But the sound was not purely in his head. He heard it again.

He opened the door and listened.

Another cry, from across the hall.

The sound half returned him to the living world.

Foggy, he crossed the corridor and knocked softly on the door. The distressed murmuring did not cease—it was harsh and tinged with fear. He cracked open the door, calling her name quietly. He was answered with a moan.

He picked up a lamp and peered inside. "Miss Cavendish?"

From the dying light of her fire, he could see she was tangled in the sheets of the bed, asleep but tossing back and forth.

"Miss Cavendish?"

Her forehead was dewy with a thin sheen of perspiration.

He moved close enough to put a hand to her damp hair. "Miss Cavendish?"

She only whimpered.

"Poppy," he said louder. "Wake up."

"No," she muttered, her voice nearly unintelligible with what sounded like anguish, or fear, or both.

He shook her gently, but she only struggled more violently with the nightmare, fighting with the air itself. He placed both of his hands more firmly on her shoulders, repeating her name until her eyes finally floated open. She flinched at the sight of him.

"No!" she cried again, putting her hands up protectively before her face.

"Cavendish. You're safe. You're at Westhaven. You were having a nightmare."

She started and covered her mouth with both hands, only half-awake.

"It's all right. I'll leave you now. Go back to sleep." He backed away, but another sound escaped from her, guttural and haunting.

Something sharp and urgent in him—the part that wanted to be dulled with brandy, gin, Elena—fell away at the sound.

He moved to the side of the bed and knelt, pulling her into his arms, and at the feel of her small frame, another scaffold within his ribs collapsed and he could not help but climb beside her and pull her to his chest and murmur nonsense, rub slow circles on her back. The motion came to him from the past, from the nights when he would comfort a small boy who couldn't sleep. The memory intensified the roaring in his ears, but he ignored it.

He held her like that until she finally stopped shaking. After some time he heard her breath return to normal. He was fairly sure she had drifted off in his arms, but he would wait until he was certain his movements wouldn't rouse her before leaving. He shut his eyes for just a moment, focusing on the steady pulse and warmth of her. The frantic edge that had constricted his own throat was less persistent with her body in his arms—reduced to a twinge. Almost bearable.

When he opened his eyes again, dawn had crept in through the window. He had fallen asleep beside her.

And something even more remarkable.

He'd grown calm.

He carefully slipped out of her bed and back across the hall.

In his study, the box was where he'd left it. It seemed less menacing in the pale morning sunlight. Not a relic of his father. Just a crate.

He would move it to the hall to be disposed of.

But perhaps first … Perhaps he should—

He took a gulp of breath and plunged his hand back in and found the threadbare bag. He took it to the seat beside the window and forced himself to withdraw the contents once again. Forced himself to look at them. To *really* look at them.

An hour passed as he sat, alone, and beheld the faces of his wife and child.

And for the first time in thirteen years, he wept.

CHAPTER 9

*B*loody laudanum.

Poppy awoke to bleary eyes, aching temples, and a rainy morning that had practically turned to afternoon.

All night she had tossed with fretful, opiated dreams laced with the old visions that had plagued her childhood. Her mother's bedside as the body in it grew cold. Her nurse struggling with a man in the shadows of the hayloft as Poppy hid, too frightened to make a sound.

Nightmares of her mother's death had chased her all her life, but she had not dreamed of the attack on Bernadette in years. At the thought of it, she shivered. Some memories were best left unexamined.

Yet plaited through those dreadful apparitions was also the memory of Archer whispering soothing words. Had he really come to her in the night, forcing the dreams back down into the depths? Or had he, too, been a figment of her restless mind?

She dressed in a drab gray gown that fit her mood and limped to the library, hoping to find a quiet corner where she could finish drawing out her plans for the parterre near the terrace doors.

Instead, she found a merry party chattering over cakes and

champagne. Two ladies and two gentlemen, elegantly dressed as though for traveling, bent their heads around Constance, laughing with the air of old friends.

"You're awake!" Constance said. "How is your ankle? I've been fretting over you all morning, but Archer forbade me from interrupting your sleep."

"I'm much recovered, thank you. I didn't mean to intrude."

"Nonsense, you must meet my friends." Beckoning Poppy toward their midst, Constance introduced her around the circle, drawing her first to a pretty brunette in a bright blue gown. "This is Miss Bastian, of the Philadelphia Bastians. Her parents sent her to England to acquire our refined ways, so imagine what they would say if they knew she'd been adopted by the likes of *moi*."

"*Quelle horreur*," the shorter of the gentlemen—a pear-shaped fellow in a primrose-colored frock coat embroidered with fanciful turquoise birds—said with an exaggerated shudder.

"And might I present Mr. Desmond Flannery," Constance said, tapping him fondly with her fan. "Editor of the *London Peculiar*, the most scandalous gazette in London and the only one worth reading."

"Charmed," the man said. "Constance tells us that you are creating a ballroom forest out of nothing but tinsel and a few strands of moss. My readers will be aground."

"And this," Constance said, moving her along to a woman with shimmering pale hair identical to her own, "is my dear cousin Lady Rosecroft." Her tone lost its warmth as she turned to the final guest, a strikingly golden young man who was nearly as pretty as Constance herself. "And Lady Rosecroft's cousin by marriage. The Earl of Apthorp."

The earl inclined his head gracefully and looked upon Poppy with smiling, amber eyes. "Lady Constance has spoken of your talents with nothing short of reverence, Miss Cavendish. It's a privilege."

Constance rolled her eyes. "Oh, Apthorp. Do stop trying to be devastating."

"What in heaven's name have I done to deserve this assemblage?" Archer asked, stepping into the room from the terrace doors.

Even on this gray day, looking so drawn and subdued about the eyes, he was handsome. His coat was damp from his walking outside in the drizzle, his lustrous hair still shiny with raindrops.

Amidst the sudden commotion of pleasantries, Poppy felt his gaze land only on her. It was just a moment, a mere flicker of an eye, but it filled her with a jolt of certainty: he *had* been in her bed last night. He had held her until she drifted back to sleep.

Her spine went rigid.

It was unthinkable.

Entering ladies' bedchambers unbidden was exactly the kind of liberty for which his late father had been infamous. She should by all rights be affronted.

Terrified of him.

She should not trust that his intentions had been kind or merciful.

And yet.

She was oddly touched.

He greeted each of the guests, lingering for a moment, she noticed, over Constance's introduction to Miss Bastian. When the conversation drifted back to the topic of the ball, he asked in a low voice: "How are we today, Miss Cavendish?"

We, he said. *How are we?*

The question was so harmless that anyone overhearing it would naturally assume he was inquiring on the state of her ankle, or her disposition, or her progress in the ballroom. Yet unspoken in his tone was every intimate thing that had passed between them the night before.

"Much improved, Your Grace," she answered softly. It was just a whisper of a bland response. But she hoped he understood that it meant *I remember.*

He didn't respond, and when she glanced at him, his eyes were no longer on her, and he had lost all color. She followed the line of his gaze to the corridor, where a little boy with a shock of white hair was toddling toward the adults inside, his shaky steps trailed by a nurse.

The boy staggered into the room with a joyous gurgle. Poppy could not but laugh at the sight of him. He was perhaps the most adorable creature she had ever seen.

Constance jumped to her feet, delighted. "Georgie!" she cried. "Look who is walking on his own two clever feet! Come here, you sly fellow!" She crouched down to hug the child, who smiled shyly and darted away to bury his face in Lady Rosecroft's dress.

"Don't hide from Lady Constance, darling," his mother said. "She isn't *entirely* wicked."

The boy peeked out, weighing the likelihood of the threat. His eyes fell on Poppy. She gave him a little wave. He beamed up at her before hiding his face once again in his mother's skirts.

Constance shot an adoring glance at her brother, as if to say, *Isn't he wonderful?* But Westmead had stood and turned to leave the room.

Constance crossed her arms. "Are you withdrawing so soon, Your Grace?"

"Excuse me," he said blandly. "I am late to meet with my solicitor."

His sister fixed him in an uncharacteristically icy gaze. "Surely your solicitor can spare you for an hour while you become reacquainted with your godson. 'Tis been a year since you last saw him." She brightened her voice and turned to Georgie. "Perhaps an adventure to the attic is in order. There's nothing like a romp through the attic on a rainy day."

The boy peered up at his godfather, hopeful.

"Not today, I'm afraid," Westmead muttered, already halfway out the door.

Lady Hilary and Constance exchanged a weighted look.

"Well, *I* should like to play with Georgie Boy," Constance pronounced, standing and taking the boy's hand. "Lead the way, good soldier."

The group dispersed, with Lady Hilary following Constance and the men retiring to dress before dinner. Only Miss Bastian lingered.

"Wasn't that an odd exchange?" she murmured.

"It was, rather," Poppy agreed—relieved that the discomfort in the air had not been her imagination.

Miss Bastian leaned in and dropped her voice. "I'm told Westmead acts very strangely around the boy—the whole family is disturbed by it. Mr. Flannery believes it's because he is in love with Lady Rosecroft and can't bear the idea that he lost her to another man." She giggled into her hand.

Poppy felt an instant stabbing of dislike, and not just because the idea of Westmead in love made her irritable.

"One finds there is often little truth to gossip," she said.

Miss Bastian gave her a coy smile.

"You can always count on Mr. Flannery to concoct the most scandalous explanation to any mystery—it is, after all, his profession. But every so often he is right about something."

Archer was drenched, bone-chilled, and exhausted.

When the rain stopped, he had ridden out with the land agent to tour improvements on the estate. Wiltshire not being known for the constancy of its weather, they had promptly been caught in a storm. When it passed, he'd lingered on the misty downs until he was certain he'd miss supper, and the excruciating task of making idle conversation with his sister and cousin while their eyes silently reproached him for the scene that had passed in the library.

He knew that Hilary could perceive his aversion to her son. His own godson. But by God, he had not yet seen the boy when he agreed to stand at his christening.

When he did, his hands had shaken through the baptism. It had taken him days to recover.

It was the hair. That otherworldly de Galascon hair—a relic from his mother's ancient Viking forebears that still graced each generation, the way other families were prone to myopia, or twins. Hair as startling as freshly poured cream in childhood that faded to a silvery blond with age. Given the chance.

The valet—a man employed at the insistence of his sister and who mostly served to annoy him—was hovering in his bedchamber, fussing with a pile of cravats.

"Would you like a tray sent up from the kitchen, Your Grace?" the man asked.

"No, thank you, Winston." He had no appetite.

"Shall I help you out of your wet—"

"No. I have no need of anything further. Good night." The man bowed and withdrew.

Archer waited until he heard the door shut before he peeled off his icy clothes. He did not keep a valet in London. He did not allow servants to see his naked flesh. The marks along his back and shoulders were not easily explained, and he had no wish to make himself the subject of gossip.

Gossip had been the province of his father.

He inspected himself in the looking glass. His otherwise hale body still bore the marks of the years when he had spent most nights on Charlotte Street. He rubbed one silver trail of raised skin along his shoulder. He had been so careless at the start, forbidding Elena to stop until he bled. There had been little pleasure in it then—only pain he craved like opium, for it pushed the sickly fog back down into his gut.

Exorcised the memory of how he'd failed them.

Allowed him to bloody well get on with the endless miserable business of being still, interminably, alive.

The joy, the rapture—that had come later. The more he shaped himself into a man who would not fail again, the more vital the release became. He no longer craved the pain itself so much as the abandonment, the feeling of her power over him, the floor beneath his fingers. What had begun as penance had become a sacrament. He was grateful for it. It had saved him. It had taught him who he was.

But he still regretted the scars.

Outside the haven of Charlotte Street, where tastes such as his were understood, the scars marked him as the sordid son of a sordid father. The latest depraved Westmead in the long and brutish line of them, their taste for violence passed down with the seed.

That he did not *hurt* anyone would not excuse his tastes in the eyes of those who would judge him. It would only make him doubly damned: weak, in addition to debased.

He tried to imagine Miss Bastian taking in the sight of him on her wedding night. She'd run out screaming, no doubt. Well, easy enough to perform the act clothed. And no need to repeat it once he was sure of conception.

Assuming, of course, that he was still able to muster the enthusiasm to perform the act at all. He'd sealed off that part of himself so many years ago that, until he'd found himself kissing Poppy Cavendish, he'd forgotten what it felt like to even want it.

How he had studied making love from books and relished mapping what he'd learned onto the woman who met him in the woods. It had not taken long to abandon the theories in favor of instinct, pleasure. He had loved the primal feeling of being the one to guide her, to leave her shaking and well cared for. It had meant something fierce to him.

This morning, seeing Georgie had been all the reminder he

needed that he didn't want to feel anything that fiercely ever again.

He *did not want it.*

It was the house. It made him behave like the fool he'd been when he had still lived within these walls.

Like he did not know that pleasure was but half of a continuum on which the other end was pain.

Like he did not know what it was to lose what was most precious.

He returned the key to its place around his neck.

He dressed and crept down the hall to his study.

He'd received a fat sheaf of documents from the counting-house in London, full of reports to read and decisions to be made. With any luck it would occupy him until he fell asleep.

A light burned beneath the door.

POPPY WAS IN HIDING.

It was absurd, but necessary.

The alternative was entrapment by a diminutive girl and her maniacal obsession with amusement.

Poppy had lost nearly an entire day dodging the demands of Constance's house party, limping from room to room with her sketchbook, evading increasingly pointed invitations to join the group in whist and singing and theatricals.

Out of desperation she had begged off supper, pleading soreness in her ankle, and tiptoed down the hall to the duke's deserted study, hoping he would not mind her using his spare table in the service of finishing her work in the only part of the house to which the guests and the servants seemed too afraid to venture.

It was peaceful in this room—darkly paneled and orderly and redolent of woodsmoke and the faint spice of dried tobacco. The walls were lined with books. She spread her scrolls and chalks out

on the table and set to work on her diagrams, growing calmer
with each hour that passed free from interruption. She looked up
only when she noticed it had grown too dim to see, and ducked
into the hall to find a candle with which to light the lamps.

Once the room was adequately lit, she lingered by the book-
shelves, stretching out her back. She ran her fingers over the titles,
most in Latin. The leather-bound books were free from dust and
well cared for but had the distinct, musty smell of volumes long
unread. Classics no doubt left over from Westmead's days at
university. She spotted a few books of poetry in English and
tomes on geometry and physics. She stopped upon an old edition
of *Systema Naturae*—Mr. Linnaeus's book, which she had read at
least half a dozen times. Could the duke be harboring a secret
interest in botany? An interest in classification would suit him,
judging by the intricate piles he was wont to leave so carefully
sorted on his desk. She reached to pull the book from the shelf,
and a slim, clothbound volume tucked beside it slid out instead.
The embossing on the cover was in French. Curious, she opened
it and saw an inscription on the blank first page.

Archer—

*I hope you will enjoy this as much as I have. I cannot look at plates X
and XXII without imagining your return. I hope when you turn these
pages, you think of me, as I lie awake and think of you.*

Always,

B

She flushed at the intimacy of the words.

They had to have been written by a lover.

She really should not read any further. It was rude enough to
invade Westmead's private study without his permission, ruder
still to touch his books, to read what had clearly been meant only
for his eyes.

She darted a glance over her shoulder to ensure she was alone
before reading the inscription again.

She ran her finger along the script. There was no date. The ink was fading.

God forgive her, but she *simply had* to know what was on plates X and XXII.

Slowly she turned the brittle, yellowed pages. It was a book of illustrations.

The first page sent a rush through her whole body. A woman lay on a blanket in a field, half-undressed, as a man stood, fully clothed, observing her. The woman's breasts were freed from her gown and her fingers clutched one nipple as her other hand disappeared beneath the hemline of her skirts, which were rucked up around her thighs. She was gazing at the man who watched her, her expression one of pleasure.

Oh.

She was not wholly unfamiliar with the activity the woman undertook, nor the pleasures of exploring one's own anatomy. But she had never heard of such activities acknowledged in the open, no less pictured in a book. Certainly she had not imagined the act might be performed for a gentleman's enjoyment. For, if her understanding of anatomy was correct, the pronounced bulge in the gentleman's breeches indicated he was as excited by the lady's explorations as she was.

She flushed deeper at the thought of it.

At the thought of it, and at the thought of Westmead being aware of such a thing.

Could it be that the stern duke, the man who had kissed her with such a guilty mix of longing and reluctance, had once been a younger man who enjoyed this licentious, private gift from a lover? She found it difficult to imagine him that way.

Lovely, rather. But so unlikely.

She quickly turned the pages to find the plates in the inscription. The images grew stranger as she went, depicting positions and assemblages she had not read about in novels and never thought to contemplate when pondering the mysteries of copulation. Plate X showed a woman with her wrists bound behind her as a man pressed his lips to her exposed breasts and his knee between her open legs. Plate XXII showed a woman kneeling before her lover, her lips locked around his very large, excitable male appendage as his hands tugged at her hair.

Oh my.

She quickly paged through to the end of the book, not wanting to be discovered spying on this so very personal relic that she definitely should not be reading and certainly should not be reading while imagining *him* reading it, yet not able to deprive herself of any additional revelations it might offer. She thought back to the first plate, the dreamy woman with her hand between her legs, and felt a pang of longing so sharp it startled her.

What is becoming of you? Thoughts such as these might be entertained discreetly in a lady's bedchamber late at night when no one was the wiser, but not in the study of said lady's host, on whom she was blatantly, unforgivably spying. She must really put this book away.

She flipped to the end, but the last page stopped her. Two plates, side by side, showed the man from the earlier pages without his haughty posture.

In the first he was on his hands and knees, his back to the lady, completely nude. Behind him the woman held her hand aloft, as though she meant to strike him. His buttocks were marked with the imprints of her hand, and his arousal made clear the assault was one he welcomed.

The second showed him with his wrists bound to the posts of a bed, his eyes masked by a blindfold. The woman, wearing stays and hose, was riding him, her powerful plump thighs holding him in place, her head thrown back in relish.

Poppy shut the book, more violently than she ought as it was fraying at the seam, then carefully returned it to its hiding place. She walked stiff-legged back to the table and the hard-backed wooden chair and her innocent sketches of flowers and stared directly into space.

What were those final images?

Was that *done*, truly?

The tableau was so different from any clue gleaned in her meager and unpleasant experience with courtship. Her years of evading unwanted leers in the market, ducking away from Tom's advances, fearing men who were capable of violence, had left her predisposed to think that men held all the power when it came to amorous matters. She'd never thought to contemplate that the roles might be reversed. That a lady might be the one to make demands. That a man might *want* it so.

Might delight in it.

How intriguing. Her stomach thrummed with a restless, churning feeling at the thought. She was half-inclined to quickly sketch those last two plates and tuck them in her ledger so that she could revisit them privately, at length. Along, perhaps, with plates X and XXII.

Instead, she forced her eyes to return to the diagram, to the wreaths that must be spun from branches and tied just so with twine. To the work that was more real and urgent than the surging feeling in her belly.

It was growing late. There would be time to consider why those prints had made her hands shake, made her breath catch in her throat. For now, she must return to work.

She picked up her chalk.

The door opened, rustling the papers on the table.

She turned around to find Westmead staring at her.

POPPY SAT AT A ROUND TABLE IN THE CORNER, SURROUNDED BY piles of drawings. She still wore her gardening clothes, and her eyes were heavy lidded. She looked intense and flushed and disheveled.

Beautiful.

No. He must stop doing that. Must chasten his reactions to her. *Hardworking. She looks tired from her labors.*

He cleared his throat. "Poppy. You're still awake."

She looked up at him with a guilty expression. "Yes. And it seems I have invaded your study—I'm so sorry. The others were playing whist in the library and I thought to finish my work in the quiet. I'm just finishing—I'll leave you."

"Never mind. Stay. Please. Show me what it is you're sketching."

She hesitated. He felt her eyes linger on his face, like she was trying to discern something about him. No doubt, her downcast expression had something to do with his invasion of her bedchamber the previous evening. He needed to address that. No woman who'd been raised in Grove Vale would be ignorant of the stories about his father. He could not have her think that he expected similar liberties of her. He had taken far too many as it was.

He stepped closer to speak discreetly and saw that she had been drawing diagrams. Each page began with a sketch of a finished design—a garland of white lilies to hang from the ceiling, a wreath of greenery to be woven through trellises—followed by steps indicating how flowers should be attached to threads and wires.

They were ingenious.

"These are for the kitchen maids?"

"Yes. There are so many designs that I won't be able to demonstrate each one myself."

Her voice was tired but satisfied—the tone of someone who took pleasure in her work.

"You're looking forward to it," he observed.

"I am. I have felt unduly idle these past days, sketching and planning in this grand house. I rather miss the feel of leaves beneath my fingers."

He smiled at this, remembering the day he had found her in

her greenhouse, her arms wrapped around a plant. He liked how she did not shy from the vitality of her body—used it to cut branches and rake fields and enjoy the sun on her back as she worked the earth. It was so different from his own work—the gray light of the counting-house, with its ever-present swish of papers and scratch of quills. All at once he wished for a different kind of labor. A physical kind, something vigorous, into which he could pour the restless, pensive memories that had left him nearly sleepless since he'd arrived from London.

"I find I am envious of your employment," he said. "Perhaps the weeks would pass faster if I took up the floral arts."

She turned her full attention to him.

"You grow restless, away from London?"

"Immeasurably."

She cocked her head to the side. "You long for your … work … there?"

"I do. You'd be pressed to find a peer who wouldn't jeer at me for keeping my own counting-house, and yet I cannot think of a single place I'd rather spend an hour."

She nodded thoughtfully. "I often find my mind is most at peace when I am at my most frightfully busy."

He threw back his head with recognition, grateful she understood.

"Indeed. This is the first time I've been away in months, and the first time at this estate in thirteen years. You, of all people, must understand that I am unraveling."

"Thirteen years," she marveled. "How have you managed to run an estate without setting foot on it for thirteen years?"

He clucked his tongue. "Do I need to repeat for you my sister's lesson on stewards?"

She gave him a sly smile. "Well, Your Grace, Maxwell's men will be out foraging in the parklands for the next few days. If you are lacking in employment, perhaps he could be persuaded to take on an extra man."

He chuckled. "I suppose you would enjoy that, Cavendish. The duke reduced to doing Maxwell's bidding once again."

"Perhaps I would." She smiled. "Perhaps it is *your* turn to be embarrassed." She wiped her hands on a cloth and began to pile up her papers.

Embarrassed. That word again. She said it lightly, but he hated the idea he had caused her distress. And he still had not apologized.

"Poppy, last night—I hope I didn't alarm you. I apologize for intruding. I would not normally disturb a lady's privacy, and I hope I gave no offense. I was concerned. You seemed quite distressed."

Her face flickered. "It was only a nightmare," she said finally. "I shan't disturb you again."

"I was not disturbed," he said quickly.

She studied his face. "When I awoke this morning, I wondered if I had dreamt you."

"No," he said, drinking in her languid eyes.

She reached up and touched his face above his cheekbone. "No," she agreed. "Here you are. Real indeed."

Damn him, but he caught her hand and dragged it down to his lips and placed a kiss inside her palm.

Her mouth parted. Perhaps in shock. Perhaps in something closer to the feeling surging behind his sternum, overriding his judgment, his propriety, his will to be the kind of person he had spent a decade refashioning himself into.

"Forgive me. I am not myself tonight," he forced himself to say, releasing her. He looked into her green eyes and told her the truth of it: "You should leave me."

He meant it.

And yet.

And yet.

He hoped she wouldn't listen.

CHAPTER 10

*H*is eyes on hers were a warning.

A warning that he was in search of some unnameable thing. That he was looking for something—some kind of solace—and if she stayed in this room, she would be what he found.

That, Poppy knew, was dangerous.

She had seen his book. There was no illusion that what he wanted would be innocent.

It would be, God help her, exactly what she wanted.

Leave him? She met his eyes and slowly shook her head. A minute gesture. A tiny rotation of the neck, left, then right.

And then, before she could lose her nerve or think too much about the thousand reasons she should not do what she wanted, she raised her mouth and brushed his lower lip with hers.

That was all it took.

In an instant he was lifting her onto the table, his forearm pushing her drawings to the floor, his mouth ragged on her jaw, her lips, her eyelashes. His kiss was not a feint or a flirt, but the confession of a body that was ravenous, starved, for another's. For a moment she was limp in his arms, stunned at the sudden revelation of how badly he wanted her. Tentatively, she put a hand on the nape of his neck, drawing him closer. Beneath her fingers, his onslaught stilled. He shuddered at her touch.

She had done that, she marveled. *She.* Her power to provoke such a reaction emboldened her. She nipped at his lip and, when he responded with his tongue, gave him her own. The growl he made in his throat nearly undid her.

"I have wanted to touch you," she whispered, "for quite some time. I wonder if I might ..." She dragged her hand down the front of his chest, letting her fingers graze the soft fabric of his shirt.

A corner of his mouth quirked up, and he leaned back to give her more of him. "By all means."

She brushed her hand down farther, over his hips and thighs, and in answer he gripped her buttocks and drew her hips against his body, where a throbbing hardness beat intently with a pulse that matched the flame burning low, so low, in her stomach.

She had never before touched a man in such a way, and the botanist in her was suddenly at full attention, rapt with the project of matching the contours of his sex to the drawings she had seen in books. Her fingers moved to feel him, grazing his erection through his breeches until he gasped.

She withdrew her hand. "That hurts?" she asked.

"No, Cavendish," he said wryly, a sheen of pleasure cast about his eyes.

Oh.

For a moment they both paused, laughing. He gripped her thighs and wrapped her legs around his waist and pulled her with him to the sofa. She felt him pulsing against her as his hands slipped inside her bodice.

He paused, his eyes a question. "Stop me if I—"

She didn't want to stop him. She did not want caution. She wanted to be consumed.

She placed her hands on his over her aching breasts, urging him onward, hoping he could sense what was inside of her, that he would know how badly she wanted this, how little she cared for proprieties. That she trusted he would know just what to do, because she didn't, and she wanted to.

"I want to feel you," she whispered. "Everywhere."

She felt him throw off hesitation like a cloak. He buried his face in her hair and breathed her in, molding her breasts out of her stays until the nipples rose above the sober gray ribbon of her neckline. They were hard and pink in the firelight, and the sight of them, feverish in his large hands, puckering for his attentions, made her feel like a rod of lightning.

She lost all thoughts of science. She instinctively pressed herself against him until the juncture of her thighs came flush with his erection. The pressure of it against her own sex was a revelation, and she gasped and moved closer, wanting to feel the shock of it again, wanting to feel the parts of him that were hard and rough against the parts of her that were soft and pliant. "Please," she whispered mindlessly, not quite sure what she was asking for.

His hand found its way beneath her gown and petticoats, until it rested on her chemise, his fingers grazing her through the linen. The feel of his hand against the juncture of her body was nearly shattering. She rocked against him, abandoning herself to the lovely pressure of his palm.

"I want to look at you," he murmured in her ear.

"Yes," she whispered. She wanted to be seen.

He grabbed fistfuls of her skirts and bunched them around her waist until she was exposed, the dark heart between her thighs bare to him. He spread her legs and sighed.

"Fuck," he breathed in softly. A declaration that should not have melted her. But did.

His gaze fell back upon her face. "So beautiful," he murmured. And indeed, she felt beautiful. Desirable and lush, an orchid blooming for the sun. Like the lady in the plate, aroused and queenly in the warmth of her lover's gaze.

He slowly stroked along her thigh, brushing his fingers up, up until they dipped inside her. She gasped. His hand lingered just below the swollen nubbin at her center, teasing it until he had her shaking. She wanted more—to be full of him. She pressed herself up against his thighs, searching for the pressure of his cock.

"Yes, move against me," he moaned, encouraging her with his own movements to follow her instincts. She opened her thighs to clench him as his hands brought wave after wave of sensation, turning her into something slick and molten and thrumming. She arched her back as the pleasures began to rise into something combustible.

But at the critical moment he lifted himself off her and pinned her hands above her head. "Not yet, Cavendish. First I want to taste you." Before she could think to be shocked, he shifted so that his mouth was at the edge of her thighs. "May I?"

His breath on her flesh dissolved anything but the desire for more of it. "Please."

He parted her, running his hand along her sex with reverence, his eyes dark with desire. Rapt, he traced the wetness there with his tongue. And then his mouth was on her fully, urging her to be wanton, to breathe him in, to use him to take what her body wanted.

The room went white. This man must have indeed spent a great deal of time studying that book.

She writhed against his lips. He took his mouth away for a searing instant and looked into her eyes. "Come for me, Poppy," he whispered. "I want to feel you."

His mouth closed around her bud and his tongue spread softly, softly, and with a mind-shattering clench, sucked right where she pulsed most desperately. She exploded, a pang spreading into a wave and cresting higher and higher until she was underwater, gasping. She buried her face into the sofa and allowed herself to moan with pleasure, heedless of passing ears, bucking against his face with each tremor, clutching at his hair. He encouraged her cries with his mouth, nuzzling gently, helping her return to herself as the waves slowed and she came, finally, apart.

Slowly, she opened her eyes. He was sultry and beautiful, his glossy hair dark and shimmering in the firelight, his eyes drinking her in from beneath his lashes. She was transfixed by him, his male beauty, his sorcery over her body. She pulled him toward her to kiss him and could taste the salt of her desire on his lips.

The luxury of holding him, with his heat and linen crispness and that way he had of trembling when she touched his skin, made her feel rich.

Curiosities she'd pondered in the dark for years flooded her head, and she scarcely knew which parts of him she wanted to linger over first. She ran her hands down his broad chest and back over the fine snowy fabric of his shirt. He was so much larger than her, and yet, in her arms, she sensed a shyness—he held himself back like he thought he might crush her. Tentatively she ran her hands over the place where the long length of his shaft announced itself. Beneath his shirt the velvet tip of it had pushed out above the waistline of his breeches, where it strained against the trail of hair at his belly. At its tip, a tear. All at once she was wild again, her hands searching for the placket to unleash him. His cock jumped at her touch. She ran her hands around it, enjoyed his gasp in response, then dragged her fingers up over his flat belly and into the hair beneath his shirt. Her hands grazed something cold.

"What's this?" she asked, finding a rather intricately wrought iron key on a leather cord beneath his shirt. She lifted up the linen farther to investigate.

His hand clamped down over hers so quickly it startled the breath from her. "No."

She dropped the key and placed her hands back on his hips, but he jerked away from her.

"Stop," he ordered. His voice had lost the husky tone of arousal. It was ice.

He moved out of reach. A tendon in his neck twitched.

She drew back, alarmed. She had never been intimate with a man in this way. There had been only the one half-permitted, oft-regretted fumbling moment in the woods with Tom. This had all happened so suddenly, a blinding burst of wanting falling upon her like drunkenness or a fit of madness. Had she been too forward? Done something to cause him offense?

"Is something wrong?" she asked.

Archer turned away from her and adjusted his clothing in silence.

She sat up. "Archer?"

He shook his head, not looking at her.

A cold wave of embarrassment was wrapping around her, but she tried again. "I'm sorry," she said to his back. "I meant no harm. I hoped to please you, as you did me."

He turned back to her, fully dressed now, the key tucked back beneath his shirt.

"You should return to your room," he said.

She stared at him. "Why?"

"Because," he drew out slowly, "I am not the kind of man with whom there is a future for you."

Her blood ran cold.

Suddenly she could see herself the way he saw her. Her breasts pushed up above the bodice of her tired, shabby dress. Her skirts bunched around her waist. Her legs open and slicked with what she'd let him do to her.

Not a goddess.

Just a spinster who forgot herself.

Hot shame came rising through her bones, and she moved urgently to cover herself, to protect her body from his eyes.

But there was no need.

He turned his back on her again and left the room.

CHAPTER 11

*P*oppy sat at the head of the long table as Maxwell's crew brought in another dozen sacks of foliage clipped from the grounds. It was a honey-gold Wiltshire morning, the mists burning off in amber rays as carts loaded with lilac, Madonna lily, larkspur, and spirea were rolled into the kitchen yard.

Inside her workroom the maids gossiped as they sewed. The room smelled of the outdoors. No one who entered it could help but be charmed by the odd creations that were beginning to take shape here. There were long, green strands of ivy and leafy willow fronds woven around sticks and wire to form dramatic bowers that would rise from urns like treetops. Thorny, fragrant bags of heather, lavender, and gorse were being tamed under nimble fingers into vibrant orbs, to be suspended in the air around glass globes lit with wax candles. Tufts of downy white bedstraw and meadowsweet were being sewn with thread into long, delicate garlands, single strands of which would hang at various lengths across the expanse of the atrium like an ethereal rainstorm of flowers, frozen in midair.

For days, Poppy had poured her anger into the making of

these dreamlike shapes. She infused it into the thorns and brambles she whittled away from stalks, into the blossoms and leaves she bent to her will until they became something grander and more unsettling than nature. Not the romantic gossamer vision of her early sketches, but something more dramatic and occult.

She did not allow her mind to drift to the man, ever awake and restless, who left his fire burning through the night in the next room. She knew he did not sleep. When she retired at the end of her exhausting days, long after midnight, his room still flickered with lamplight and she heard him pacing. When she awoke, she would often see him already up and working with Maxwell's crew, hauling branches in the coarse linen of a laborer. Often she heard him leave the house in the middle of the night, slipping out onto the terrace and into the dark woods on foot. Where he went, she did not know.

The few times she had seen him in passing, he had been all polite solicitude. *How is your ankle recovering, Miss Cavendish? Constance tells me your designs are a thing of beauty, Miss Cavendish.* As though they were distant acquaintances passing unexpectedly in a crowd. There was no acknowledgment of that last fevered hour they had spent alone together in his study. How he had called her to the wild and left her there, shaking and alone.

At supper she watched him leaning toward the empty conversation of Miss Bastian. Politely following along with her accounts of Parisian modiste shops and fashionable personages she had once seen in the crowd at the theater. Even Constance could not hide her boredom, yet Westmead nodded attentively, kindly, until Poppy could barely swallow her soup.

Not the kind of man with whom there is a future for you. Her blood grew thick as venom at the words. When she allowed herself to recall them, she felt like the Furies of Greek myth, those godlike women animated purely by their lust for vengeance.

Her anger was overblown, she told herself. His words, after all, were not *inaccurate*. And yet it was the deployment of them just precisely then, while her body was still vulnerable, while her heart was still prized open from her chest. The precise humiliation he had inflected and the flash of shame that had pierced his eyes exactly as he did so left her no doubt he had done it intentionally. He had coarsened what had awoken between them and made it tawdry. He had taken down her defenses and punished her for letting him.

A fluttering among the girls broke her concentration. She looked up from the wreath she was weaving to find Tom Raridan standing in the doorway.

"Poppy," he said. "A word?"

Tom had always had a habit of appearing without notice. Since her girlhood she would look up to find him suddenly in her midst, as though he had traveled through the ether and landed in the Bantham Park stable yard, or in the middle of a clearing where she'd been picking bluebells. It had never bothered her in childhood, but it was becoming unnerving, how he trailed her.

Ignoring the staring maids, she beckoned him to follow her outside to the kitchen yard.

"How did you get in here?" she whispered.

He gave her a roguish smile. "Strolled in through the service door."

"You are bold to come here after the things you said to Westmead about me. I can't imagine what you were intending, but I will not soon forget it. You should leave."

He made a great show of not understanding. "You have no cause to be cross-tempered. Someone needs to protect you now that there's no sensible man to keep you out of trouble."

"I'd be grateful to be spared any further attempts at protection. Why are you here?"

"I have news for you. I was at the Angler and Fin having a pint this afternoon."

She frowned at him. He knew she did not approve of his habit of spending his days at the public house. It was drink that had been the undoing of his father.

"Don't fuss. Just a pint to pass the time. Robins came in. Said he saw a couple that called themselves Hathaway at the inn at Ploverton."

Bollocks. Eliot Hathaway was her uncle's heir and Ploverton was only an hour's ride away.

"But they aren't due for days. And why would they stop there? Robins must be mistaken."

Tom came close and attempted to take her hand.

She pulled her fingers away and stepped back. It would not do to have the servants see her touching a strange man in the Westhaven kitchen yard.

His features turned harsh—for a second she thought he might grab her again. "Tom, mind the servants," she hissed under her breath.

His face returned to its usual affable composure. "It would be a shame if Mr. Hathaway were to hear whispers of your scheme. Wouldn't be surprised if the magistrate were called. You ought to marry me for your own good. I won't let anyone insult you."

"It seems to me, Tom, that the only person insulting me is you."

"I come here to warn you out of charity, and you accuse me? But then that's our Poppy," he said, his voice overloud with what she suspected was the easy amusement of the slightly sauced. "Never showed a lick of gratitude."

Any trace of solicitude he had shown her when her uncle still lived was gone. Had he ever been her friend, or had he merely been a man with expectations?

A pair of maids heading toward the icehouse glanced at them.

"Go," she said. "Someone will see you here."

With an impish expression he grabbed her hand again and placed it to his lips. She jumped away with such force that she tripped over a sack of flour, sending a fine spray of dust up around her. The maids stopped what they were doing and stared.

"Go," she whispered between clenched teeth.

ARCHER HAULED A BUNDLE OF BRANCHES INTO A SACK, A PASTIME for which he had developed quite a skill of late. It was amazing the pursuits a man could develop an affinity for when he no longer had the capacity to sleep, or eat, or think.

Abilities he had lost when he walked out of the room on Poppy Cavendish trailing a sickening string of words that would not have been out of place in the mouth of his father. *I'm not the kind of man with whom there is a future for you.*

The words were true, of course—he wasn't. But not for the reasons she would hear. She would see a duke, taking what he wanted and withdrawing his interest. Reminding her of her place.

It was behavior worthy of the benchhouse, and he knew it. He had nothing but contempt for wealthy men who treated women poorly, and even less regard for aristocratic snobbery. He had alienated half of London's drawing rooms with these qualities, earning himself the nickname "the humble Mr. Stonewell" among the swells and lordlings who spent their days at White's and never dirtied their boots with the coarse commercial dust of the City of London. The man he had been in that room in that moment with Poppy was not the man he wanted to be, and he was ashamed. He owed her an apology.

But every time he saw her, the hollow look on her face arrested him. What could he possibly say when he could hardly account for it himself? It was as though when her fingers had touched Elena's key, he had woken from a trance. The heat of her skin had been within a finger's reach of the marks on his shoulders—angry scars that would have left her shocked. Shocked enough to ask him questions that he might have been just raw enough, had her hands been on him, and his mind full of her, to answer. And so instead he'd fled the room, and made very sure she wouldn't follow.

He slung the finished bundles over his shoulders and trudged along the sloped path, and two maids carried silver buckets to the icehouse. Off to a corner a flash of movement caught his eye. A cloud of flour rose up around a woman in a muslin dress. It was Poppy. And that hulking wantwit Tom Raridan, standing over her.

Bloody bully.

He dropped his branches.

"Raridan," he shouted, striding down the hill. "What are you doing in my kitchen yard?"

Raridan paused and stepped back, his face a sour smile.

"Good afternoon, Your Grace. I was just calling on Miss Cavendish with some news from the village."

Archer leaned in, making his taller stature unmistakable. "If I see you slinking about this house like a common thief again, I'll see that you're treated like one. And trust me when I say that if I should ever see you lay another finger on Miss Cavendish, I will not bother with the magistrates."

Raridan folded himself into a mockery of a courtly bow. "Of course, Your Grace. Good day."

With a parting wink at Poppy, he sauntered out the gate.

Archer's fingers twitched to grab him by his neck and give him his due for that bit of insolence. But Poppy moved between him and Raridan's departing back.

"What exactly," she asked with deadly quiet, "was *that* intended to accomplish?"

"My apologies that you were disturbed, Miss Cavendish. Are you injured?"

He knew the words were wrong even as he said them. The phrasing was too formal, as though she were some forgettable drawing room miss he'd once spoken to of her dog, or her water-colors. As though she were Miss Bastian.

"Certainly I am not injured. A better question is, why you are interfering in my conversation?"

"Conversation?" he repeated. "I saw him nearly knock you to the ground."

"Not unlike your own introduction in my greenhouse. It seems one needn't be a gentleman to lack delicacy."

Defiance flashed in her eyes. He drew a breath, willing himself not to match her temper.

"Not a week ago he was here dissembling as though he was betrothed to you and insulting your integrity," he said, aiming for a calm tone of voice. "I thought you might wish to see him set down."

Her lips twitched into a rueful little smile. She leaned back a bit, nodding slightly to herself.

"Ah. Indeed. You have great skill for that, haven't you, Your Grace? Putting people in their rightful place."

Oh, but that stung. Landed exactly in the spot where she'd meant it.

"Since we are elucidating where things stand, Your Grace, let me be clear. You seem to be under the impression that I am a woman in frequent need of rescue. You are mistaken. I have looked after my own affairs quite competently for well nigh on a decade. I would ask that you stay out of them."

"Poppy," he said softly, "I have every confidence in your abilities. But you can't expect me to stand idly by and watch that lurking knave try to manhandle my—"

"Your *what?*" she hissed. "Your *sister's hired gardener?*" She turned in disgust and walked toward the house. At the door, she paused and turned back. "Please try to recall that my life is not a diversion to distract you from your boredom of the countryside."

She disappeared into the house.

CHAPTER 12

*J*t had taken all night, but every last garland was hung. Every last sculpture was mounted. Every last blossom was in its rightful place. The house smelled like sunshine and shadows and moonlight and earth and flowers and beeswax and grass.

She'd done it. She'd brought a forest to life inside a ballroom.

Servants crept carefully through the rooms with brooms and ladders, sweeping up fallen leaves and petals and positioning candles inside crystal.

Poppy led Constance by the hand from the atrium and through the colonnade and finally to the ballroom. For once, the girl was silent.

All around them were trees. The tall, verdant structures made a canopy of the ceiling and lunged down dramatically, casting shadows on the floor. Garlands of delicate flowers drifted from above, some pale yellow like rays of sunlight, others dazzling white, like rain.

"You must be some kind of sorceress," Constance breathed.

She was not a sorceress. Merely a woman who had forsaken sleep for most of the past three days.

Constance put an arm around her waist. "It is an enchantment, Poppy. It's going to make you the most fashionable gardener in England. I shall see to it myself."

Constance was right. Tonight would make her reputation. And tomorrow she could return home and begin the rest of her life.

There had been no further sign of the Hathaways. Grouse had met with her this morning to inform her that her plants were safely situated at Greenwoods, and the grounds at Bantham Park were restored to rights. The slapdash plan had worked. The sheer relief of it exhausted her. And now, at long last, she could go home.

"I'm so glad it's what you hoped for," she told Constance. "If you don't mind, I am going to retire for a few hours before I travel."

"Yes, of course," Constance said. "But first there is something I would like to give you. It's waiting in your bedchamber."

Constance followed her to the ivory room. The enormous mahogany bed was piled with large scarlet boxes wrapped with striking golden ribbon.

"What is all this?"

"Valeria finished your things."

Poppy bit her lip. She had asked Constance to cancel the order and to excuse her from attending the ball, pleading lingering weakness in her ankle. Constance had agreed.

In retrospect, she had agreed far too easily, making almost no fuss.

"I know you said you would rather not attend, but truly you should. It would be a great favor to me."

"Constance, I don't want to argue with you, but I am quite exhausted."

"Would you at least open the boxes?"

"Very well."

She removed the ribbon from the largest box and sorted through layers of delicate paper to find a lustrous gown of pale green silk inlaid with tiny drops of opal. She ran her hands along the garment, hardly able to believe the beauty of it. The next box contained a set of stays to fit below the stomacher, panniers to lift the skirts up and out around her hips, and a fine sheer muslin chemise embroidered with flowers in pale green thread. She clutched the garment to her chest and shook her head at Constance's generosity.

"This is beautiful. I've never seen anything like it."

"Please wear it tonight. Please come. As my guest of honor. You have worked so hard, and I know that the benefits to you in attending will outweigh the discomfort."

She met Poppy's eye. "To your ankle," she added after a brief pause.

Poppy wondered how much she had guessed about what had passed between her and Westmead. Surely, she could not know the full extent of it. And yet there was a glimmer in her eye that implied that little had escaped her.

Constance helped her open the remaining boxes, laying out gold slippers, fine stockings, and satin gloves. "I shall send my maid, Sylvie, to come and dress you and help you with your hair. Say you'll come. Please."

Poppy sighed.

"May I think about it?"

"Of course. Oh, and I almost forgot, there is this." She pointed at a small, unopened box in plain white paper, overlooked in the pile of scarlet trimming. "It was here before. You must have another admirer."

She kissed Poppy on the cheek, and turned to go. "Send word up to me if you decide to stay. I hope you will."

Poppy waited for her to leave before opening the final box.

Inside were a clasped case and a folded note pressed with ruby wax—Westmead's seal.

Cavendish—

Let the final humiliation between us be that I could not find adequate words to ask for your forgiveness. Know that as you ascend to ever-greater triumphs in what shall no doubt be a long and storied life, somewhere a rueful friend smiles, wishing you every happiness.

All regret.

Archer

Inside the velvet box was a crown of perfect white plumeria blossoms. She knew these flowers. They were from her greenhouse. From the very plant he had toppled the day that he'd burst in on her.

Later, after she had sent word to Constance that she would accept the invitation to stay after all, and Sylvie had come to dress her, the maid lifted up the delicate wreath of buds with a wrinkled nose.

"Well, is that all you plan to wear in your hair?" she asked, looking skeptical. "With the other finery, you'd be better with a tiara. Shall I see if her ladyship would loan you one? She has a set of emeralds that would suit you."

Poppy shook her head.

There were no words for what she felt.

Only the sight of her image in the mirror: a woman with a modest headpiece and eyes that glowed like thawing ice.

ARCHER TRIED NOT TO WINCE AS THE YOUNG MISS BASTIAN continued to prattle blandly in his ear. How he was going to summon the force of will to offer for her he didn't know. At least his secrets would be safe with her as his duchess. In the many days of their acquaintance, she had yet to ask him a question.

"Lady Constance has made this place so beautiful," she enthused, gesturing at the lushness that surrounded them. "You must be very proud of her." She plucked a rope of flowers from a trellis and wound it around her neck—a gesture meant as flirtation that succeeded only in giving her the aspect of some dairy maiden's favored milch cow.

He glanced over at his sister, glittering in an appropriately ludicrous pink confection that nearly swallowed her and her crowd of admirers whole.

"I am always proud of Constance. Though I suspect the credit for the beauty lies largely with Miss Cavendish. She has an unusual talent."

Miss Bastian smiled in a way that was not kind. "She certainly seems to think so. How fine she looks, in that gown. A gardener in Valeria Parc. Imagine."

He followed her gaze to the assembled crowd below.

She'd come.

He'd been informed she had declined the invitation, but there she was, standing beside Lady Rosecroft, who was introducing her to a group of elegantly dressed gentlemen.

Her lean frame was molded and stiffened into the curvier style of fashionable society, her skirts billowing out around panniers, her bust uplifted with stays. Her hair, for once, was not a riot, but was coiled elaborately around the sides of her head, drawing attention to the elegance of her long neck. She looked every bit the sophisticated London lady she might have been through a different accident of parentage.

Except for one detail.

His breath caught.

She had worn his flowers in her hair.

The simple wreath of plumeria was the only item that gave a hint of the woman she was beneath the finery—the waif in her smudged gardening gowns who stayed up all night drawing plants. The woman who had seen in a patch of wildflowers the makings of this verdant fantasy. No one would mistake her for an eccentric spinster in this crowd. No one would dare take her for an object of pity. And yet, he preferred her in her breeches, lugging plants in the sunshine. Not Miss Cavendish, but Poppy. The brilliant and singular Poppy.

Constance tapped him on the shoulder. "It is time to commence the dancing. I trust you will lead us in the first minuet?"

She gave him a meaningful look. Given he was widely known to eschew dancing, his participation would set the whole room atwitter. His choice of partner would no doubt be scrutinized like tea leaves for some sign of his intentions. There was one clear choice for whom he should ask, and she was standing next to him, fluttering her eyelashes in expectation of being made the envy of the room.

"Excuse me," he said, nevertheless, to Miss Bastian.

He turned and walked toward Poppy. The gentlemen surrounding her greeted him with the grudging respect that marked his relations with London's grandees. He rather enjoyed their incredulous expressions when he interrupted them to address the nurserywoman.

"Good evening, Miss Cavendish."

She arranged her face into a polite, if chilly, smile. "Your Grace."

"It's a triumph, what you've done here," he said. "I can't fathom how you've managed it."

"You're kind. I'm glad I was able to help your sister make her mark."

He felt the other men watching him with interest. "I trust," he drawled, grasping for a neutral topic, "that you are satisfied with the work at Greenwoods House? Constance tells me that her steward finished transporting the last of your plants."

"Indeed."

"What will you do next?" he asked.

"I shall use your sister's influence to expand my custom and attempt to launch a subscription scheme for my nursery." She paused and lowered her voice. "And endeavor to do so without falling off my horse."

He laughed, wishing he could hug her for that acknowledgment of their brief friendship. He'd missed the rueful way she had with words.

"I must make my farewells, Your Grace," she said, moving as if to turn away. "And I can see Miss Bastian has grown anxious for your company."

He glanced back at the young lady, who was regarding them with an expression of profound distaste.

"I don't suppose, Miss Cavendish, that you remember how to dance?"

She looked up in surprise, her eyes guarded.

"I am not certain I do, Your Grace. If you recall, I had a terrible teacher."

"You deserved better," he said in a low voice. "Would you do me the honor anyway?"

She accepted his hand.

He felt hundreds of curious eyes following them as he led her through the open terrace doors and down the candlelit path to a dance floor lit by torches at the edge of the lake.

As the first strains of the music began, he bowed and took her hand. She held herself crisply, on edge.

He focused on the pleasure of her hand in his, in watching her swirl about the floor. When the movement concluded, and other dancers joined them, she stepped away.

"I must bid you farewell," she said with a curtsy. "I am to leave early in the morning. I wish you well, Your Grace."

"I beg you, sit with me for a moment?" He indicated a bench overlooking the lake a few paces away.

She glanced skeptically at the bench.

"Please. There's something I owe it to you to say, and I am weeks remiss in saying it."

She relented and followed him to the bench. She settled her

skirts around her, careful not to allow them to brush against his person, and looked at him expectantly.

"Poppy, I want to apologize to you. Properly. For what happened in my study."

She looked out at the lake beyond him, avoiding his eyes. "Let's not speak of that unpleasantness. We have both made mistakes. We part amicably."

He shook his head, hating this polite, circumspect dismissal.

"Cavendish, the mistake was mine. I should not have put you in that position. It was dishonorable of me. I flatter myself a better man than that."

"Put me in that position," she repeated, narrowing her eyes. "Is that what you thought you were doing? And here I thought I put myself there. If you wish to apologize, do so accurately. The way I recall it, your injury to me was not in bestowing your attentions, but in withdrawing them. And in so doing, informing me that I was the wrong kind of woman on whom to bestow them at all."

He winced. "What I said was nonsense. My words were rude and ungracious and I have spent the last week at a loss for how to tell you how deeply I regret them."

She was silent for a moment. "Nevertheless, you were not wrong when you reminded me of the order of the world. You are a duke and I am the proprietress of a modest nursery. I shan't forget myself again."

She made as if to rise once more. And so to stop her, he let the first words that came to him pour forth.

"I did not mean to imply you are the wrong kind of woman, Poppy. I meant that I am the wrong kind of man. And not in the way you might think. I don't customarily conduct myself that way. I don't … *bestow* my attentions in that fashion. On anyone. I haven't for years, and for good reason. But I simply wanted you too badly to stop myself. And when I came to my senses, I fled. *That's* the truth. It was cowardly. I regret it. And I'm sorry."

He fully expected that these would be the last words he ever said to her.

That she would turn on her heel and walk away from his admission.

Instead she looked at him with an expression that was half-amused and half-intrigued.

"Really?"

~

THE EXPRESSION IN THE DUKE OF WESTMEAD'S EYES WAS SO astoundingly, resignedly unguarded that for one moment she could have mistaken him for a different man. Not the one who held himself with such intense control. Someone else. Someone who held a hidden depth of feeling he chose not to reveal.

She had misjudged him.

These past weeks she had assumed his listlessness was the pouting of a bored aristocrat, deprived of his clubs and women. That his unkindness to her was the inborn arrogance of Norman bloodlines. That she was one of many women who found themselves disrobing in his study, and he had found her lacking.

One could not reside in Grove Vale without hearing the rumors about his father. The women he'd kept here, despite the presence of his suffering wife. The unsettling conditions in which they'd lived until, inevitably, he'd tired of them.

It was said the son had sought out the injured women and made what reparations he was able. But were sons not made in the image of their fathers? Was the man who'd invited her to call him Archer not still Westmead?

And yet tonight she had seen the way that the men and women of his rank looked at him. The way powerful men went quiet when he came near, and ladies ceased to laugh and flirt, growing sober and uncertain in his presence. He was clearly a legend in this world. And yet, just as clearly, he was not a member of it.

He was something more intriguing: an impostor.

Now that she had seen a glimpse of the man that he was hiding, she wanted to see more.

"I wish you had simply told me this before," she said.

"It's not something I relish discussing."

"Nevertheless I should have liked to have your friendship."

He sighed and looked away. When he looked back, his eyes were once more strangely luminous. "Poppy. You have it."

"Westmead?" a voice behind them said. They both turned to find the silhouette of Lady Rosecroft.

"I'm sorry to interrupt, but I need your help," she said. "Georgie has gone missing."

CHAPTER 13

*A*rcher stared at his cousin, stricken.

And then he was off the bench and leading Hilary back to the terrace, where a small crowd of family and servants had gathered discreetly.

Poppy took a moment to collect herself. Had Lady Hilary not appeared at that exact moment, she would have leaned in and touched his face and kissed him.

Why was it that he made her do exactly what she knew she shouldn't?

How many times did she need to learn this lesson?

She stood and smoothed her gown, letting the cool nighttime air do the work of coaxing the blood out of her heart and into her head. A *child* was missing. She knew these grounds as well as anyone. She should offer her help in finding him.

On the terrace, Lady Hilary was speaking to the small crowd in an anxious murmur. "Sometimes he wakes up in the night and wanders from his cot. At home his nurse sleeps with the nursery door locked, but here there is no bolt." Her voice broke. "I fear he may have slipped outside."

Archer put a hand on his cousin's shoulder. "We will find him.

I promise you." He turned to the nurse, an older, kind-faced woman hovering nervously at her mistress's side. "Where has he gone in the past, when he wanders?"

The old woman gathered herself with a shaking breath. "In London he often heads for the mews. He's fond of horses. But he doesn't know his way around these grounds." She glanced with dread at the lake. "And he doesn't know how to swim."

"Miles," Archer commanded the underbutler, "gather the footmen and see that they surround the perimeter of the lake with torches at once. And send another group out to search the pleasure gardens. He couldn't have gone far."

Poppy took a torch from a footman. "I will check the garden outbuildings. Maxwell keeps animals there. Perhaps he saw them from his window."

"Miss Cavendish," Lady Rosecroft objected, "thank you, but you mustn't walk out alone."

"Don't think of it. I have been over every inch of these grounds. I daresay I am as equipped as anyone to find the boy quickly."

"I'll accompany Miss Cavendish," Archer said. "In the meantime, Hilary, stay here in case he returns."

He took his own torch from a footman and together they walked briskly away from the lights and music, following the path to the outbuildings west of the house. A single mule stood loose before the stall, munching on grass. The door to its pen was ajar.

"Christ," Archer swore, and broke into a run. She jogged along behind him, fearful of what they would find inside. If the tiny boy had indeed made his way in and managed to open the pens, he would be in danger of being kicked or bitten.

"Georgie?" Archer called, ducking under the low roof.

Inside the dim building she could hear the breathing of sleeping animals. It made her uneasy. The calm rhythm of their breath in the moonlit pen brought back memories of her own childhood, when she'd crawl up into the loft of her uncle's stables when she was terrified and missed her mother.

"He's not here," Archer said, shining the light across the stalls.

She leaned up on her tiptoes, looking for the smallest, darkest spaces.

She could still feel that child's fear, that primal urge to burrow into the darkest, smallest nooks. Hiding in the shadows, listening to the breath of animals the way she'd once listened to her parents sleep when they had lived, had been the only way to outrun the nightmares. She had sorely tried the patience of several relatives before her uncle had taken her in, for no one knew what to make of a lonely little girl as liable to be found at dawn trembling in a manger as asleep in the nursery. No one knew what to do with a child who screamed through the night, stricken by terrors no one could account for. Her parents' deaths, after all, had been so ordinary—weak lungs, a fever following the loss of a child. The visions that had tormented her—her father's coffin, the tiny, wizened baby, the deluge of maternal blood, the soiled sheets—had struck her aunts as ghoulish and unnerving, out of all proportion to her loss.

Only Bernadette had understood. Bernadette, the nurse her uncle had hired at Bantham Park, had lost her own parents. She'd sensed innately what Poppy had really wanted when she'd hidden herself away.

To be found.

For to be found was the only way of knowing you were wanted.

In the farthest corners, she saw a recess under the roof, just low enough that a child might clamber up the stall beside it and tuck himself inside.

"Georgie?" she called out. "Georgie, darling, are you about? You mustn't be scared. We're here to bring you home. Your mama misses you very much."

A small voice laden with tears whispered from a corner stall. "I'm frightened."

Poppy raised her torch.

The boy was tucked up in a pile of straw, his frilled nightdress and cap covered in bits of hay. Archer handed her his torch and lurched for him. "Come here, my boy," he murmured. "It's all right. You're safe." Georgie snuggled against him with a frightened sob, his blond ringlets crushed against Archer's neck.

She watched as Archer rocked the child back and forth and whispered soothing words to him. His face was poetry, haggard with quiet devastation. She stared at it. That face was one she knew. She *knew*.

That fierce slash of a nose, the tousle of dark hair. The torchlight in the near blackness of the stables, the grassy smell of manure, a whispered voice amidst the murmuring of sleeping animals.

The wind fell out of her.

She knew exactly who he was.

Why she had recognized him that first evening when he'd driven her to Greenwoods House.

Why, in the grips of laudanum, the man in her bed had seemed no more real than the figure in her nightmares.

Why lately her thoughts had turned so frequently to that night when no one had found Poppy hidden in the stables, because Bernadette had disappeared.

She had sensed Westmead had a secret. But never, ever, had she imagined it was something like this.

He was indeed his father's son.

She'd been a fool.

It had grown late. The last of the guests were making the sleepy walk to their chambers or carriages. Outside, footmen tiptoed across the shadowy lawn, removing abandoned flutes of champagne.

Archer had meant to use this night to find a wife, and instead he'd spent it on the floor of the nursery, watching his godson build and destroy towers of blocks until the dying notes of the orchestra had faded.

Not that he minded. He felt curiously aloft. He had forgotten the way that children of that age smiled and laughed at the slightest provocation. How their large eyes looked at you with the purest kind of trust, the darkness the world could bring not yet impressed upon their minds. The clean and milky smell of them as they drifted off to sleep.

He grabbed a bottle of chilled wine from a silver ice chest and snatched two crystal glasses from the tray of a passing footman. Now that the ball had concluded, festivities were in order. And he knew just the person he wanted to toast.

He strolled to his wing of the house and glanced down the hall. Firelight flickered beneath the door. He gave it a light tap. "Cavendish?" he said quietly, through a smile. "A word, if you're awake?"

There was no answer. Perhaps she had gone to his study.

But that room, too, was empty. The fire was nearly dead in the grate and her things were no longer on the table. All that was left of her pile of drawings and chalk was a single slip of paper and the crown of plumeria he'd had made for her—torn now, as if she had ripped it from her head without removing the pins.

He picked up the note.

I once asked you how it was I seemed to know you. I now understand why you lied.

Stay away.

He stared at it blankly. When she'd inquired if he'd known her late uncle, he had answered truthfully. Of course, he had been to Bantham Park once or twice, if furtively, during the years when she would have been a child. But certainly never as a guest of the house. Certainly not in any circumstance in which he would have been introduced to a little girl.

He strode back to her door and knocked on it firmly, not much caring who heard. When still she didn't answer, he tried the handle. It wasn't locked. He poked his head inside, averting his eyes in case she was indecent.

"Poppy, what is the meaning of this?" he said, holding out the offending slip of paper.

Silence. He scanned the room.

She wasn't in it.

Her fire was lit. Her gown was laid out on the bed. Her shoes, cleaned of mud, were drying on the windowsill.

But she was gone. On her dressing table she had left a note to his sister. Furiously, he scanned it— *Summoned suddenly ... Have my things sent to me in the morning ... Most affectionate regards.*

Lies. There was no one to summon Poppy Cavendish. She was as utterly alone in the world as a young woman could be.

Which meant that she had run away.

From *him*.

In the middle of the poxing goddamned night.

CHAPTER 14

*I*t was madness to walk through the forest alone in
the dark.

She had been overwrought.

She had made the wrong calculation.

And now she was trapped. Too far to go back to Westhaven.
Miles yet from the safety of Greenwoods House.

She crept through the woods in her boots and breeches,
cursing herself for the decision to flee with every heart-stopping
snap of a twig. *Breathe. Now would be a very bad time to fall apart.*
She need only locate the stream that bordered the edge of the
Westhaven lands. From there she could extinguish her lamp and
follow the water by moonlight. She would be safer without the
glow of the candle alerting passersby to her presence.

She crept onward through the fine mist. Clouds shuttered the
moon and trees rose up around her in every direction, tall and
menacing. She paused again, disoriented. It would not do to walk
in circles.

Her heart sank when she heard it. The distant *clip clop clop* of
an approaching horse. She had only a moment to make a decision:
she could leave her lamp burning and be certain to be spotted by

whoever approached, or extinguish it and attempt to hide, which would leave her in complete darkness once the rider passed.

She chose the occlusion of darkness. The pale flame of her lamp died just as the rider's own came into view. She darted under the cover of a thicket but chose her berth badly—thorns sank into the thin fabric of her breeches. Pain shot through her knees, so sharp she had to bite her hand to keep from gasping.

The rider slowed within a few yards of her hiding place. He must have seen her lamp.

"Poppy," Westmead's voice called from a few feet away. "Come out."

She felt a momentary flood of relief that it was only him, not some vagrant or poacher prowling in the woods. And then she remembered what she had to fear from him and felt foolish.

She kept quiet.

He jumped down from his horse and shone his lamp into the trees.

"I know you're here. Please come out. This is absurd."

She said nothing. She would wait him out.

"I can hear you breathing," he sighed, after a pause. She held her breath.

"I will wait here all night if I must."

He was only a few inches away.

He hung his lamp lower, shining light into the underbrush. And then its soft glow was on her face, and his eyes were on hers.

"What is it?" he murmured. "You're shaking."

"Stay away," she barked. Her voice had gone raspy with exhaustion and fear.

Looking more bemused than dangerous, he rose to his feet and backed away a few paces.

"Why did you follow me here?" she hissed.

His brow knit together. "What choice did I have? Did you think I would really leave you to wander the woods alone? Do you have any idea what could happen to you?"

The question was so absurd, so offensive, that her better sense disappeared, and she answered it.

"Yes. Perhaps something like what you did to *her*."

"Did what to whom?" he asked, running a frustrated hand through his hair. "You aren't making sense."

"Bernadette," she cried out. "My God, you don't even remember her? Bernadette Montrieux. My nurse."

He did remember, clearly. The fact that he remembered was written in every line of his body, which, in the moonlight, had gone rigid.

"Ah, so you *can* at least recall the name of the woman you ravished. I suppose that's some small comfort."

For an agony it was just their ragged breathing in the woods.

When he spoke, his voice was deadly, deadly quiet. "How dare you say that to me?"

"How dare *I*? Because I saw what you did to her. I saw everything. To think what I have allowed between us." She shivered. "It makes me ill."

"Enough," he said.

"Enough? I saw you, Westmead. I *saw* you."

"Whatever you think you saw, you were mistaken." He spoke with such force his words echoed in the night.

But she would not be cowed. She *had* seen it. It had haunted her for years.

"Deny it if you haven't the honor to confess, but I assure you I was there. I was hiding in my uncle's stable. Bernadette came in with a man—with *you*. He pushed her up against the wall. She was whimpering and crying out, but no one came to help her. And the next morning she was gone. She never returned."

He stared at her with such contempt she felt it like a physical blow, despite her fury. The gall of him, playing the persecuted man after what he had done.

"Admit it, Westmead," she said. "Admit it was you that night."

He threw back his head. "What you accuse me of doing I have

never done. Would *never* do." His voice was unlike any sound she had ever heard. He paused and blew out a ravaged breath. "We—that is, yes, Poppy: I am guilty of having once made love to Bernadette Montrieux in your uncle's stable. Eighteen-year-old lads do such things, I'm afraid. When the lady is *willing*."

Oh. That, she had never considered.

Was it possible that her child's eyes had misconstrued what she'd seen? The note of despair in his voice sounded to her like the truth. But how could she believe him, when for years she'd replayed a different truth in her mind?

She struggled for some question that would lead her to an answer—some sign that she could grasp upon for clarity—but before she could speak, he broke the silence with a string of words he uttered like she had cut them from his throat.

"I would never have hurt Bernadette. She was my *wife*."

HE FELT LIKE HIS THROAT WAS RIPPING AS HE SAID THE WORDS. THEY were fossilized now. One could not expect to excavate them without shattering away layers of calcified rock.

Even Constance knew nothing of the gap in his life. His father had never told her of his marriage in the years he'd lived abroad, and had sent her to an aunt's upon their mother's death, when he'd returned with his family. She only knew that there was darkness in their family's dissolution that he refused to speak of.

"I don't understand," Poppy said. She looked at him like a bewildered child. "You have no wife."

"She passed. Many years ago." Some perverse part of him, the part that found some sick relief in saying it out loud, could not stop himself from adding the final note of horror. "Along with our son."

Poppy put a hand to her mouth. He simply watched her, numb.

He wished he could summon some stronger emotion than the

sense of defeat that suffused him—some low-simmering anger at her accusation. But he felt only empty. He knew what was coming. He felt it rising up, closing around him. Filling the place where the rocks and fossils had been. Emotion. Pure and sickly and unstoppable as flowing water.

"You're telling the truth?" she asked, her voice sounding small.

"Do you truly think that I would invent such a thing?" He put his free hand to a tree trunk, the torrent within him closing around his organs from inside.

He struggled for breath, but it was choked beneath the weight in his chest, crushing him.

Damn her, she could see it. Even in the darkness, she could see.

"You *are* telling the truth," she murmured. "Oh, Archer." She stood helplessly and moved beside him as he strained to breathe against the fog in his lungs.

"I'm sorry," she whispered.

He tried to answer, but what came out was something like a sob. Fuck. *Fuck*, but he was going to succumb to it.

She tentatively put her hands down on his shoulders and brought him toward her until he was enclosed in her embrace.

An age passed while she breathed with a slow forceful rhythm, as though she could model for him the proper working of lungs. *I'm sorry. Breathe with me. I'm here. Slowly. Just breathe.*

Finally, excruciatingly, he found the strength to straighten up and break away from her.

He was soaked through with sweat, and the breeze in the air sent such a chill through him she could likely hear his bones rattle above the rustle of the trees.

"Apologies," he murmured, mortified at the display she had just witnessed.

She reached out and put her fingers lightly to his hand. "Please. It's me who is sorry."

He turned back to his snuffling horse. "Come. We should return. You can leave in the morning."

"Archer," she said quietly, staying rooted where she stood.

He turned back to her, impatient to put this all behind him.

"It's a great comfort to know that she simply had a love affair. I feared for her all these years. I'm so relieved to know that she was loved. And by someone like you."

The words were kindly meant, but he'd rather she stay silent than congratulate him for the pain he'd wrought so long ago.

"Do not be tempted," he said, "to cast me as some romantic hero. The story is not a happy one."

SOMETHING IN HIS MANNER MADE HER THINK HE WANTED TO TELL her more, but couldn't make himself.

"But you married," she said softly. "And you had a son. What was his name?"

His eyes looked fixedly just beyond her. "Benjamin."

She had always found his eyes remarkable—their essential gentleness, which he could never quite mask even at his most lordly and imperious, was what had endeared him to her, made him handsome. Now they clouded with an anguish she could hardly stand to look upon.

"I'm sorry," she whispered. "I won't make you speak of it."

But instead, he drew a ragged breath and began to tell the story of a boy who met a girl and fell in love.

How one summer afternoon in his eighteenth year he wandered into the woods on an afternoon's aimless stroll and discovered her with her bare feet dangling in the stream.

She was six years older, a nursemaid employed by Poppy's uncle to care for his recently orphaned young niece. She'd grown up in Paris, the daughter of a merchant who'd died when she was young. She'd been sent to a convent for an education, and to find work, she'd come alone across the sea to Wiltshire.

He knew he could never have her. His father had made clear it was his duty to secure a wife who would enhance the family's crumbling finances, despite the fact he was the second son. She was alone, foreign, a Catholic, in service—unsuitable to a family that had carefully tended its bloodlines for generations.

Poppy was silent as he told his tale. How they'd met in the woods for two summers until he'd convinced her to run away with him—taken her to France and told his father of his marriage only months later. How the duke had sent solicitors to Paris threatening annulment, disinheritance. How little they had cared.

How Bernadette had painted while he apprenticed with a merchant trader who specialized in wine. The arrival of their baby. A laughing, merry boy with a mane of golden curly hair who loved to ride on his father's shoulders to the market, babbling nursery songs in French.

How they'd been happy. Until one day a letter came informing him of the death of his mother and elder brother in a carriage accident. *You will be Westmead,* his father wrote. *Whatever our differences, your responsibility to this family outweighs them. You must return.*

"He told me to leave them in France," he said bitterly. "He wanted an annulment, or at least discretion. But I was defiant. Determined that if he wanted me, he must accept my family. I brought them here. *I brought them here.*"

Suddenly she knew with sickening clarity how this story ended. Westhaven's west wing had been ravaged by a fire many years ago. The old duke had died soon after the blaze and the family had not returned. The official cause had been a dirty chimney. But local legend had always had it that the duke had set the blaze himself, in a drunken fit after the death of his wife and eldest son.

"Oh, Archer," she breathed. She reached for his hand, but he waved her away.

"He waited until I was out with the estate agents. By the time I saw the smoke, we were a half hour's ride away. By the time I made it back, the stairs had collapsed. It was too late."

She could not think of what to say but knew she must say something. "You couldn't have known. He'd have to be mad."

"No. He wasn't. For all the talk of my father's insanity, it was never him who succumbed to madness. It was me. For weeks, I couldn't rise from my bed. By the time I came to grips, my father was dead of a bad heart and I couldn't bear to speak of what he'd done. So he accomplished what he wanted. And that's my fault."

"You can't blame yourself," she said softly. "You were grieving."

"I was weak. Out of control. Unable to go about the basic tasks of living and frankly better off had I been among the dead. I spent months that way. And when I did come half to rights, I couldn't stand to remember. I threw myself into investing with a kind of single-minded madness and I let my wife and boy … just disappear. And for that, I can't forgive myself. I have no wish to."

His face rearranged itself as he said these words. The pained light in his eyes went cold, and he straightened his face back into the aloof veneer of the duke who strode around and never slept and kept his papers in exacting little stacks.

And so she completed the story for herself. About a man who had shut himself up very tightly, and assumed control very rigidly, to pay an act of penance.

She wondered if he could see, like she could, that it wasn't working. That the mask that he wore was beginning, little by little, to slip away.

She wondered what would happen when the inevitable occurred.

When it fell away entirely.

～

THE EXPERIMENT WAS OVER. HE HAD THOUGHT A DECADE'S ABSENCE from this place was enough to cauterize the wounds.

It was not.

His mind was fog, his chest a chasm, turning septic.

He had not told her the whole truth of it. It was not just his labors that saved him. It was also pain, and with it strength. The possibility of a place inside himself that bore no relation to the house of Westmead. A place he longed for now.

What he needed was in London. What he needed was not kind words but a cold stone floor beneath the balls of his hands, branches snapping on his skin, fingers in his hair. Sharp commands pulling him back into himself. Bracing him into the man he chose to be instead of the one that he'd been born.

Poppy stood quietly, observing his effort to collect himself with an expression she might have worn upon discovering a wounded fawn.

Intolerable.

He turned away from her and glanced up through the trees. The sky was beginning to change from darkness to the deep purple preceding first light.

"We should return to the house before the sun rises. Better no one know you left."

He lifted her up onto his horse and swung himself behind her, tucking an arm around her waist.

He rode quickly to beat the light. The sooner they were parted, the sooner he would recover.

But to keep balanced, she pressed her body back against him, and with every movement of her form along his person, he felt a pang of want.

He *hated* himself for it.

The proper thing would be to loosen his grip on her waist. To wall off this desire for her touch.

Instead, he held her tighter.

She snuggled back against him, indulging his mad desire for affection, not reproaching him for his flesh wanting what it wanted. For being still damnably alive.

As the forest parted and the house peeked into view, he crushed his nose into her hair and placed a kiss on the crown of her head.

"Thank you," he whispered, loosening his grip on her. He was grateful she could not see the longing no doubt written on his face. It would not do to let this need be what she remembered of him.

But she was no longer paying attention to him at all. Her gaze was trained on something in the distance.

"Bollocks," she murmured, shielding her eyes against a ray of sunlight sketching the rooftop of the house in blinding orange.

"What is it?"

"Nothing. I thought I saw someone in the window. But it was only a trick of the light."

"Constance's set is not known for their early hours. I expect they won't begin ringing for their breakfast trays until twilight."

"I have noticed you have no surfeit of affection for them. Will you return to London?"

"Yes. This morning."

"You won't come back here."

"No."

Not ever.

His sanity was a skittish creature that required a climate of grayish light and ordered papers and rooms that bore no memories. Sheep-speckled meadows and lichen-spotted elm trees and dewy dawns breaking with a wild-haired girl tucked under his arm fed an ache inside him he was not in the business of indulging. It needed to be slaked into submission and fed a diet of solitude.

There was only one thing he would miss here.

He helped her down onto the terrace mounting block.

"I suppose this is farewell, then," she said.

Christ, but she was beautiful, looking up at him beneath those long black lashes with the morning sun bouncing off her eyes.

He tried to summon words that could adequately express his depth of feeling without descending to the mawkish. The silence between them was the sort that cried out for some kind of declaration of attachment or gesture of affection. But he was not the kind of man who had those to give away.

"I am all gratitude for your friendship, Cavendish," he said. Feebly. "I shall think of you ... most fondly."

You insufferable clot. The words landed with a thud, so insufficient as to be ludicrous.

Poppy, lovely Poppy, spared him the indignity of acknowledging their unsuitability as she accepted his hand one final time.

She squeezed it.

"Be well, Your Grace."

He made his hand let go of hers, finger by reluctant bloody finger.

And then he memorized the sight of her as she disappeared into the house.

CHAPTER 15

*H**oxton Square, London*
      August 2, 1753

Archer had nothing but contempt for gentlemen who drowsed away the day in bed and lingered over their toilette. Any man who was not at his desk in the counting-house by the stroke of seven was not long for a position in his concern.

But it was well past eight by the time he had dragged himself from his bedchamber to his dressing room, squinting at the gray light pouring in from Hoxton Square. He ate porridge without tasting it and scalded his mouth on strong black coffee and felt as though his coat were made of lead. The day rolled out in front of him like a death sentence. He would go to Webb's and buy a ring. And then he would call on Miss Gillian Bastian and offer to make her a duchess.

It was exactly what he wanted. Why the thought of it was making him so miserable was, therefore, confounding.

"Your carriage is waiting outside, Your Grace," Gibbs said.

He nodded at the butler and dragged himself up from the table. He shrugged on his overcoat and walked to the door.

"Your Grace, I should warn you—" the butler said, but he was not paying attention and pulled open the latch himself.

"Your Grace!" a chorus of voices called at once. Fifteen or so men huddled in front of his house, waving their arms and calling out his name. The path before his front gate was littered with them.

"Westmead, what say you of the Beau Monde Botanist affair?" a particularly strident specimen shouted above the rest.

He recoiled and slammed the door.

"As I was saying," Gibbs said blandly, "a crowd has gathered outside."

"What, pray tell, is the Beau Monde Botanist affair?"

Gibbs gestured at a pile of newsprint neatly folded on the sideboard. "I believe it refers to some chuff in today's *Peculiar*."

He rifled through the papers on the table until he found Desmond Flannery's frivolous gazette.

A sketch of Constance under a cloud of blossoms dominated the page. THE TRIUMPH OF THE HOUSE OF WESTMEAD—*London's most mysterious family set the latest fashion in the country.*

Constance would be pleased. It was exactly what she'd hoped for. But hardly the stuff of scandal. He looked up at Gibbs, who was staring grimly at the page over his shoulder.

"Further down, Your Grace." He located a bolded square of text at the bottom of the page.

SCANDAL BLOOMS?

The sylvan scenes of the glittering ballroom were designed by Miss Poplar Cavendish, of Bantham Park, granddaughter to the sixth Viscount Mallardsly. Miss Cavendish's brilliant blossoms are sure to be fashionable in the coming season. But whispers have it that it is the elegant figure of the Beau Monde Botanist herself that has caught the eye of the Duke of Westmead. The duke began the evening's first dance with his garden nymph in arm, and, if roving eyes can be trusted, he may have ended the night with her as well. His Grace was spotted at first light in the company of fair Miss Cavendish, no chaperone in sight! Could it be the flower of love that blooms? Or is it the scent of a budding scandal?

"Desmond *fucking* Flannery."

Gibbs nodded. "Indeed, Your Grace."

Archer took great pleasure in crumpling the paper in his fist. He took greater pleasure still in writing a note to his sister instructing that Flannery be ejected from his property immediately, or else line up a second time for his imminent return. He rather hoped the man chose the latter. He would relish the opportunity to shoot him.

But Christ. What was he going to do about Poppy?

He'd tempted her to Westhaven with the promise that her nursery would flourish, and instead her prospects were as good as destroyed.

To be a woman in business was difficult enough with a spotless reputation. She'd be ruined by this.

Unless, of course, he married her.

As soon as he thought of it, he realized it had been the answer all along.

There was an elegant kind of logic to it. Who, better than Poppy, understood the nature of a transaction? Who, better than Poppy, would understand that there were aspects of his life that simply did not bear looking into?

Was it not precisely the scenario he sought? A woman who needed his name? A woman who understood the advantages of a fair exchange and could be counted on to extract terms that suited her? A woman who would no doubt find far better uses for his fortune than amassing jewels and dresses? Who would contribute to his offspring's intelligence and spirit, rather than a tendency toward indolence and gossip?

He ignored the part of himself that objected that he felt many, many things about Miss Cavendish, and not a one was indifference. That the last thing she was to him was *safe*.

Instead, he strode outside, ignoring the shouting crowd.

"Throgmorton Street," he told the waiting coachman.

The proprietor of Webb's brightened at the sight of Westmead on his doorstep, anticipation blooming in his eyes at that rare customer who bought generously and paid readily.

"Your Grace." He bowed. "What an unexpected surprise. I hope Lady Constance admired the parure. Such a fine set of emeralds—exceedingly pure in quality. What can I help you with today?"

"I need a ring."

Webb's eyes glinted with promise. "Of course, Your Grace. Something for a lady? I have recently acquired a cluster of diamonds in a brilliant setting, nine large stones in fine silver. Dazzling by candlelight. Lord Westing has had it in mind for his mistress, but given the weight on his line of credit, I could see that it be released to Your Grace instead."

Anything coveted by Westing's mistress was sure to strike horror in the heart of his intended recipient. "What have you that's ... simple?" he asked, trying unsuccessfully to locate an appropriate word for Poppy's humble, unaffected taste.

Webb assembled several trays of baubles, each one gaudier than the next. These would do for Miss Bastian and his sister's set, but not for Poppy.

Sensing his client was on the verge of departing empty-handed, Webb rummaged in a drawer and produced a box.

"I have a few older pieces, yet to be reset. Perhaps something like this?"

He held out a ring of six teardrop pearls arranged like petals around a small yellow diamond. It looked like a plumeria blossom from Poppy's greenhouse.

"Quite elegant, if modest, Your Grace. But of course I can add more stones if you desire."

"No need. I'll take it now."

With the ring carefully tucked in a leather box, and the box tucked away in his pocket, he returned to the carriage.

"On to Mayfair, Your Grace?" the coachman asked.

"Change of plans. Grove Vale. And please make haste."

CHAPTER 16

*P*oppy leaned down to inspect the fragile pink petals of a bee orchid. The humble local flowers, which crowned Wiltshire's chalky meadows in the summer like enormous, fuchsia-winged bumblebees, had been much admired at the ball. She had thought to grow them in large enough quantity that her fashionable new customers might order them for their gardens next summer, at a tidy profit to herself.

Now she wondered if she would have any customers left at all.

It had scarcely been a day since the dreadful story was printed in the *Peculiar*, and already her new relations, the Hathaways, had withdrawn their invitation for her to dine with them at Bantham Park. Sir Horace Melnick, dear friend to her late uncle, had written to cancel his autumn planting, just as Mrs. Elizabeth Ellis had sent word that she no longer required new hedgerows for the vicarage.

The only positive word Poppy had received was from her loyal correspondent Mr. Carpenter in Virginia. For the first time, she was grateful for the slow and irregular interchange of information between England and the colonies. Rumors of young ladies'

ruined reputations were unlikely to penetrate the wilds of
Virginia for some time.

Her friend began his letter, as always, lamenting the difficulty
of obtaining suitable European cuttings for his nursery and
requesting any help she could provide.

Perhaps all was not lost. Plants could still be her salvation.

She sorted her disorderly boxes of letters into tidy piles in her
makeshift workshop, drawing up a list of her contacts at nurseries
from Carolina to the Continent. She had well-placed friends in
the world of botany and eight hundred pounds of ready money. It
was enough to purchase a few acres of land closer to London,
where she might establish a larger nursery near the river, with
access to the ports. Her reputation would not matter so much if
she controlled the prevailing means of horticultural exchange
across the Atlantic.

But. There was always a but.

The trouble would be in arranging adequate funds to pay for
transport and entice other nurseries to participate in the scheme.
She would need to loan out a great deal of her capital, and take on
a great deal of credit, in order to engage partners abroad. But to
secure a loan without a male sponsor, she would need, at minimum, her good name.

Which was a difficult thing when one was utterly ruined.

She pushed her papers to the side. It was a trap, this business
of being a woman. The simple truth of it was that after all her
efforts to secure her independence, she was still stuck. To accomplish what she ought, she need not have bothered with years of
being single-minded and industrious. She needed only to have
been born a man.

She knelt on the floor to sort through a stack of crates that had
yet to be unpacked. At least now she would have ample time to
cultivate her neglected cuttings. A lifetime, the way this week was
unfolding.

She was in the midst of unwrapping a parcel of bulbs when a tapping sounded at the window.

She looked up, expecting the bustling intrusion of some prying village busybody.

It was Westmead.

He'd come back.

He entered the room tentatively, as if unsure of his welcome. Fair be that, for in truth, there was no sense to the relief she felt in looking at him. If they were seen together, it would only add to the rumors. She needed him to leave immediately if she wasn't to be ruined twice. Which was unfortunate, as she had a sudden pressing desire to launch herself into his arms and spend the next quarter hour recounting her misfortunes into the comfort of his chest.

"Your Grace," she said instead.

"Archer," he corrected her.

"Archer," she echoed.

It was a mistake to use his Christian name. It brought back the unsteady feeling she had felt at their last parting, like her limbs were made of churning water.

"I thought you had returned to London."

"I had. I turned back as soon as I saw the *Peculiar*. It seemed I was needed here. To murder Desmond Flannery."

She allowed him a rueful smile. "Slowly and without mercy, I hope."

"May I help you with these?" He crouched down to join her on the floor amidst her muddle of crates and trunks.

She allowed herself a moment to look at him in wonder. For all that her relations with the Duke of Westmead had invited the occasion of her downfall, she could not help but like the fact that he was the type of man who wore his title in such a way that kneeling on a countrywoman's humble workshop floor came to him as naturally as breathing.

"No. It's growing late. And given the rapid desertion of my

clients, I shall scarcely need such an immoderate number of seeds."

He frowned. She instantly wished she hadn't said that. There was nothing to be gained by making him feel guilty for the position she was in. She had, after all, left his house in the middle of the night all of her own volition. He hadn't compromised her reputation. She had managed that on her own.

"If only there was something that could remedy that."

He reached inside his coat pocket and removed a small, round leather jewel case. Meeting her eye, he slid it across the floor.

Oh no. The churning drained from her limbs as though someone had let out a stopper at her feet.

"Open it?"

Squinting with dread at what she would find inside the box, she opened the lid. Inside, a ring shivered in the fading light.

It was small and shaped like a flower. A plumeria. It would have been the perfect ring, just right, had they been lovers. The sweetness of it made her falter. She looked up at him, trying to find the words to say that the gesture he felt honor-bound to make was neither required nor welcome. But before she could get them out, he took her hand. Only in looking down at it, clutched in his own, did she become aware that she was trembling.

She shook her head, wanting him not to say whatever it was he meant by giving her this ring. "Archer, please, there is no need—"

He cleared his throat. "When I saw that headline yesterday, I was instantly filled with regret—"

"Stop there. You are not responsible. I did not intend to imply—"

His face lost its tentative expression and fell into a grim-set line. "Cavendish, let me finish. I don't mean I regretted that I would be forced to offer for you. I regretted I hadn't got it through my skull to think of it before I left. You see, I think we can be useful to each other."

"Being useful to each other is how we arrived at the current predicament, if I recall," she said, careful to offer him a rueful little smile to show she meant no ill will. "Truly, you are kind to offer, but you need not."

He looked at her unhappily, as though deciding whether to pursue this further. "Cavendish," he drew out. "No one wins at business by rejecting a proposal before she's heard it."

She didn't need to hear it. He could contend what he liked about his reasons for returning, but she knew why he was really here and she couldn't stand to be the recipient of charity. She hated to be beholden. To be beholden to a man like him would be a special kind of torture.

"You may call it what you like, Your Grace, but I have no desire to marry. And while we're giving lessons, need I repeat mine on rescuing women who do not desire it?"

Again, he rearranged his face. She could see whatever response he had been expecting, this was not one he had imagined.

"If you would give me a fair hearing," he said drolly, "you would see that I don't intend to rescue you. I merely perceive a way to use the circumstances to our mutual advantage."

His tone had no chivalry to it. It held the brisk tone of calculation she had become accustomed to hearing whenever the topic of conversation found its way to his dearest subject: commerce. This meant he was honest in his protestation that he was not here strictly out of misplaced honor. It also meant he simply did not understand the stakes of what he asked. And why would he?

"I'm sorry, but it would not be to my advantage to marry."

"Forgive me for being blunt, Cavendish, but I fail to see a single advantage for you in remaining unwed."

"Well, of course *you* wouldn't see."

"I am not *entirely* stupid. Perhaps you might explain."

She rubbed her temple. How to explain to a *duke* that marriage made women vulnerable? That she had arranged her affairs to protect herself from such a fate? That she wanted to be her own protector, her own provider? That it kept a person safe?

She looked at the contents of the room around them. The pots and bulbs, the rows of orchids, the mud-stained ledger. They would not look like much to him. But to her, they were not merely objects. They were tokens of something incalculably precious.

"If I were to wed, my nursery—everything I've worked for—would be surrendered to my husband. I would lose the right to conduct business in my name. I would lose my independence. My ability to decide for myself ..." She trailed off, unable to express the magnitude of the loss, the inherent vulnerability of wives. "I suspect you will tell me that it amounts to little in pounds sterling. But to give it up would be to lose my finest self."

She waited for him to dismiss her as hysterical.

Instead he tapped his knee and mulled her words.

"I suppose," he said after a long pause, "that were our roles reversed, I might share your hesitation."

"Oh, good," she said with relief. She spared a moment's appreciation for the way he understood her. "Nevertheless, thank you for your offer. I'll see you out."

"I'm afraid I'm not done negotiating, Cavendish. For while I might share your instinct, following it would be a mistake. Forgive me, but surely you must realize you are in a dreadful situation. You have your independence, that is true, but you lack certain critical resources for maintaining it."

Her gratitude was replaced with the urge to hit him over the head with a trowel.

"Yes, thank you for articulating the nature of my plight so succinctly, Your Grace. I can see you've missed my point completely."

"Insult me if you wish, but a clever businesswoman might ask herself not what she stood to *lose* by marrying me, but what she stood to *gain*."

"A husband. That very thing I have spent my entire life trying *not* to acquire."

"A partner. I can't in good faith deny that as my wife you would lose the right to enter contracts in your name. But what if I offered you the power to enter them in mine? My lands, my capital, my credit, my ships—whatever you need—all at your disposal. You could build the finest nursery in all of England."

If there was one lesson she had learned in the last fortnight, it was that when things sounded too good to be true, they were.

"What generous terms. And just what precious thing is it you are after in return?"

He locked eyes with her, and the smile left his lips. "An heir."

Oh.

Their conversation no longer seemed like a puzzle she must solve before she could dismiss him and retire to her bed. It was as grave as life itself.

"A child," she said, more softly than she ought to. "You want another child."

"No," he said crisply, his manner growing icier by the second. "Not *want*, precisely. I have a responsibility to produce an heir. And given the status of the succession, I need one quickly. A man with a history of brutality has recently become next in line to my title. I have a duty to protect these lands and the people who depend on them. What I want has nothing to do with it."

She felt her face grow rosy with offense. "Ah. You need a broodmare. And I am the most desperate candidate."

He stared at her unhappily. "It really isn't quite so crass as that, Poppy. I do require a woman who is able and willing to bear a child. But more specifically, I desire a wife with whom I can be honest about the fact that I have limitations. I lack capacity for the attachments and expectations that inevitably arise from marriage. I intend for my private life to remain private and free from obligation, and I want a wife who desires that same freedom and will respect my need for it. The fact that you *don't* wish to marry me is what makes you a desirable candidate. That, and the fact that I think highly of you and can offer you something of value in return. It would be," he concluded, "a cordial business arrangement affording independence to us both."

A cordial business arrangement. She regarded this chilly figure, finding it strange that the more he spoke of matters of grave importance—marriage, life, death—the more remote and formal he became.

"And what of the matter of conception?"

He shrugged. "We would go about it in the usual way. I should hope, given our history, it would not be so unpleasant. And I should not ask for your favors once conception is assured, nor object should you grant them elsewhere."

He said this all so bloodlessly she wondered if there was something truly wrong with him. Had she not seen the depth of feeling he was capable of in the woods, she would have believed he felt so blithely of such matters. But she didn't. Not at all.

She would leave him to his fiction. *She* did not feel blithely.

"No," she said.

"No?" he asked, visibly thrown by her refusal. "Is it the terms that bother you? Or perhaps you don't desire children?"

"It isn't that." There was a part of her that had always mourned that the price of her independence was losing the chance to have a family of her own. The part of her that grew uncomfortably wistful around babies and large families. That saw small children toddling with their mothers and thought ... *that.* Someone who belonged to her. To whom she belonged in return.

But she could bear not to have a family. What she could *not* bear was to inflict the paltry, distant kind of upbringing that she'd endured on her own child. An "heir" was no less a person than any other baby, and she would not subject a child to a life of being treated like some dreaded obligation.

And what if she had daughters?

"Perhaps I don't strike you as maternal, but I lost my parents as a child—"

He cocked his head before she could go on. "What in my

suggestion that you bear my child makes you think you don't strike me as maternal, Cavendish?"

"The fact that this view is shared by everyone in Wiltshire? Even you call me Cavendish, like a man."

"Cavendish," he said softly, his coldness melting away all at once. "Trust that I have never doubted you are every inch a woman."

She crossed her arms. "You are evading the point. I know what it is to be unwanted. I could not in good conscience agree to a scheme that would deprive my own children of a loving family."

His eyes bored into hers, unflinching. "Our child would have as much a family as any other. I will of course look after my own issue, to the extent it is required, and you may be as tender and devoted a mother as you wish. My only requirement is that we afford each other space for private lives."

His meaning was clear. She could love her child, but he would not. Just as he would not love her. She looked at him for a long time, trying to understand him. Trying to make out what he must think of her to believe she would accept what he proposed.

"And what guarantee can you provide that you will honor your word? Wives have no recourse from husbands under the law."

He met her eye. "No," he said. "You are correct. I suppose you will simply have to trust me."

Trust him.

But that was just the point. She had no faith in others. She trusted just one person: herself.

A bit of shadow fell about his face, and the longer she hesitated, the more he seemed to falter. Finally, he let out a breathy kind of laugh. The kind one allows to escape when one has done something embarrassing, and one is the last to realize it. He quietly snapped the ring box closed.

"I understand. And I sincerely regret that your excellent work at Westhaven has caused you this inconvenience. I will not insult you by offering 'rescue,' but please know that should you require any assistance or funds, you need only write to me in care of Grouse."

He gave her a tight smile and a nod and rose on his knees to stand, and the sight of it was so grim and terminal and sad that her heart made the decision for her, and she knew it was the wrong one even as she said: "Wait, Archer."

He paused, half-crouched.

It seemed as though any number of futures danced in the air between them, and regardless of the choice she made, all of them were colored with shades of loss. Only one glimmered with the possibility of new-budding, springtime things. Of joy rising up amidst the sorrow like a weed.

God forgive her, she seized it.

"What if I wanted to build a nursery on the Thames?" she blurted out.

She avoided his eyes, as shocked as she had ever been by her own conduct. Despite her every instinct to the contrary, she was considering this notion he proposed. She had her scruples and her fears. But she also had a dream. Perhaps what he offered was as good as any other way of getting it. Perhaps she might get even more than she had ever dared to hope for.

He smiled. "I would see that you had every resource at your disposal to build a nursery wherever you desire."

"I would not want you or anyone else interfering in my vision. I would insist on total control over my affairs."

"This may come as a surprise, but I haven't the slightest interest in plants."

She found it within herself to meet his eyes. They were smiling.

"No one else has stumbled yet on the promise of an international subscription scheme for exotics. There is a hefty advantage to be won in being first. I want to break ground in time for winter planting."

He raised his eyebrows at her. "Then we shall find a way. I'll put my best men on it, at your direction."

She closed her eyes and abandoned herself to fate. "I will require a ship fitted with compartments of my own design capable of transporting plants efficiently across the Atlantic."

"I imagine you will get it."

"And a conservatory in which I can grow exotic trees, with an unlimited budget for glass."

"Then ours shall be notable among marriage contracts for enumerating the bride's portion in windowpanes. Or mulch. Or whatever else your heart desires."

It occurred to her that he would accede to everything she wanted. That she could think of nothing else to demand.

She opened her eyes. He offered her his outstretched hand.

In it was the ring box.

She took the only option she had left herself.

She plucked the ring from its nest of satin and put it on her finger.

ARCHER WALKED INTO THE DRAWING ROOM TO THE SOUND OF HIS sister singing to her guests. High and determined and not within a trace of being in tune.

Her fingers landed on the keys with a discordant thwack at the sight of him.

She rose, nearly knocking the elegant hand of the Earl of Apthorp out of the way with her shoulder.

"Archer!" she cried with a clap of her treacherous hands. "And here I thought you were never coming back so long as you lived."

He scowled at her.

She grinned at him. "Well? Tell me you have news for us!"

"A word, Constance. In my study. Immediately."

She smiled indulgently at her guests. "Excuse us."

He strode down the hall to his desk and poured himself a generous slug of brandy.

She perched beside him on his desk. "Are we toasting to your betrothal?"

He examined her slowly, in the way he might inspect a lurid crop of algae that had bloomed on his lake and killed his fish. She looked every inch as colorful and guilty.

"Before you say another word, I would like to make it clear that one simple fact became apparent to me today as I was riding here. And that, Constance, is the location of your bedchamber."

She sucked in her lips with a guilty pop.

"Desmond Flannery—and, indeed, all of our guests—slept in the east wing the night of the ball. I know, because, if you recall, you plagued me for a fortnight with their sleeping arrangements. The eastern rooms lack views of the forest. In fact, only one person has such a stunning vista from her window. You."

He watched his sister's face flicker from guileless denial, to feigned offense, to acceptance of her doom, and finally placation.

She flopped down into an armchair, caught.

"I will not contest your deduction, Archer. I will merely say in my defense that if meddling is what I have to do to make you see there are less depressing possibilities than the utterly preposterous notion of marrying Miss Bastian, then I congratulate myself for my success. There are plenty of Lord Apthorps in this world for its supply of Miss Bastians. But there are not so many Archer Stonewells, and precious few women like Poppy Cavendish who might, dare I say, have some chance of making them happy."

She looked tempted to bow, so pleased was she with the fluency and touching nature of her oratory.

He was not moved.

The sight of Poppy crouched around her seeds and crates, trying not to be disconsolate at the fact of her diminished future, had been unbearable. He never wanted to see a sight like that again.

He slammed his brandy on the desk.

"You could have destroyed Miss Cavendish's life irreparably with that gossip. Do you understand the magnitude of what you've risked?"

She made her eyes into hostile little slits. "I understand far more than you think I do, Your Grace."

"Then I hope it has not escaped your notice that our name is synonymous in this country with the hurt and pain our father caused by doing exactly what he pleased with no regard to the cost on others. I will not see that legacy continued. Decency is the highest and only value I have ever asked of you, Constance, and I'm appalled at what you did. Appalled."

She folded her hands demurely in her lap. "I never could live up to your standards. Not even as a child. God forbid one simply *live*." She looked up at him, her face impassive. "Did you offer for her or not?"

His mouth fell open at her audacity. How it could still have the power to shock him, he could not reckon.

"Of course I did."

She raised an amused brow at him. "And she accepted?"

"What *choice* does she have?"

The truth was that he was offering Poppy less than she deserved, and they both knew it. She had made no secret of her clear-eyed views of his inadequacies. He had never felt less wanted nor less deserving in his life, and he was half-sure she would change her mind yet.

Constance's smile bloomed into an all-out beam. "Oh, good. Your mood was so dark that for a second I thought she declined. What a relief. I shall accept my thanks in the form of a niece or nephew."

"I am not offering you my thanks. I have no desire to marry Miss Cavendish."

She squinted at him. "Is that *truly* what you think? You poor, daft man. You've been wandering around this estate like a condemned man ever since she threw you off."

The undeniable truth of this observation did nothing to decrease his anger at having to listen to it.

"Hear this, Constance. You are forbidden to have anything further to do with Desmond Flannery."

Her mouth fell open. "What?"

"I forbid you to feed him information. I forbid you to set foot on Grub Street. I have given you far too much liberty and I can now see that you are not mature enough to inhabit it gracefully."

"Archer! You can't forbid me."

Oh, he could. He should have done so ages ago.

"I am your guardian. I have a moral obligation to prevent you from harming the lives of others—or your own—with actions that are cruel and reckless. If I catch wind you have given Flannery so much as a loaded *stare*, I will move you into my house in Hoxton, where I can keep an eye on you myself. Do you understand?"

"I understand you perfectly, Your Grace. Now may I return to my guests? I was just in the midst of a very moving country ballad, and they are no doubt in an agony awaiting its conclusion."

"Go."

When she had completed stomping down the hall, he sank back against the edge of his desk and tried to catch his breath, thoroughly shaken.

With the crisis settled and the future resolved, all the urgent clarity that had compelled him to race back to Wiltshire in a furious all-night lather deserted him.

Perhaps he had embarked on something foolish.

For Constance, despite her recklessness, was a preternaturally observant person. If she thought she'd engineered some kind of love match, perhaps she saw something that he didn't.

He recalled Poppy's face, arranging itself in mute horror at his ring box.

No. *Her* views were clear enough.

Could Constance have perceived some unsuitable fondness in *him*?

He took a swig of brandy and tested the theory, worrying the key around his neck.

Certainly he thought highly of her. He would see to it that the arrangement suited her wishes and addressed her scruples.

And yes, he had felt reduced when she greeted his offer with dismay. Had found himself making arguments he couldn't precisely defend in order to convince her to agree despite her better judgment.

Then again, had he not done that same thing a thousand times in negotiating with reluctant sellers, and made them all rich?

He had, without a quibble of conscience.

He felt his shoulders relax.

Constance was a twenty-year-old girl who acted rashly and thought she knew more than she did. That did not make her correct. He held Poppy Cavendish in high regard because she was clever and steely and unlikely to get the wrong impression.

And as with any valuable asset, he would invest in her, for their mutual benefit.

His plan held. Nothing was at risk.

He tucked the key back inside his collar and sat down to write to his solicitors about a wedding contract sealed in panes of glass.

CHAPTER 17

*P*eerage marriage settlements were meant to be drawn by solicitors in austere London offices and signed by the signet-banded hands of noble relations in plush drawing rooms. Brides took no part in these activities. Surely they did not do so in the flickering light of a tallow candle in a drafty outbuilding that smelled of moss and soil.

But Poppy Cavendish had no intention of leaving her fate in the hands of others. If marriage was to be a business, she would see that her interests were protected. Whatever Westmead proposed, she would begin by doubling it.

Except. *Oh.*

The figures on the page made her eyes water.

Thirty thousand pounds would transfer to a new concern, under the direction of the Duchess of Westmead. She would be granted signatory rights over her husband's capital and made a principal of Stonewell Holdings, his investment concern. She would receive her ship and land and glass in addition to a lavish personal allowance, her own carriage and six, agents to run the ducal homes. It went on and on, in such sumptuous and implausible detail—imagine, her, needing eighty pieces of millinery in a year, needing livery for her private servants. It seemed she had not understood the scale of her future husband's life, or his wealth.

Archer meant these pages as a message to her: if he could not wield the power to preserve her independence under law, he could transform her—an orphaned, grass-stained spinster with only a shambling farmhouse and a hundred pounds of seed debts to her name, save for a banknote from his sister—into an unfathomably wealthy woman.

It was chilling in its exactitude.

Was this what her autonomy was worth?

She walked slowly through her dark workshop, remembering her excitement at finding the shillings to purchase each tool pegged to the wall. She fingered the waxen leaves of hybrid plants she had imagined and brought to life like a demigod. She would lose all this. She would lose the fine feeling that every box and packet and leaf and flower on this small property had been earned outright and against the odds. That she owned it free and clear.

She would trade it for a man who saw her as the solution to a problem. A bill of goods.

Why, then, could she not dismiss him? What tempted her?

Blast him. Blast him and the molten feeling that had risen in her chest when he had walked into this room five days before, unsure if he was wanted.

The truth was that she did want him. She had wanted him since the day he had stood outside his house in the sunlight waiting for a carriage and told her the truth about herself. And that made her doubly foolish. For she wanted the only thing he wasn't offering her: his heart.

Wrong, Cavendish, he would surely lecture her. *A clever business-woman does not base decisions in emotion.*

She had a predicament indeed. She wanted to preserve herself, and she wanted to unravel him. She wanted to be fierce and fearless, and she craved to be undone.

I suppose you will have to trust me, he had said.

Don't do it.

The thought came pure and unbidden from a place so deep inside her it must have been her soul that spoke. For her soul had kept an eye on him, when her heart was too fluttering to see clearly.

Her soul was not seduced by promises. It knew that wives had no legal rights and no recourse against their husbands. It knew that she had no power once she signed. This bargain was hers to lose.

She returned to her desk and began to write a letter.

Your Grace,

After much consideration of your generous offer, I regret I cannot accept it.

"Poppy."

She whirled around.

Tom Raridan was standing in the doorway, leering with a smile that made her want to cover up despite the heat of summer.

That so large a man could move so silently must defy the laws of sound.

She did not move. "It is much too late for calling."

"That's no way to welcome your future husband. I've come to say my offer for you stands."

There was an insolence to his tone that she remembered in his father when he'd been drinking.

He reached in his pocket and produced a thin, gold ring. She recognized it—he must have plucked it off his mother's finger. He reached out and snatched her hand.

"Stop it," she snapped, wrenching backward. He persisted, all but pinning her against the wall as he fumbled with her finger. His breath smelled of gin.

"Stop." She used all her strength to whirl away from him, maneuvering so that there was a table between them and a spade in her hand in case she need fend him off more forcefully.

"Understand this, Tom. If you wish to remain my friend, you will leave here now without another word save for an apology. And you will never, ever lay a hand on me again."

He waved this off with the expansive, unsteady gesture of a man deeper in his cups than he'd originally appeared.

"Meant no offense. Wanted to give you a betrothal ring. I won't have the town thinking I've mistreated you just because you're ruined. Besides, I've gotten my new posting in London. We'll live well now, we will."

His speech was slurred with the effects of alcohol. Just as his father's had been on those days when he'd talked himself into a merry rage and gone about the town looking for the nearest person on which to pour it with his fists. Uneasiness pricked along the back of her neck.

"As I made clear before, I cannot accept your offer. Please, I would like for you to leave."

"Oh, enough with the coy talk. You'll not find better than me, being compromised."

She stared at him. His face was a portrait not of anger but of certainty. He thought he had her.

Rage sparked in her toes and fingertips and shot up her arms and legs until it tingled behind her eyes, hot as a beam of light.

This would be the life that she had to look forward to if she returned Archer's contract to him unsigned. Men who thought they could do what they wished to her because her name had once been printed in a gazette. Men who smelled the stink of vulnerability and chased it.

She came to a decision.

"I'm promised to be married to the Duke of Westmead."

"Wot?" Tom's eyes flashed from disbelief to wounded pride to something more like hatred.

"I am pledged elsewhere. And the duke will be displeased to find you lingering here. Go." She pointed out the door with her spade.

Tom turned and stalked toward the door. He stopped at the shelf holding the delicate shoots of her magnolia plants. He snatched the most promising of the cuttings, which just this morning she'd carefully planted in damp soil in a pretty painted pot. He took the time to meet her eye before he hurled it at her feet.

Shattered glass and soil erupted around her shoes.

"Cunt."

He kicked the pile of dirt and glass toward the hem of her dress as he walked out the door.

She waited until she was sure he was gone before she moved. Shaking, she bolted the door and shut the windows. She got on her knees and swept up the shards of glass. She found another pot and carefully transferred the plant into fresh soil.

And then she returned to her desk and crumpled up the letter begging off. She dipped her quill in ink and wrote *Poplar*, after the tree, *Elizabeth*, after her mother, *Cavendish*, the last of her father's line, and signed the last contract she would ever conduct in her own name. The name of a girl who had fought and fought, but who had lost the battle.

It was a gamble, to retire Poppy Cavendish.

But the fine fight wasn't over yet. She would simply have to wage a war.

And she would do so under the banner of the Duchess of Westmead.

CHAPTER 18

The Westhaven chapel being one of the few ancient buildings that had yet been spared Constance's zest for renovation, the air that greeted Archer as he entered the nave was damp and musty.

Outside, a crack of lightning rent the charcoal sky in shades of jaundice. The old stone building shook with thunder. A bead of water dripped from an eave above his head, hitting him on the forehead with a smack.

"How auspicious," he muttered to the vicar.

He had slept badly. He had had to see to business in London and consequently had not set eyes on Poppy since the day he had cajoled her into marrying him. And though she had signed the marriage contracts and consented to his sister's rush to outfit her in nuptial finery, he could not shake the feeling that she would not show up this morning. Nor the feeling that if she didn't, he would be rather more crushed than was proportionate to the kind of marriage he had meant to arrange for himself. The kind one did not stand at the altar fretting over when the bride was three minutes late.

He refrained from checking his watch, refusing to make a

public spectacle of his nerves, but he keenly wished he knew the precise hour, minute, and second of this day, the better to recalculate the odds he would conclude it still unmarried.

The guests shifted, no doubt making the same grim calculations.

But no. They were only looking toward the door, where Poppy dashed inside flanked by Constance and Valeria, who held cloaks above her head to shield her from the rain.

She was stunning.

She wore a simple ivory bodice with a low neckline and long sleeves. Below it delicate skirts swirled around her over airy petticoats, like one of her gardening dresses had been respun from magic and fine silk.

This was how she should look always.

This was how she should look, at least, until he took it off her.

A sedate march played as she walked toward him down the aisle. It tugged at him that she made the walk alone—that there was no one to whom she was precious enough that her hand must be given away to her husband in marriage.

He would be that person, he decided.

If he could give her nothing else, he would be the person to whom she was precious. He was not capable of love. But he had a gift for recognizing value.

She walked toward him with such confidence that it was only when he took her hand, and felt that it was damp, that he realized she was nervous. He locked her in his gaze.

"Cavendish. You came," he murmured, only for her ears. "I woke up convinced you wouldn't."

She shook her head. "Of course I came."

He turned to the vicar, determined that she would not live to regret it.

≈

As the storm raged on through the wedding breakfast, Archer turned grim with growing certainty that the houseful of guests due to depart in the afternoon would decide to stay on, pleading impassable roads.

He wanted them out.

Apthorp stood to make yet another toast to the happy couple. Archer groaned. Beside him, Poppy listened politely, raising her glass, smiling, laughing as required. She looked exquisite in her dress, her long neck rising swanlike from the low bodice, her hair frilling sweetly around her face below her crown of flowers, even curlier from the rain.

The godforsaken fucking rain. Would it never bloody end?

As yet another round of glasses drizzled champagne on the table, a ray of sunlight crept in through a window. Archer smiled for the first time in hours. The storm had finally exhausted itself. He abruptly rose from his chair and thanked the guests, concluding the meal. A flicker of amusement passed between several of the men at his eagerness to have his bride alone. Well, let them have their chuckle. But let them have it privately, in their coaches bound speedily away from this house.

Within the hour the good-byes had been said, the happy tears shed, and the guests departed. Only Constance and the Rosecrofts remained to say their last good-byes. They were off to Paris, where Constance and Hilary intended to spend the autumn buying jewels, gowns, and furs for the coming season.

"How happy I am to call you sister," Constance said, wrapping her arms around Poppy. "We are so fortunate to have you as our own."

She moved to Archer next. As she hugged him, she whispered something in his ear that sounded like *you're welcome.*

At last, the door closed behind them. He turned to Poppy. Save for the footman, they were alone.

"It's sweet, how much you'll miss them," she quipped. He laughed, surprised that she could read him.

"I missed you," he said, drawing her close to him and inhaling the rosy smell of her hair and realizing it was true.

Out of the corner of his eye, he saw the footman sweep silently away. His new favorite. He didn't want to be watched doing what he wanted to do to her. Which was to press her back against the mighty wooden door and bury his face exuberantly in her neck.

It was just a marriage of convenience, he reminded himself for the fourth time in as many hours. It wouldn't do to get carried away. He must keep his head. He had talked her into this, against her better judgment. He had a responsibility to ensure this day went well for her.

And yet the smell of her skin was like a balm, soothing the tension that had been mounting in him for days. Here, with her in his arms in the entry of this house in which he'd always felt unwelcome, he had never felt more extraordinarily the relief of home.

WHEN POPPY LOOKED BACK ON HER WEDDING DAY, SHE KNEW SHE would never forget how Archer had smiled that morning when he first saw her. One of his lazy, glimmering smiles, like a light opening behind his eyes. There were no words for what it felt like to have his powerful attention trained on her. She had been well and truly frightened in that moment. She could not afford to lose sight of the fact that the vows they were making were a pretext. She could not let herself look into his face and mistake it for what it plainly looked like.

She had to guard her heart.

But it was difficult, when his undisguised relief to be with her, the pleasure he took in touching her, even smelling her, was making something well up deep inside her stomach.

Difficult, when his lips had migrated somewhere beneath her hairline, and seemed to be nibbling at her neck.

"Shall we go for a stroll?" she asked on sudden impulse, her voice brittle with artificial cheer.

"A stroll," his lips repeated from their vantage point beneath her ear, his voice dripping with amused dismay. He tore his mouth away from her and laced his fingers inside hers. "Yes, my dear wife. *Just* what I was thinking."

"I must change first, of course. My gown will be ruined in the muck."

"Were you planning on needing your wedding dress a second time?" he asked airily, steering her directly out the doors to the terrace.

"Archer," she protested, gesturing at the impossibly delicate fabric of her skirts. "I refuse to ruin this. I could never look Valeria in the eyes again."

He twitched his lips, considering, and then whirled her around, his fingers deftly finding the tapes that attached the skirt to her bodice and releasing them. The fabric fell to the ground around her, leaving her standing in her many layers of fine petticoats.

"Much better." He nodded, squinting at her. "Just the ensemble for a stroll."

She laughed helplessly as he led her down the terrace and to the path around the lake. The unfriendly pair of swans for once ignored the human interlopers, floating picturesquely near the Pantheon at the end of the gardens. For a while they walked in silence, she unsure of what to say, but happy just to enjoy the sensation of his fingertips brushing against her own.

Oh good heavens, what had she done?

Without conversation to distract her, the intimate event that must take place to ratify the oath they'd made loomed large ahead.

She had spent the last three weeks worrying over just this moment. Oscillating between excitement and dread until she lived in a permanent state of queasiness and couldn't eat. On a visit to Constance, she had slipped back to his study and retrieved his secret book. It was wrong, and no doubt shameful, but at night, alone, she looked at it. Pondered the possibilities. Thought of what he'd think if he knew she was picturing them inhabiting those poses. She'd lingered over the ones in which the lady seemed imperious. She imagined them that way until she was flush and impatient for his hands on her, for hers on him, for the way he had made her feel the last time he had touched her.

Until, inevitably, her thoughts turned to the teeth-clenching way that evening had ended, and her stomach turned sour and she wanted to beg off entirely.

I suppose you will simply have to trust me.

Oh God, what had she done?

She'd resolved that she would not touch him. She would submit to the act, but no more, unless he specifically instructed her. That was how it was properly done, was it not? The way men expected women to conduct themselves?

"What is it?" Archer asked, the fine playful gentleman having retreated as he noticed her becoming lost in worry. "Do you regret it?"

"Regret marrying you?" She looked up at him, at the magnificent hair that fell over one eye, which her fingers had itched to sweep aside all day. His remarkable jaw, where a faint hint of dark stubble was beginning to appear. His eyes, which were constantly tricking her into feeling things that she shouldn't.

"I don't know yet, Your Grace."

"I appreciate your honesty, Cavendish," he said, the corners of his mouth rising up in a smile. Oh, how she liked it when he smiled. She wanted to make him smile again, and so she stood on her tiptoes and pressed her lips to his mouth.

Bollocks.

She froze and cringed, her eyes shut, waiting for him to recoil. *Why* had she done that? Mere *seconds* after telling herself not to? If she was to survive this, she mustn't, mustn't touch him.

But he did not demur at the brush of her lips. He drew her

against him and deepened the kiss, threading his fingers through a lock of her hair. Noticing she had grown rigid, he froze, then broke away, looking down at her in question.

"I'm sorry. Too much?"

"I keep forgetting not to touch you."

He cocked his head. "*Not* to touch me?"

She nodded. Oh, but this was miserable and embarrassing. Couldn't they just go inside and find the bed, and he could tell her what to do and have it done with?

"Because of ... before ..." she muttered helplessly.

Understanding dawned and the gentle humor left his face.

"Of course. I'm an idiot, Cavendish."

He picked up her hands and put them to his chest. "But trust that I'm an idiot who wants, *very badly*, for you to touch him. However much you like."

Tentatively, she raised one of her hands to his jaw and guided his mouth back down to hers. He murmured approval, taking her lower lip in his front teeth.

Feeling bolder, she nipped back at him, eliciting a growl from his throat. She wriggled, gaining purchase on his body, and he threw back his head at the feel of her. "Very, *very* badly," he said in a low voice, and she felt her skin prickle awake.

A crash of thunder sounded as a single drop of rain landed on her hand. She looked up at the sky to find it had gone sallow. With another crash, beads of hail began to pebble the ground.

Archer grabbed her hand and dashed toward the Pantheon. The lawn off the path was spongy with rain, erupting with every step to soak through her slippers and splatter her petticoats with a thick spray of mud. As they dove for cover, the sky erupted in violet threads of lightning and hail rained down harder, in bits the size of marbles that scattered on the ground and stung her ankles through her stockings.

Laughing and out of breath, she sank back against a column. And suddenly his mouth was on hers again. He took her hands in his and raised them above her head, dragging his mouth from her lips and down her neck to the tops of her breasts.

She loved the luxury of his mouth on her, his hands on her, the way his eyes went dark and far away as he touched her.

"Untie me," she whispered, wanting freedom from the heavy silk bodice, wanting to feel his hands on her skin. He unthreaded her gown and pulled it down, drawing her breasts up from the loosened stays and pressing his mouth to her nipples. She grabbed at him impatiently to rid him of his waistcoat, running her hands up and over the impossibly perfect contours of his back and shoulders. Finally her fingers freed him of his outer garments, leaving only the linen shirt below. Inordinately pleased, she kissed him along his jaw and down his neck and grabbed the ties that held his shirt and greedily unlaced them so she could run her hands along the bare surface of his chest.

GIVEN HE HAD NOT MADE LOVE TO A WOMAN IN THIRTEEN YEARS, HE had imagined he would take his time with it. Maintain some husbandly modicum of restraint. He had not imagined it happening this way, urgently, outside, in his father's ludicrous Pantheon.

Poppy ran her hands along his bare skin and he closed his eyes and surrendered to the feeling of her warmth, her girlish satisfaction in his body. Until it filtered through his consciousness that she was taking off his shirt.

He could not let her see his naked flesh.

His hands came down on top of hers to stop her. But at the look on her face, tentative and trusting, flushed with curiosity—he couldn't bring himself to do what his better sense demanded. He could not jump away. He would not hurt her that way again.

He let her go about her task and braced himself for what he knew she would discover.

And indeed, when she saw it, she gasped.

SCARS.

Running down the tops of Archer's shoulders and down his back like a patch of soil in her garden, fiercely raked.

Poppy's hands froze. Neither of them breathed.

She took a shaky breath and caressed his damaged flesh. He cringed.

In that small gesture she saw the real reason why he had run from her that night in his study. It was this. He did not want her to see these marks.

One more of his secrets that unfurled only to reveal another mystery. For these scars had been made by human hands.

"I'm sorry," he repeated, gruff. "I meant for you not to see that."

His voice was so subdued that she couldn't stand to hear it. She put her head on his bare shoulder and drew him near her with everything she had, pressing her hands into the small of his back to bring him closer.

"It doesn't matter," she said. "You're the most beautiful thing I've ever seen."

And he was. In the rain-dimmed twilight, his shoulders were broad, his stomach taut and trim, his chest dusted with dark hair that grew darker around his navel and trailed maddeningly below. Her fingers wandered down to trace the path it led, drawing up the courage to dance below his waist. She paused, waiting to see if he would shrink from her, as he had done before, but instead he threw his head back and thrust forward at her touch.

HE CLOSED HIS EYES AND FOCUSED ON HER FINGERS CLOSING around his shaft, on the animal shock of it. And suddenly he didn't have to try so hard to concentrate because she was grazing his erection with her impossibly soft cheek. She was placing her lips on the tip of him, brushing him lightly with her mouth, running her tongue experimentally around the underside. Christ, but where had she learned to do that?

He heard a noise like a growl escape from himself, and all at once he knew exactly what he wanted and it was not to put his shirt back on.

He gently broke away before he lost himself entirely and spent in his innocent young bride's mouth.

"My turn," he said. "May I undress you?"

In response she smiled and lifted up her arms.

He unpeeled her from her shift and stockings, unveiling at last the long and lithe and winsome whole of her. A slip of a girl, pale skin made paler by her long black hair. And then a womanly thatch of dark curls at her entrance, such a shockingly erotic counterpoint to the girlish slopes of her hips that for a moment desire nearly choked him. Oh, he could do *this*. *My God, could he.* His body wanted this. Was starved for it.

Too aroused for delicacy, he leaned her back against a marble column and knelt before her, dragging his lips along her hip bone and down between her thighs, teasing her with nothing more than breath until she parted wider and began to move for him, searching for the relief of friction. Precious, precious girl. He let his fingers fall gently on her hip bones and parted her with his mouth, letting his tongue at last find purchase against her hot, slippery skin.

She was so soft and wet and salty sweet. He lost all track of time, feeling a pang of pure possession every time she writhed or shuddered or dragged her fingers through his hair or whispered his name. *Archer. Archer.* Christ. He had never had such profound affection for the sound of his Christian name.

He swirled and suckled her until he could feel the tension

rising in her body, on the verge of crisis. He invaded her passage experimentally with his tongue.

"Yes," she said, all breath.

He had meant to make her come with his mouth, but now he wanted to feel it with his cock. He dragged his lips away and rose back up, edging his body so his erection pressed at the entrance of her quim. Her eyes flew open. Her lips pulled up in a grin.

"My bride, I did mean to undertake this in a bed."

She snuggled closer, so that his cock was nestled just between her thighs. She closed her eyes at the sensation and pressed her face into the hollow of his neck. "Never mind beds."

He took her hand and pulled her down atop the discarded pile of her skirts. He owed her dressmaker a debt of gratitude that there were so very many of them.

She landed beside him, laughing as their mouths met and stroking his foot with hers as they fell back into the tangle. What she wanted with his instep he could not say except that it delighted him and she could have it, though his hips were moving of their own volition to reunite his cock with the blessed sultry heat between her legs.

She wrapped herself around him. He could feel that she was yielding, eager.

"May I?"

"Yes. Please," she breathed.

He edged inside with a slow, shallow thrust and waited for her to adjust.

"All right?"

She sighed and put her forehead against his shoulder. "Yes."

He placed his fingers against the bud above her quim, stroking her, hardly moving inside, though the effort nearly killed him. She moved, urging him closer still. He gently withdrew and thrust back in. She gasped. He looked to her eyes for clues as to her pain, or pleasure, but they were closed.

"I'm not hurting you?"

"No," she whispered. He let his hand work lazily in tandem with his thrusts until she began to quake beneath him, uttering a helpless little sound that made him smile. She cried out in earnest and contracted around his cock with such surprising force that she brought him with her.

And as he spilled his seed inside of her, he had a shockingly mutinous thought: *I hope it doesn't take.*

Because now that he had had her once, how was he ever going to stop?

CHAPTER 19

a light supper had been laid out in Poppy's bedchamber,
but she ignored it, wanting only to soak off the remnants
of the mud and rain in her—*her*—copper bathing tub. By the time
Archer rejoined her, she was still immersed in the warm water,
enjoying how her hair floated up around her like a mermaid's. No.
Like a proper duchess.

"Well look at you, Cavendish," he said.

Cavendish, he called her still. As though she existed exactly as
she always had. It made her inordinately fond of him.

She flashed him a saucy smile and rose up so that the tops of
her breasts poked above the froth of fragrant water. She wanted
him to see her. She wanted to make him hard and shaky again.
She wanted to make him drunk on her.

He looked rather taken aback.

And then very, very pleased.

She liked that.

She liked that simply by existing, she could wrest a response
from him. One even he seemed surprised by.

She was glad, she decided, that she had stolen his book. She
was glad she knew what was in it and that he did not know that

she knew. She liked that subtle imbalance in the knowledge between them. It gave her the advantage of surprise.

And now that they had covered most of the acts in plates I though VI this afternoon, there were a number of others she wished to try.

A cordial business arrangement, he had called this.

Given what she had planned, they might need to revisit that classification.

"I've been waiting for you," she said, beckoning him nearer. "A hundred servants in this castle of yours and not a one to wash my back."

"I should dare my servants to try it."

He let his eyes linger on the stretches of her body that were bared. She stretched out, so that her ankle rose above the water, and smiled to herself at the way his lips curled up in appreciation for her provocation. He wanted her. She could see it in his face.

"Join me?"

He undressed and climbed into the bath behind her, arranging his knees around her thighs. He found a flannel and ran it down her neck and shoulders, around to her clavicle and breasts. She sighed with pleasure innocently, and then less innocently, leaning back to let him hold her. She pressed her slippery back and buttocks against his solid heat and amused her fingers by tracing them over the tops of his thighs. He placed a shuddering kiss behind her ear and she wriggled back, teasing his erection with the cleft of her buttocks until she could feel that his arousal was urgent and her only goal was to make him mindless with it.

"Are you sore?" he asked, tracing her from nipple to belly to the wet, soapy curls between her legs.

She was perhaps slightly sore, but the more pressing sensation was that she wanted to mount him, claim him.

He had made love to her outside. Now she wanted to make love to *him*.

She lifted her hips back until she felt the blunt, slippery pressure of his cock against her tender, swollen flesh. She rubbed herself against it for a moment, enjoying the simple tactile pleasure that shot through her. She was rewarded by a ragged sigh from her husband. She wanted more of that. She reached down, adjusted her hips, and put the head of him inside her.

For a moment they were still, a bolt of heat between them. She shifted her hips to draw him in, and he let out a gasp. He reached around and placed his hand on her most sensitive part. She momentarily lost her concentration. The man had a way with his fingers. Such a way that if she let herself, she could shatter right down to her bones this instant. But she wanted to take him with her. She shifted her hips again, guiding him inside.

"Christ," he whispered in her ear.

She moaned and gripped the sides of the copper tub, slowly taking more of him, using her body to control the angle of his entry, teasing them both with the unbearable slowness of it. She could feel his breath catch. Feel him losing his control. Oh, she wanted that. To make the strong duke shudder. She was pleased with her unladylike body, so strong and sinewy from her exertions out of doors, which could be used in the service of assuming this exquisite little sovereignty. She bore down on him—then up, and down again, not a bit of her withheld.

He put his forehead to her nape and ran his thumb against her lips, and she bit it, hard. He hissed. "*Fuck*, Poppy."

The hoarse, unmediated crudeness of his cry took her over the edge.

A pang of white heat unfurled through her body, and she sank down until she fell entirely apart, her body a fugue, insensible to words.

Later, after she had regained her powers of speech and he'd admired the sight of her in her new lace dressing gown and they'd picked at the food and she'd grown sleepy, she had a private thought.

She was not, in fact, a proper duchess.

And that was fine.

Her husband clearly didn't want one.

"I MUST SLEEP, ARCHER," HIS NEW WIFE SAID, RISING FROM THE SPOT before the fire where she'd been lying with her head on his lap after he'd once again made love to her.

He took her hand and kissed it. "Dream sweetly, Cavendish."

She squinted at him. "You're not *leaving?*"

He had not intended to share her bed. It was too intimate a habit to establish.

Consummation of their marriage—the act required to beget the child they'd agreed to conceive—was unavoidable. Doing it in a way pleasurable to them both was only sensible. But he owed it to his wife and to himself to establish the proper boundaries, lest there be confusion on the nature of their purpose here.

But the look of Poppy, sleepy and sated, made him waver. Surely a single night would make no difference. He rose and carried her to bed.

With her in his arms, he slept easily and dreamlessly for the first time he could remember.

He woke up to the sound of his wife laughing.

She was standing in her shift at the door to her dressing room, hip cocked, having a quiet chuckle to herself as she examined the contents of her wardrobe. His mouth quirked at the sight of her. How bloody adorable.

He climbed out of bed and padded across the rug to stand behind her, wrapping his arms around her shoulders and resting his head on top of hers. She fit him nicely.

"What could possibly be so amusing about your gowns?" he asked, breathing her in.

She leaned back against him and gestured at the shelves and hooks, overflowing with pretty, costly new items. "Have you ever seen anything like it? You'd think your sister expects me to open a shop in Mayfair."

"Just her way of welcoming you to the family." He stroked her hair, which ran gloriously free all the way to the small of her back. "What are you doing out of bed so early? It's practically dawn. Couldn't you sleep?"

"Practically dawn is when we decent working people rise for the day, Your Grace."

"Then I shall have to make you indecent," he said, dropping his lips to her earlobe.

ARCHER GRIPPED HER HAND AND LED HER TO THE BED, AS LIGHT AND free as she'd ever seen him, and she could not help but be startled by the sight of his back and thighs, which she had yet to see in daylight. His body was so visibly strong that the angry lines on his skin were like a sharp rebuke to his vitality.

He turned back with a smile in his eyes and caught her staring. She tried to correct her expression, but it was too late.

His face went blank.

"I'm sorry," she said.

"Pardon?" He kept his voice carefully neutral, as if he had not understood her.

Oh, God. She had embarrassed him. How excruciating.

"I didn't mean to stare," she said softly. "I don't mind. It's only that it looks painful."

"It isn't," he said dismissively.

She moved closer and put her hand to his arm, expecting to be drawn into his embrace, but the ease with which he'd touched her moments before was gone. She could feel the tension in his muscles, the way his pulse beat faster. It was costing him, to show himself to her.

"Poor man. What happened?"

He sighed and removed his arm from the vicinity of her hands. "It doesn't matter. It was a long time ago."

It didn't look so very long ago. A few of the scars had not yet silvered.

She could not resist giving him a skeptical expression.

"I assure you, it's not painful," he said stiffly. "I'll cover up."

She grabbed his hands as they went rummaging about on the floor for his discarded shirt, stopping him. She would dig them out of the discomfort of this moment if it took her six more tries. He was her *husband*, after all.

She gave him her largest, most earnest smile. One that lived mostly in her eyes, and which she usually reserved for babies and especially delightful dogs. "You don't have to. *Truly.* I only want to understand."

He closed his eyes and tilted his head back. Several seconds passed, during which she could see him gathering his thoughts. Engineering just the right response.

He opened his eyes and met hers, his expression gentle. Very, very nicely he said, "Poppy, if I wanted to talk about this, I would have sought a different kind of marriage. I'd like to keep this private. Please don't ask me again."

Oh.

She rose from the bed, about as leveled as she could recall ever having been. To be put in one's place with such kindness. How singular.

"Cavendish," he said, so very, very gently. "Come back?"

Such delicacy, he had, with her feelings.

She *despised* it.

It meant that he could see how much he'd hurt her.

She granted herself a moment to gather her frayed dignity into some semblance of order before ironing her face into a smile and turning back to him.

"I must finish packing. The carriages are to leave for London at noon."

He stared at her, clearly struggling to read her tone. "Very well."

He rose, collected his discarded clothing, dressed, and left the room.

As soon as he was gone, she closed the door of her dressing room and sat on the floor and did what she'd wanted to do for the last ten minutes: wept.

She cried for the plants and soil she would leave behind today. She cried for the loss of her parents, so many years before, and the loss of her uncle, not yet fully mourned in the chaos that his death had triggered. She cried for the loss of her girlhood, which was well and truly over now, if she'd ever really had one. She cried for the dull ache between her legs and in her heart, and for her stupidity, for taking risks she'd always flattered herself she was too smart and too clearheaded to venture, risks as old as womanhood itself.

She was not so misty-eyed she had deluded herself into thinking this was courtship. She knew he didn't love her and didn't plan to start. But she'd been vain, thinking she possessed some kind of sultry female potency strong enough to melt away his scruples.

Yesterday, with all his nerves and affection and tenderness, it had been possible to imagine it was working. That the connection she felt to him was returned, in some small way.

And today he had been so polite and bloody *sweet* in letting her down gently that her foolishness was compounded, because he must have seen how she had *hoped*.

It was mortifying, the amount of care he took. She would rather he had simply said *That's not what I bought you for, Cavendish,* and slapped her.

Well, she had learned her lesson just the same.

She had entered this marriage to protect her ambition. She must not risk *herself* in the process of saving it.

She slumped against a rack of shoes. How could she protect

herself when he held all the power? He had secrets; she did not know what he might be hiding. He had wealth; she had only what he gave her. The imbalance was striking, and dangerous, and it galled at her. Until her nursery was built, the only asset she possessed in their arrangement was her womb.

The door cracked open, revealing the kindly face of Mrs. Todd, whose eyes widened at the sight of her. She must look every bit the sloppy, tear-soaked mess she felt.

"Oh, Your Grace, my poor dear. Whatever is the matter?"

At the woman's sympathetic, motherly tones, Poppy cried harder.

"Shall I summon His Grace?"

"No!" she cried.

"Ah, I see. Not the wedding night you'd imagined? Few of them are, lass. Well, worry not. The act is painful at the start for some, but a body adjusts. Some even come to enjoy it. Shall I make you a simple, for the pain?"

Poppy was not sure whether to laugh or cry harder.

"Oh, Mrs. Todd. I have no need for a simple. But I wonder, have you any pennyroyal?"

The housekeeper's face went flat with surprise. A country-woman, she would know well what the plant was used for.

"Your Grace," she said gently, "such remedies are not typically prescribed *after* a wedding."

Particularly, she did not add, a wedding to a duke. What more were duchesses, after all, than vehicles for the begetting of heirs? Was that not what Poppy was? What she had explicitly agreed to become?

"I grow a bit in the walled garden," Mrs. Todd admitted, glancing about as though she might be caught in the act of domestic treason. "I make a tea. For the maids."

"Would you please have several doses packed in my trunk?"

The woman stared at her like she had lost her mind. Penny-royal brought on the monthly courses. High doses could trigger a miscarriage—or worse—but a smaller one was thought to prevent conception. It was used by anxious maidens who'd allowed a gentleman too much liberty, or women with a house of children who could not afford another one.

Some said it didn't work. But Poppy believed in the mysteries of botany. They'd always served her better than prayer alone.

Mrs. Todd relented. "Aye. But if His Grace were to find out …"

"He won't."

Her husband was not the only one who could keep a secret.

CHAPTER 20

*O*h God, his heart.

He had known he would hurt her feelings by declining to discuss his scars, but that didn't make it any easier to watch. Archer stood outside her door and listened to the muffled sound of his wife crying. It took every drop of self-control to stop himself from returning to her room and taking her in his arms and answering her questions—and the inevitable, excruciating corollaries—one by one.

He was not ashamed of his private lusts. Their awakening had saved him, returned him to himself, and that discovery was precious. But the truth of his desire was between himself, God, and Elena. Explaining the painful, freeing acts that kept him sane and strong to Poppy would be like handing her his soul and asking her to treat it tenderly. He did not *want* Poppy's tenderness. Tenderness made one vulnerable, and evading that was the *point* of this arrangement. They had an agreement, after all, and his end of it had not come cheaply. He had done nothing he had not warned her he would do when he'd offered her his hand. He had done, in fact, the very least of it.

And would knowing make her any less upset?

Inevitably: no.

He did not wish to imagine what his country nurserywoman, with her scent of grass and dewy skin and twenty-five years of self-discipline and moral rectitude, would make of a man who sometimes longed to tremble on his knees. What was solace to him was to the greater world perversion. A laughable depravity that would make him seem to outside eyes as dissipated as his father. Men had been destroyed by far less.

Besides, he did not wish for terrified acquiescence from his wife, nor some wan, disgusted tolerance.

He wanted the bloody privacy he'd paid for.

So he did not return to her bedchamber. Instead he slipped across the hall to his own room and found the leather cord and iron key he'd discarded the morning of his wedding and returned them to their place around his neck.

He gathered his few remaining effects from the bureau and packed them in a trunk bound for his house in London. He went to his study to gather the books and papers that he'd left there. He paused only when he looked down at the drawer of the desk where he'd stored the threadbare bag.

He debated.

But it felt wrong to leave them here now that he had found them.

He gathered the portraits along with his books and papers and packed them in the trunk and rang for a footman to load it in the carriage.

When Poppy joined him in the grand salon to depart for their trip, he was relieved to see his resolve to keep her at a distance was not necessary. She regarded him the way she might a leech that had attached itself to her ankle.

They departed, and an hour passed in silence. She sat erect and wrote notes in her ledger, behaving as though she shared a mail coach with a stranger. At her purposeful remove, she was more beautiful than ever, self-possessed in a traveling dress of fine navy silk that made her skin look like milky tea and her pale eyes glow like seawater. He feigned the act of reading and attempted not to let her catch him gazing at her. The trip from Grove Vale to London, undertaken at a respectable pace with luggage and servants in tow, would take two days. It was going to be torture, staring across the carriage at her beauty all day in that correct, immaculate dress.

"Would you care for a game of chess?" he asked her finally, when he could no longer stand the tension. She lifted her eyes slowly from her papers to give him an acutely uninterested look.

"Chess?" Never had so harmless a word been uttered with so much disdain.

"We have hours yet before we reach the inn. I thought we might amuse each other."

"I'm terrible at chess."

He grinned at her. "I don't believe that for a moment. I do believe that that is precisely what someone as clever as you would say when they are brilliant at chess but do not wish to reveal their advantage to their opponent."

"No," she said flatly. "I am, literally, terrible at chess."

He bit his cheek for forbearance. "Indulge me anyway?"

Her mouth, gratifyingly, bent in the slightest hint of a smile. He would take it, that smile, even if it was a begrudging and annoyed one.

"Very well, Your Grace. I am at your service."

He dug out the board and pieces and assembled them between them on the traveling table.

He proceeded to lose several games in rapid succession. This, despite the fact that *he* was masterful at chess.

"Checkmate," she said in a puzzled tone, for the third time that day.

He looked down. He hadn't even noticed her pawn approaching his king. He'd noticed little beyond the delicacy of her features and the swell of her figure beneath that navy dress and the wrinkle of displeasure knit between her brows—evidence that she still had not forgiven him. He could not recall ever wanting more fervently to be forgiven. Particularly for a crime of which he did not believe himself to be guilty.

"For a putatively clever man, Your Grace," she said, "you have markedly little skill at games of strategy. I was not lying when I said that I was terrible. But you, I'm sad to say, are worse."

She plucked his king off the board and held it up in a cold salute of victory.

He couldn't stand it, her wintry poise. He wanted to restore the easy harmony they'd shared until this morning. He leaned forward and detached her fingers from the ebony figure one by one. She breathed in, startled.

"Poppy," he said quietly. "Forgive me."

She looked at him inscrutably.

"For this morning," he clarified. It was as far as he could make himself go, but he infused the words with everything he couldn't bring himself to say.

She stuck out her chin and drew her shoulders back.

"Forgive you? Nonsense. Nothing is amiss. I've beaten you at chess three times."

BY THE TIME THEY REACHED THE OLD CROWN INN, IT WAS NEARING eight o'clock. Though there was not a chill in the air, the dining room was lit with a welcoming fire, and the public rooms had a convivial buzz that was rather a relief to Archer after the strained atmosphere of the carriage.

The inn, in the little market town of Faringdon, was not particularly luxurious, but it was clean and well maintained, with a reputation for its food.

"Ah, Your Grace," the innkeeper said when they walked in. "My felicitations on the happy news. Your house sent word that you and your duchess were to be expected. We have reserved our finest room for you, and my wife, Mrs. Wiscomb, has prepared a feast. Pheasant, jellied eel, a joint, hare pie. You will not go hungry here."

He was exhausted, and not at all hungry, but he thanked the man for his kindness. Poppy, however, seemed plagued at the notion of enduring a long meal.

"I'm so very sorry," she told the man. "I hate to disappoint your wife after she has gone to so much trouble. But I believe I will retire early. I am not accustomed to long hours of travel and I'm afraid it has not agreed with me."

The man's face fell so low that Archer felt inclined to embrace him—he, was, after all, a fellow new initiate in the pool of men who knew what it was like to feel the chill of the Duchess of Westmead's indifference.

"Well, I, for one, could eat the whole spread and still have room for cake," he assured Mr. Wiscomb.

In Poppy's absence he invited their personal servants to join him for the meal, treating them to the inn's best wine and ale and accepting their toasts to his nuptials. But he ate lightly and left them quickly to their private revelry. He wanted, despite himself, to return to his wife's side.

In their room, Poppy had already readied herself for bed. She was under the covers with a book.

"I brought you a tray," he said, gesturing down at a slice of pie and a mug of ale he'd charmed from the innkeeper's wife. "Are you hungry?"

"No," she said, not looking up from her tome on botanical remedies.

"You are not feeling well?"

"Only tired." Her voice was a study of politeness.

Her careful distance was beginning to aggravate him. How long was she going to punish him for doing what she'd known all along he would do?

He undressed and refreshed himself—leaving on his shirt—and made order of their things for the next morning, dragging it out to prolong the time before he would need to do the awkward thing of getting into bed with her.

When he ran out of clothes to fold and hairpins to assemble, he cautiously approached the far side of the bed.

Poppy didn't look at him as he climbed in.

He lay there, staring at the ceiling, listening to her turn a page in her book.

Finally he rolled up on one elbow and looked at her.

"Cavendish?"

"Yes?"

"Come here?"

He held out an arm to her. Since words of apology had gotten him nowhere, he thought perhaps simple human warmth might help restore their rapport.

She eyed him, then obediently edged a few inches closer until her shoulder was just below his own. He pulled her firmly against him.

She held herself rigid.

At least she was touching him. He could work with touching. He leaned down and placed a kiss on her head. Then her right cheek. Then the left one. By the time he ventured to her mouth, his motives had become less purely congenial.

"Let me make love to you again," he said huskily, running his hand down to her breast. He smoothed his way lower, over her shift, until his fingers touched the lowest perimeter of her stomach.

"Very well," she said. She reached down and lifted the hem to give him crude access to the lower half of her body.

Like she expected him to pop himself in and swive her while she lay there reading about botany.

It was childish, and plainly rude. He groaned, out loud, and not with desire.

"I shall infer by this display that you would prefer to decline." He flipped her gown back down to her knees.

She looked at him evenly. "If I recall, our arrangement was meant to be procreative in nature. I see no reason why I should need to feign undue interest in the act of conception."

"Feign undue interest?" It annoyed him that she would pretend the hours they had spent the day before were somehow not real. They had been real enough to him. They had been some of the better hours of his past decade.

It had aroused him unmercifully, how her eyes grew glazed and hot at a simple kiss behind the ear. How wet she was when he put his hand between her legs. How quickly he could make her come, and how often he could repeat it, eliciting furtive little quakes or splintering orgasms that had gripped her so fully she had left marks on his skin with her nails.

To diminish all that—it hit him exactly where she'd meant for it to: in the gut.

Because perhaps she was right.

Perhaps he *was* trying to have it both ways. And perhaps that was unfair of him.

"I had hoped that to the extent we must be intimate, we might enjoy it," he began to say, trying to make sense of his own thoughts, but she cut him off with a raised hand.

"Our arrangement is of your own design, is it not? Either take what I have offered or leave me in peace."

He rolled over and blew out his candle.

But it was many, many hours before he slept.

Poppy lay awake in the unfamiliar bed. She did not like the inn, with its public smells and raucous noises. She missed the loam of the greenhouse. She missed the crisp, mossy air of Grove Vale. She missed the comfort of Archer's arms.

There was a piercing kind of emptiness in being cold to someone who was trying to be kind to you. She had thought it would be satisfying to trouble him, but it made her feel more bereft.

He was only inches away from her. All she had to do was roll over, and he would take her in his arms. But in the darkness, what would stop her from indulging her desire for his touch, and, worse, his affection? She stared up at the beams in the ceiling and felt a sickening certainty that if she let down her defenses even one more time, he would see what was happening to her.

How she felt about him.

And what would she have left then?

She tossed and turned and barely slept.

In the morning he was already awake and gone when she opened her eyes.

She smelled rashers, grease, and yeasty buns wafting from the dining room. She was ravenous. She could not recall going so long without food in all her life.

Archer sat alone in the breakfast room, reading a gazette as he sipped a mug of tea. Beside him were a plate of toast and a tureen of creamy butter. She descended on it, barely pausing to greet him in her haste to fill her stomach.

He stared up at her over his paper with a faint look of amusement.

"Hungry, Cavendish?"

She could only moan in response, as her mouth was busy chewing.

A well-built, aproned woman came to the table and offered her tea.

"Yes, please, with cream and lots of sugar. And have you any eggs? And perhaps some bacon?"

The woman gave her a kindly smile. "I see Her Grace has recovered her appetite," she said to Archer. She was too polite to leer, but her implication could not have been clearer had she added the words *in bed*.

Archer bestowed a sly, sideward smile on the woman. "I must confess, she *does* appear rather ravenous."

The lady gave a hearty laugh. Poppy ground her heel into Archer's toe beneath the table for his outright insolence. He merely sipped his tea.

"Well, Duchess, I shall bring you eggs and bacon both," Mrs. Wiscomb said.

"And I," Archer said, putting down his paper, "will leave you to it. I must settle with the innkeeper before we leave."

He walked across the room to the innkeeper's counter, sidling against the bar while he waited for the man to serve a small queue of customers ahead of him.

A well-dressed pair of gentlemen were chatting to Mr. Wiscomb. By the nature and volume of their laughter, Poppy could only gather the subject was ribald. Behind them, a woman with a baby in her arms and a little girl beside her made a pained expression at their talk. It seemed the men's laughter had roused the infant, for he suddenly began to wail. The baby's shrieks startled the older child, who, in her distress, dropped the bun she had been eating on the floor. When her mother told her not to pick it up, she began to wail as well. The woman crouched down, trying to soothe the angry baby and the offended child all at once, while the gentlemen in front of her turned and glared at the racket her family made.

Archer, taking all this in, bent to his knees and said something to the mother. The woman nodded and he addressed the little girl. She stared at him warily, still crying, and he bent down and collected her discarded treat and then picked her up and set her on a stool. He plucked another pastry from behind the counter and set it on a plate for her, doing all this with the workmanlike alacrity he might have shown had he owned the inn himself. He then set about wiping away the girl's tears with his handkerchief as he said something that she found amusing. By the time her bun was devoured, the two of them were laughing like old chums, to the astonishment of the harried mother. Having made a bosom friend, and waited out his place in line, he bowed to the child, winked at the mother, tossed a few coins to Mr. Wiscomb, and then exited the inn to confer with the coachmen outside.

Poppy observed all this while munching on bacon and working her way through two deliciously sweet and milky cups of tea.

"Anything else, Your Grace?" Mrs. Wiscomb asked.

"No, thank you," she said. "But it was delicious."

She walked back up the stairs to her room to prepare herself for the remaining leg of the trip. At her request, her maid had left a small satchel of her personal effects and a mug of boiled water on the dressing table.

She poked around inside the bag and found the small glass jar prepared by Mrs. Todd. Pennyroyal tea. According to her book on healing, she would need to take a small dose daily to produce the desired effect.

She hesitated, tapping her fingernails against the glass.

I suppose you will simply have to trust me.

No. It wasn't right.

He had done only what he said he would do: treat her with kindness, make their marriage friendly. It was petty to hold her own desire for some stronger form of attachment against him, given she had explicitly agreed to its absence.

He was not the problem. *He* had not gone against his word.

She had.

She shoved the bottle in her pocket unopened, closed the satchel, and returned it to her trunk.

Outside, the two carriages and accompanying luggage coach had been readied for their departure. Archer leaned against the door of their private vehicle, looking tall and handsome in the morning light. The scene she had made the night before must have left him less disturbed than it had her, for he looked like the living male embodiment of a refreshing ocean breeze.

"Ready to depart?" he asked her.

"Just one moment." She popped around to the coach and located a trunk secured just inside the doors. She slipped the bottle from her pocket and threw it in with her books and seeds and other items from her workshop desk.

She smiled at her husband.

"I'm ready."

CHAPTER 21

*P*oppy grew ill at ease as the carriage wound its way down the narrow streets of London.

Something was different about Archer.

All day he had been buoyant and unruffled, like the previous day had never happened. He had beaten her savagely at chess. When she protested, he taught her five-card loo and beat her savagely at that. With every mile they drew closer to the city, he became more polished, more blandly debonair. It was as though London were a shield he wore, and he was putting it back on.

Now the city rose up around them in an ominous miasma, as gray as Wiltshire was green. The streets were clogged with hackney coaches, carts, sedan chairs, and pedestrians darting through the muck and the rush of traffic. As they wound their way past Cheapside and through the throng of the Exchange, she could feel London on her tongue and in her nostrils, a gritty, sooty air that smelled of coal and dung and damp. She coughed, and shut the window of the carriage.

Archer raised an eyebrow. "Had enough so soon?"

"I knew the air was bad here, but no one mentioned you could chew it."

"One doesn't come to London for fresh air, Cavendish. Look, we're here."

The carriage drew to a stop in front of a row of terraced houses that lined a small square northeast of the Exchange. Archer led her inside the tallest of them, a four-story town house with a basement kitchen and an artless garden to the rear. Though the house was modern in its comforts, the rooms were dark and the furnishings were spartan. It was as unlike Westhaven as any home she'd ever seen.

Left alone in her husband's study to refresh herself while the servants brought in her trunks, she examined his desk and shelves. They were immaculate and spare, not a paper out of order. So unlike the cheerful chaos in which she worked that she wondered if all he ever did was alphabetize his files and square papers into ninety-degree angles.

And now she was alone with him, in his tidy, ordered kingdom. Trapped.

Stop that, she commanded herself. *You are being absurd.* Her behavior these past days had been dreary and wholly unbefitting of her character. What did it matter to her if his home was unwelcoming? This was *London.* The center of the world. The only place where her dreams made any sense. A woman of her constitution did not arrive in *London* and reproach it for lacking the scenery of Grove Vale. She must rise to the occasion, not slump around and mourn the countryside, as she was doing in this chair.

"You dislike it here," Archer said, returning before she had quite followed her own command.

"No I don't," she said, just to argue.

"I admit it's not fashionable. The advantage of Hoxton is only its proximity to my counting-house. I can set you up somewhere grander, if you wish. Westmead House in St. James's Square is much more lavish, if rather oppressive for my taste."

"No need. Your home is lovely." Her voice came out bright and hard at the notion that he would so casually suggest she decamp to a separate residence three days into their marriage.

He crossed his arms and stared at her for a moment, and then his shoulders dropped and the unemotional and somewhat frightening personage that had emerged in the carriage softened, just a little. His face said that he plainly did not know what to do with her. She shared his bafflement. She did not know either.

He touched her shoulder lightly. "Poppy, if this is about yesterday—if you're still upset—"

"I am *not* upset," she said primly. "Only tired."

"I don't believe you," he said softly. "Poppy … while our arrangement is based on business, that does not mean we cannot be allies. Friends. I want that. And I want you to be happy here."

His face held so much concern for her. So much *bloody* earnestness. This was his damnable skill—he looked at her like that, said things in that tone, and made mincemeat of her caution. He lured her to be that most dangerous of things: honest.

He was like a chimera. A man who didn't care, wearing the face of one who did.

She shrugged off his touch. "I believe I shall take a nap. I assume I am to have my own room?"

He dropped his hands to his sides.

"Of course. Gibbs has prepared the chamber downstairs across the hall from mine."

She turned to go, but he cleared his throat.

"I need to go to the counting-house for a few hours. I'll be back by half nine."

She tried to keep from gaping.

"But it's late."

"There's something I must attend to."

She felt her composure slipping once again. It was her first evening in his house. In his city. And he meant for her to spend it *alone*.

"Perhaps it could wait until tomorrow?" she ventured, forcing her voice to remain steady.

He glanced at the clock.

"I'm afraid not."

Seeing her pitiful expression, he softened his tone, but only slightly. "Rest. We can have a late supper if you like. But don't wait up for me if you'd rather sleep. It's been a trying day."

He turned and left without a backward glance. She heard him make some quip to Gibbs, positively jaunty to be rid of her. And then she heard his carriage drive away.

Where he was really going, she couldn't say.

But no part of her believed that his destination was a counting-house.

ARCHER STROLLED INTO HIS COUNTING-HOUSE TO FIND GORDON, his secretary, waiting at his desk with the maps and papers he'd sent word to get in order.

"The deed is signed?"

"As of this morning," Gordon said.

"Thank Christ," he muttered.

"Is something amiss?" Gordon asked.

"Not anymore."

He had realized this morning why his marriage was not working: he was conducting himself *exactly* the wrong way.

Had he married Gillian Bastian, and not Poppy Cavendish, it would have made sense to spend his early days being as courtly and gentle as he was able. Attending to her small comforts, easing her into the demands of the marriage bed, plying her with compliments. Making her feel secure in the irrevocable, lifelong decision she had made by marrying him.

But Poppy was as much like Gillian as a ship captain was like a ball gown. She had not entered this marriage expecting wooing.

She had entered it expecting property and manpower. In her position, he would be anxious and irritable too, waiting to see if he had made a rotten deal.

He did not need to assuage her with affection. He needed to assuage her with an act of good faith.

He glanced over the plans. The property was perfect. As soon as she saw it, she could have no doubt of his intentions. Then, surely, the easy way between them would be restored.

"You've done well, Gordon. I'll bring Her Grace here tomorrow. Have an architect on hand. She'll not wish to waste time."

"Very well, Your Grace. These came for you." Gordon handed him a stack of letters.

He sorted quickly through correspondence, not planning to linger, and paused at a note from the Marquess of Avondale that did not look like a formal congratulation on his nuptials.

Westmead— In light of your recent happy news, a word of caution: the rumors are intensifying. Elena and I have an investigator looking for the source. Until the matter is resolved, utmost circumspection is advised. (But then, that shouldn't be a problem with a new wife to distract you.) My best wishes for your happiness, if you are capable of such vaporous emotions. (Really.)

Avondale

This was not good news.

Avondale was his fellow investor in Elena Brearley's club. In the past two years there had been rumors of its existence, despite the precautions Elena took to ensure discretion to her members. They had stamped down whispers before, but speculation now was especially ill-timed, with zealous evangelicals making thunderous condemnations against vice in every page and pulpit, kicking up sentiment that could make exposure ruinous.

He wrote back to Avondale offering the services of his private tracer, lingering longer than he liked. By the time he descended to the street, his coachman was idling with horses at the ready.

"On to Charlotte Street, Your Grace?"

He hesitated. He had planned to make the second stop. *Needed* to make the second stop.

A session with Elena would restore his mind to order. Purge the uncertainty that rose in him when his thoughts turned to Poppy.

And yet he found he had lost his stomach for it.

It was too great a risk to go there with the club facing renewed speculation.

Hang the speculation. That was no excuse. He had always found ways of arriving undetected when the need arose. Fear had never stopped him before, only made him cautious.

What was stopping him was Poppy's distress at being left alone.

You're being bloody sentimental.

But no, surely it was only decent to offer his wife company until she was comfortable in his home.

His coachman was waiting for an answer.

"Back to Hoxton, please."

In the darkness of the carriage, he rustled Elena's key from under his cravat and worried it against his thumb until it hurt.

He would find a discreet way to go tomorrow.

He'd make certain of it.

Poppy paced her husband's study, too restless and aggrieved to sleep.

Where had he really gone?

If she had been properly immune to him, it would not matter. But she wasn't.

If she only knew what he was hiding, perhaps she could harden herself to him. Avoid this miserable feeling of wanting more than she was due.

She'd wandered around his house all evening, hoping the

furnishings might bear clues as to his secret self. But the rooms were tidy and impersonal, offering little evidence beyond neatness.

Gibbs, the butler, appeared in the study with a tray of tea she had requested.

"Is there somewhere I might put my things?" she asked him, looking at her husband's orderly shelves.

Gibbs gave her a nervous look. "His Grace keeps this room just so. Perhaps you would like me to have your things moved to the sitting room? There is ample space and it has lovely views of the garden."

She looked around. It would indeed gall her husband to disturb this space. She would take her childish solace in her ability to irk him.

"I prefer this room. Better light. I'm sure Westmead won't mind."

A vein in Gibbs's forehead pulsed. Nevertheless, he nodded. "Of course. There is an empty cupboard there. Would you like me to help you unpack?"

"No, thank you."

She sat down with her trunks and began to sort through her things. At the top of the pile was her old, fraying copy of *The Gardener's Dictionary*. She opened it to the front page. *Elizabeth Cavendish, 1731.* She traced her mother's pretty script with her fingernail, then put it aside and found her ledger. Still odious. She smiled. It soothed her to see and touch these relics of her life in Wiltshire. She did not limit herself to the cupboard but scattered them all about the room.

When she had emptied the first trunk—and satisfied herself that she had assailed Archer's study thoroughly enough to irritate him—she began looking through the crates for her botanical correspondence. She opened a trunk marked only *Westhaven* and saw it was not one of her own, but was filled with Archer's things. Neat stacks of books. Reports from stewards. Sheaves of correspondence bound in gleaming leather. Rather discordantly, an old muslin bag was tucked in among these items, ripped at the corner and coming apart. It did not look nearly expensive or well cared for enough to be something Archer owned. Curious, she plucked it from the case and opened it. From inside she pulled out a miniature portrait in a wooden frame. It was a pretty child, two or three years old, with curly blond hair. Georgie.

The likeness was not quite accurate—the eyes weren't right and Georgie's complexion was pale, not sun-kissed—but she smiled. It was rather sweet that Archer kept a portrait of his godson. She fished out a second portrait from the bag, wondering if it was Constance.

The face that looked back at her was not the deceptively angelic visage of her sister-in-law. It was the image of a ghost.

Bernadette.

Her guilty, prying fingers froze. She should not—*should not*—have seen this. But now that she had, she could not stop herself from looking back at the other painting. The little boy was not a poorly rendered Georgie.

He was Archer's son.

Benjamin.

For a long time she sat there, looking.

Suddenly the desolation of his loss was real to her. Two living, breathing people who had once been precious to him now lived in a worn bag in the corner of his trunk.

She tried to picture him at the age of one and twenty faced with such a loss. To imagine the long expanse of years in which he'd borne that grief alone.

For two days she had resented him for holding parts of himself in reserve. But looking at these faces, she understood why such a man might analyze the risks of marriage and determine he could not afford them.

She could not fill a hole that was the size of these two portraits.

And he had not asked her to.

She was ashamed.

"You're still awake," Archer said, walking into the room at precisely the wrong moment.

She froze, caught.

There was nowhere to hide what she held in her hands.

Poppy was crouched on the floor of his study in a messy pile of her belongings. Drooped so, she looked like a bird who had returned to its nest to nurse a broken wing.

"What is it that you've got there?" he asked, trying to keep out of his voice his irritation at the hundreds of objects of miscellany she had seemingly spent the evening strewing about his pristine room.

She finally turned to look at him and he realized she was not ignoring him. She looked stricken, hunched over something in her lap.

His frustration with her curdled into an urgent, melting need to make it better. He should not have left her here alone all evening. He was an arse.

"Poor girl, what is it? Surely London is not as bad as that."

He reached down to take her hands and found there was a hunk of something hard in them. Wood.

He glanced down and froze.

The object she'd been examining was a portrait.

Of his son.

For a moment he could hardly see. The stab of his boy's face was still so physical. It hurt to look.

He made himself set the portrait aside. He found its pair in her lap, and took that too. And then he slumped beside her. He did not know what else to do.

"I'm so sorry," she sighed.

"It's all right," he said, not quite sure that it was, but helpless to say otherwise.

She looked up at him, her eyes tired and glassy. "I was angry at you. And you've done nothing wrong. I'm sorry."

He leaned back against the cupboard.

He did not know what to say.

He did not know how to feel.

She sometimes made him feel so much. So much.

She picked up the portraits and studied them. He averted his eyes. He wished she would put them away. It ravaged him, to look at them. It ravaged him to remember them at all.

"I forgot how beautiful she was," Poppy said.

Her words were like a stab in the chest. Because so had he.

"I wish she was here," she said. "I wish they both were."

His heart came dislodged and landed somewhere in his knees. "So do I."

And it was true, though he had long ago learned to live in the aura of their absence.

"Your son," she said shakily. "He looks *just* like Georgie."

He could barely get the word out. "Yes."

She edged out from beside him and turned to look at him with her lovely, solemn face and wrapped her arms around his neck.

The gesture was so simple, so childlike, that he felt himself breaking. No one had ever consoled him quite like this. He supposed no one had ever known he'd needed it. He had turned to different forms of solace.

He looked up and placed a kiss on her lips. She tasted of salt, the way she had when he'd first kissed her in the forest.

She returned his kiss tenderly. No biting, no jostling for control. Just her tongue meeting his, letting him lead where he wanted. Letting him draw life from her.

"Archer, take me to bed," she whispered.

He lifted her from her nest of papers and carried her down the stairs to his room.

Slowly, he undressed her. He took his time.

When he went to undress himself, she stopped him. Drew his shirt above his head and dropped it on the floor, not pausing to fuss about his scars. Without a word of question she dragged the leather cord from around his neck and dropped it too. She simply dropped it all in a messy pile and pulled him with her toward the bed.

He lowered himself on her lovely, moonlit body.

And when she took him in her arms, the feeling of her skin was something he wanted with a ferocity that scared him.

CHAPTER 22

*A*rcher waited until breakfast to ask her to the counting-house. After she'd shyly kissed his temple and left his room to dress. After he'd gone into his study to find that she'd tidied up her mess and put his family's portraits in a place of honor on the mantel.

By the time he handed her down from the carriage and onto Threadneedle Street, he'd begun to doubt himself. He so badly wanted to make her happy with this gesture. But a desk at an investment concern was not most women's dream of wedded bliss.

Still, he enjoyed leading her inside, through ground-floor rooms that buzzed with conversation and the clinking of expensive china. Though he was known as an investor, the core of his business was accruing information. His stewards did the work of intelligence officers, cultivating networks whose knowledge could be stitched together to make predictions on supply, demand, and price. Over the years, he and his partners had honed this to an art, methodically working their sources to reveal a hidden map of markets—serge, porcelain, timber, ore—that others couldn't see.

He was proud of what he'd built here. Many of his stewards had risen from apprenticeship to become powerful figures on the Exchange in their own right. With his backing they made fortunes, employed hundreds. And the concern collected dividends, and used them to expand.

He took Poppy to the top floor of the building, where each of his senior stewards had a private desk. He led her to an empty one in the sunniest corner of the room. Behind it was a map of England, plotted with pins in different colors.

"What's this?" she asked.

"Your wedding present, Cavendish."

She smiled. Truly smiled. "My own desk. And look, you went to the trouble of decorating," she said, gesturing at the map.

Her quiet pleasure made him almost bashful. "The pins are the nurseries of southwest England. The blue lines are waterways; the black dots are ports. Based on our research, the most suitable parcel of land for a trading nursery would be just west of London, near the large red pin, at Hammersmith. We made some inquiries and found a two-hundred-acre plot with access to the river."

"Very good intelligence, Your Grace. I shall look into it."

He took the deed from his pocket and held it out to her, nervous as a boy. "No need. It's yours."

She scanned over the lines. "It's mine?"

She looked at him queerly. Perhaps he had overstepped.

"That is, if you want it. I don't mean to intrude in your affairs. Though, if you expect me to build you a nursery by winter, we're going to need a piece of land to build it on."

Her face softened, and he was embarrassed that she had seen his flash of nerves.

"I'm touched. I had no idea you had paid such attention to the specifics of my plans."

"Well, Cavendish," he said gruffly, "a clever businessman knows that when a woman is so struck by the brilliance of an idea she falls off her horse, it may be worth further inquiry."

She laughed. "Thank you. You are very thoughtful."

"There's one more thing. The property came with a house. It's in an indifferent state of repair but rather lovely. I thought you might prefer it to the town house."

An odd expression flashed behind her eyes, and the pleasure in them vanished. "Oh?" was all she said.

God's toes, but it was torture, maintaining her approval. He'd hoped she'd be pleased, given her obvious dislike of his terrace in Hoxton.

"Would you like to see it?" he ventured nonetheless.

"Now?"

He nodded.

Poppy tried to hide her apprehension as Archer led her past the crowd of men loading goods bound for lighters and down the narrow footpath to his wharf. "The river is the fastest way of getting west," he said, helping her onto his wherry. "And I thought you might enjoy the view."

She had never been on a boat. This one was as finely made as any carriage, black lacquered with handsome silver fixtures and deeply polished wood.

Archer tucked an arm around her shoulders.

At his touch, she felt like she might weep. After the way he had made love to her last night, she'd been so sure she was not imagining he cared for her. And yet here he was, making the distance between them official: installing her in a separate house. She should not be surprised. He had as good as said this was his plan the day before. But still, it stung.

The oarsmen slowed the boat at a tall iron gate built up along the riverbank. "A private wharf," Archer said. "You'll not need to pay for access to the quays. And we can build a warehouse here. I've already seen to it that our best builder is made available."

She tried to muster some enthusiasm for this. But the truth was that she could scarcely concentrate, because her heart had spent its puppy-love years sighing over plants and was unaccustomed to such violent surges of emotion.

Only when they alighted and she saw the grounds did her mood improve. The empty stretch of land looked nothing like London at all.

The grass was green and rose up to her knees. She reached down and removed a glove, burying her fingers in the soil. It came up easily, dark and thick with roots and fungi. Earthworms writhed about in the hole she'd made, an auspicious sign that trees would grow.

Suddenly, she could *see* it. The sloping ground where she would build walled gardens, the places for potting sheds, force houses, an arboretum. She walked deeper onto the property, imagining how it would look buzzing with builders and masons, humming with the work of hired gardeners dragging up the soil to prepare for the first planting.

She had made the right decision.

Her dream was going to come true. She itched to get to work. She moved quickly through the property, making plans. She nearly forgot that Archer was with her until he tapped her shoulder and pointed out the pathway to the house. Through a grove of trees, a large Italianate villa stood near a quiet, pretty flower garden, still colorful with the fading blooms of August. Standing on the empty land, shrouded in its pleasant garden, it looked like a piece of her beloved countryside. If you ignored the musky river breeze, the place could be Bantham Park.

Still, she didn't want it.

"Would you like to tour inside?" he asked.

Not really.

Nevertheless she nodded.

Archer led her through wide, airy rooms, blessed by high ceilings and pleasant lines, even if the paint was peeling. She tried to admire the plasterwork, the birdsong drifting in from the garden, the good air and strong light. But all she could think about was the size. How she would bear to live in it alone she could hardly fathom.

"There's room enough for you to conduct your business here, if you choose," Archer pointed out, smiling like this was excellent news. He was correct, and yet all her heart heard was the word "you." Not *us*. Not him, whom her heart desired despite her better sense.

"Do you like it?" he asked her, as they stood in the largest bedchamber on the top floor.

"It's beautiful."

He must have heard the note of sadness in her voice, for he cocked his head at her.

"When I saw it, I thought it suited you. It reminded me of your home."

The sweetness of the sentiment stabbed at her. She turned away from him.

"We can have it renovated any way you like."

"I like it as it is."

"What's wrong? What aren't you saying to me?"

"Only that you're very kind, and I'm very grateful," she said, striving for a joyful tone. It would only confuse things to say any more. It was she who kept allowing herself to mistake his kindness for something more. He had never been anything but clear in saying what he wanted.

In the corridor she noticed a door they had not entered. "What's through there?" she asked.

"The attic," he said.

"I wonder if it's too damp for seed storage." She opened the door and found a staircase lit by skylights and painted in pastel scenes from fairy stories. The sunlit room above was filled with wooden toys and little cots—some previous family's nursery.

She turned back to look at Archer, but he hadn't followed her up the stairs.

He was waiting at the landing, drumming his fingers on the banister, his face troubled.

"It's a nursery," she told him. "A beautiful one."

"Yes," he said, like she'd discovered something he'd rather she not see.

"You called it an attic."

He stared at her.

"I was going to ask the architect to move the nursery downstairs," he said finally. "I would never be able to sleep with them helpless above us."

Now it was her turn to stare at him.

"In case of fire," he went on weakly.

He didn't wish to leave her here.

He wished to live here *with her*. In this gorgeous, rambling, romantic house.

Where he might worry after the safety of his children in the nursery as they slept.

Children he claimed meant no more to him than ink on the pages of a contract.

Her loneliness flared into something brighter, harder, more like anger.

At herself, for being moved by him. And at him, for making gestures that meant everything and insisting that they meant nothing at all.

Cordial business arrangements did not feel this way. *Cordial business* did not make one feel like one's heart was constricting one's throat, depriving one of breath.

She sank back against the door.

"*Oh,*" she said.

"OH," POPPY SAID, LOOKING AT HIM ODDLY.

Archer shifted on his feet and looked away from her, hating to be observed feeling as he did.

She made an odd sound in the back of her throat. It sounded like ... *laughter*.

He glanced up. She rested her head back against the wall with her eyes closed, some private amusement taking hold of her until she was actually *shaking* with silent mirth at the apparent absurdity of what he'd just admitted.

He gaped at her, unbelieving.

Something about that nursery, when he had seen it, had ripped him open. Something in him was unable to walk into that room and think merely about "heirs." He thought of family. Of what it would be like to have one. With her.

He didn't want to think about it. He had hoped she wouldn't notice the nursery door at all.

Clearly, he had been foolish to think she might see the hope and fear that overtook him at the thought of something so fragile taking root here.

She hadn't noticed anything. He spoke of fire, and she *laughed* at him.

"May I ask what you find so amusing?" he asked.

She opened her eyes. There was no mirth in them. "Only that I now see you intend to live here too."

He stared at her in disbelief. "That *is* traditionally the way that marriage is conducted," he said, not bothering to keep the edge out of his voice.

"Perhaps. But this isn't a traditional marriage. Or so you keep insisting."

He had had enough of this.

"I insist on nothing more than what you agreed to."

"Yet I find myself confounded by what exactly it is that you want from me. You wish to make love in the rain, yet you rebuke me for asking questions of your health? You say we are no more than polite associates, that you will have no interest in your heir, and yet you wish to live with me in a family house with fairy pictures in the nursery? Forgive me, Archer, if I find your notions of a business arrangement maddening."

"Maddening. I do apologize, Poppy. However, I fail to see what you find so difficult to understand. I told you we would attempt to conceive a child, and we have. I told you I would enable you to build the business you desire, and I have. If my attempts at fulfilling these commitments with some concern for your pleasure and comfort are too *maddening*, I will leave off of them forthwith. You have my word."

Never mind that it was puerile and that he was a man of four and thirty, he turned on his heel and marched downstairs.

Maddening. *She* was maddening.

He had spent days tiptoeing around her unhappiness, weeks scouring half the country to find exactly the right gift for her, making his men half-deviled with his demands for briefs on horticultural trade and agrarian economics. He had lain awake at that godforsaken inn racked with guilt for hurting her, more guilt still for, even in his state of shame, not being able to shake the memory of how their bodies fit together—for being obsessed with how she tasted, how she sounded as she came, that precise moment she had sunk down on his cock and bitten his thumb and ridden the very life from him.

And then, last night.

He was, indeed, *mad* for her. Sick and foolish with it.

He had to stop this.

He had to draw a line.

He should have done it yesterday like he'd intended.

He'd let the threat of rumors make him cowardly.

"Make sure Her Grace is seen home in the wherry," he said to the architect waiting downstairs with a steward. "I have business elsewhere."

He strode down the country lane to the nearest thoroughfare and flagged down a hackney. "Charlotte Street," he ordered.

He sat in the dark, enclosed vehicle and closed his eyes, picturing Elena in her severe black gown, a raised eyebrow at seeing him in such a state in daylight, with no appointment and the threat of whispers circling. How furious she'd be. What she'd do to him.

His cock stirred, and he grasped it through his breeches, throwing back his head in anticipation. Fuck, but this was what he needed. He clenched his jaw and stroked himself. God, the relief it would be, after these weeks of denying himself. The pure, bracing pleasure of it. Without it, his control over himself was slipping. He was becoming far too bloody *soft*.

Poppy's face broke into his thoughts. His innocent young wife going glumly about her business in the pretty family house where he'd left her as he stroked himself to a frenzy in a hackney imagining the crack of leather on his back.

It doesn't matter. He had promised her a greenhouse and a ship —not the loyalty of his body. Not his private, most intimate self.

Of course it does.

He thrust his hands away from his groin and into his hair. He wanted to rip it from his skull. He wanted to scream in frustration.

Instead he stuck his arm outside and pounded on the side of the coach.

"Change of address. Threadneedle Street."

CHAPTER 23

*T*en minutes.

Ten minutes she had wandered the empty house alone, searching for her husband. Ten minutes she had poked around in corridors and closets before it finally dawned on her that he had *left her there*. An indignity confirmed by the sheepish architect and steward waiting in the parlor, where they had no doubt spent ten minutes listening to her disbelievingly calling out her husband's name.

"His Grace asked me to see you home in his wherry," Mr. Partings mumbled, flushing.

"I see," she said.

And she did. She finally saw.

She saw the image in this man's eyes of the pathetic, abandoned figure she was cutting. An object of pity. The Duchess of Westmead, once again, crushed.

She saw this woman, and she had had enough of her.

For this creature, the Duchess of Westmead, whose fine clothing she wore, was insufferable. Poppy was bored senseless of this lady, with her ever-injured feelings and fits of bloody unrequited *longing*.

Poplar Elizabeth Cavendish did not behave this way. Poplar Elizabeth Cavendish had no patience for ladies who acted foolishly, so deep and sure was her scorn for the practice of making oneself vulnerable to men.

Poplar Elizabeth Cavendish was smart enough to recognize that Westmead was neither her friend nor her ally. He was merely her *husband*. Husbandry, in the purest definition of the word, was the nature of their connection. And somehow, she had let this fact escape her despite her training as a botanist.

In the greenhouse there was no romance to the act of reproduction. She did not grow misty-eyed as she swabbed pollen from a stamen and applied it to a pistil with her brush. One crossed two hearty specimens to produce a third. That was all he'd asked of her. Why she had allowed herself to imbue the act with so much fretfulness she could not say.

Except that unschooled countrywomen from the land where she was from sometimes whispered of a spirit called the devil in the road. A sprite who waited at the juncture of wooded paths and offered riches for a maiden's soul. There were many versions of this story, but the moral was always the same: the temptations the man offered were damnation in disguise.

In other words: she should have known.

Which is why, as soon as she stepped back into the Hoxton town house, she marched upstairs and summoned a maid and rid herself of her stiff Valeria Parc day dress, with its bustle and embroidery and its suffocating stays.

"Such a pretty gown, Your Grace," her maid enthused.

"Do you like it, Sophie? Why don't you keep it?"

"But you've only worn it once. I took it out of paper just this morning."

"I find it doesn't suit me."

She went into the back of the dressing room and searched a trunk. Here it was. Old gray muslin with a mended hem. Her favorite.

Once dressed, she went to the study and sat at her husband's desk. She regarded his neatly sorted papers and expensive kit of writing implements. She pushed them aside and smiled as they fluttered to the floor. She placed her tattered ledger on her right, her botanical correspondence on her left, and a stack of blank pages in between.

And Poplar Elizabeth Cavendish set to work.

If she had indeed traded her soul, she intended to get what she was promised for it.

The devil could hang.

~

ARCHER CLIMBED THE TOWN HOUSE STAIRS AT MIDNIGHT, HAVING worked in the counting-house until the boiling feeling in his blood simmered into something less likely to cause burns to passersby. He intended to finish sorting his effects from West-haven as late into the night as it took to achieve a state of calm that might allow him to sleep.

But that would be impossible. Because his wife was in his study basking at his desk, upon which she had created a mess so disordered it resembled primordial chaos.

"What are you doing in here?" he demanded, at a volume that was not civil.

She glanced up at him, as though annoyed at his intrusion into *his own* study in *his own* house. "Working."

"I did not give you permission to colonize my desk," he snapped. "Nor did I invite you to use my study. This house is filled with empty rooms. Pick one."

"I don't believe I *asked* for your permission, Your Grace," she said, unmoved by his aggression. "And you have no right to shout at me. Do go away."

He stared at her, so serene in her disorder. He noticed papers at her feet.

She had pushed his papers to the floor.

A man aspired to be rational and levelheaded. He aspired to meet his responsibilities, to be a river to his family. For some, perhaps, this came naturally. For him, it came by rigor.

His wife could mock his stacks of paper, his lists and calculations. But these things had never failed him. They proved that turmoil could be ruthlessly sorted until it was brought to order. Control was the only antidote to the unseemly, chaotic force of passion.

Which was why he could not seem to make his tone anything but menacing when he parried back, "In fact, I am your husband. I have *every* right to shout at you, or do whatever else I wish. As you are undoubtedly aware, given your uncommon familiarity with law."

Her chin somehow found a way to look even more contemptuous than usual.

"Ah yes," she sighed. "There are so many means of protecting male authority. The law … inheritance …" She reached across the desk and tapped a single disdainful finger to his chest. "*Brutish shows of strength.* We ladies lack such facile means. We must rely only on our wits. So please, Archer, invoke the law if it brings you comfort. But do so with the knowledge that you reveal yourself as weak."

She smiled at him serenely and resumed scribbling at her letter.

He tried a different tactic.

"Leave my fucking desk and go to bed, Poppy," he shouted.

Catlike, she smiled.

"I'm not *fatigued*, Your Grace."

If she meant to goad him, she had picked the wrong night to test what he was made of.

He was not unaware of the belief that he had no depth of feeling. That he was all hauteur, a domineering prig. When he heard these things about himself, he smiled, for it meant that it was working. It meant that the rafters he had built within himself to stanch the overflow of temperament were structurally sound and visually unassuming. The truth was that he did *not* lack feeling. He overflowed with it. It was a bloody labor to be the bloodless Duke of Westmead. There was nothing effortless about it.

And he allowed himself one release from this exertion. A town house on Charlotte Street where one could, at last, drop the demands of authority and the pretense of self-control. Where one could drop one's very self to the floor and be used accordingly. Without this relief, his true self bubbled over—all disorder and sentiment and grief.

And sometimes, like tonight: rage.

"If you aren't tired, I believe you have duties to perform," he said, knowing it was vile and not caring. "Come to bed."

Poppy reached out and ran a finger down his cheek. Her eyes were cold.

"Ah. You wish to lay claim to your marital rights?" She smiled with false sympathy. "I suppose I would be eager to exercise them too if I had had to pay so handsomely to secure what decent men can get by simply asking."

He stepped closer. "I did try the 'making love' approach, if you recall. My wife claimed she has no taste for it."

She raised a brow. "Judging by the nature of the book I found in your study at Westhaven, one wonders whether you have a taste for it yourself."

He froze. He knew exactly the book she meant.

At the idea of her reading it, his cock roused instantly to life. So, too, did his anger at the idea that she was once again *nosing through his private things*.

He leaned in so his face was an inch from hers. "Be careful what you might discover, Poppy. I cannot promise my tastes confine themselves to books."

He waited for her to ask him what he meant. But she only drew up with that feline smirk.

"Ah. Is that why you had to buy yourself a duchess? No one else would have you?"

She was provoking him. And it was working.

"As I recall, I rescued you from ruin when I could have had a *proper* lady. Not this"—he ran his hand down the dingy lace trim of her dress, letting his thumb crudely linger on the flesh above her breasts—"*mess.*"

Her expression went so black he worried she might slap him.

Instead, she barked out a mirthless laugh, as though she found even his attempts at cruelty ridiculous.

"Ah. The gallant man. How *heroic.*" She walked around the desk until she was flush with him and smiled. "Is that what you need to hear me say to enable your virility? What a strong and *fearsome* lord you are? Is that what you have wanted all along, Your Grace?"

She slid her hand down to the swelling in his breeches.

"Oh, my, I can see that it's working. You're so eager I don't know that we'll have time to get you to a bed."

They locked eyes. Hers flashed with challenge. She was waiting for him to deny it. To apologize. To retreat.

He wasn't going to.

He spread his thighs, making his arousal plain.

If she wanted the truth she could have it. Nothing made him harder than a woman who saw him for the wretch he really was.

She reached down and took the falls of his breeches in her two hands. Not breaking her stare, she smiled. Then she ripped.

Tiny buttons scattered quietly to the floor, the only sound in the room. Other than the one that gave up the game: he moaned.

She smirked and wrapped her fist around his cock.

"I suspect, Archer," she said, running her hand along his length, "that you are about to embarrass yourself with how pitifully you want me."

It was certainly a tempting thought.

"You want to, don't you?" she asked, taunting him with long, fluid strokes. "You want to spend right here on your precious papers."

She thumbed the tip where, indeed, the likelihood of such an event was presaged by a leak of male excitement.

"But then, that would violate the terms of our agreement, wouldn't it, Your Grace? Isn't that why you *saved* me? Because you knew I was adept with seed?"

Even as she said it, she was lifting up her skirts.

She pushed him back, so he was not just leaning against the desk, but was splayed on top of it.

She spread his thighs to make a berth for her knee and poised herself above him, her quim a hairbreadth from his shaft.

Could she *smell* how badly he wanted this? Could she *read his mind?*

"Fuck," he cried out, because he had to say something to keep from coming at the *thought* of what was happening. He jerked up, to feel her with his cock. But she was faster, flitting out of reach.

"If you want it—beg."

"Please," he got out, dying for it.

"Please what?"

"Please *fuck me*, Poppy."

She adjusted his cock until the angle pleased her.

And then, as she had once done in the bathing tub that had a place among his fondest memories, she sank down and took him in.

It was then that he realized there was more to her than she let on.

For she was so wet you'd have thought she'd been sitting at his desk teasing herself for hours. Imagining using him just like this.

She *liked* it.

And so she won the game. For that was all it took for him to explode inside her, barely one thrust deep.

"Fuck," he yelled again. He smacked the side of the desk with the force of it. "Fucking hell."

She did not release him.

"Don't move."

She put a hand beneath her dress to feel herself and rocked against him, hard, until she buckled with a shivering, shaking sob that rang out in the quiet house.

She slid slickly off him and primly returned her dress to rights, while he lay there, panting, paralytic.

"You may have your desk back, Your Grace," she said. "I've taken what use I had from it."

POPPY LEFT HER SPENT HUSBAND SPLAYED OUT ON THE DESK AND walked blindly to her bedchamber, where she bolted the door behind her and stood in shock at what had just transpired. At what he'd said to her. At what she'd done to him. At how he'd thirsted for it. And how she had.

Numb, she removed her clothing and got in bed.

Since she had known the Duke of Westmead, he had been tightly coiled. His manner brought firmly into line.

Only that first night that he'd touched her, in his study, had she ever seen him waver. Even when he'd told her of his wife and child, he had fought so hard to keep a grip on himself that grief had had to exit him by an explosion of force, unbidden.

Tonight the mask had finally slipped.

He'd been filthy. Disrespectful. Mean. He'd deserved the contempt he'd gotten.

And if she was not mistaken, he'd relished getting it.

He'd given her a clue. Another sight of something he kept hidden. A darkness in him that spoke to something equally dark in herself. A part of her that had been waiting all her life to see the pictures in that book, because it answered instincts deep inside of her she did not trust or understand.

They could not go on like this.

Because the darkness of that scene was hateful. Its pleasures, such as they were, a slinging of anger back and forth.

The words he'd said to her were cruel.

The things she'd done to him were insulting.

They would not have felt so vital were they not a symptom of a bitter war that she was losing.

The fact that she'd *enjoyed* it left her lonely and afraid. She longed to knock on his door and apologize. To curl up beside him in the dark and say that she was sorry and confused and sad and ask him what that coupling had meant and why this marriage *hurt* so much.

She could not imagine what he'd say.

They'd done altogether too much talking. Whatever this ragged thing between them was, conversing served only to make it worse.

And yet, despite all that, she touched herself, remembering how he'd shuddered as she'd grabbed him. How his eyes had flashed with something dark and raw and wild she'd never seen in them before.

She brought herself to satisfaction twice before she slept, remembering.

And when she awoke, it was with two words burning bright in her mind, like a lighthouse viewed from a roiling sea, the only hope of her salvation.

Never. Again.

CHAPTER 24

*C*ity of London
       December 5, 1753

"My sister and the Rosecrofts are back from Paris," Archer told his wife one cold December morning as they shared a carriage to the counting-house.

Poppy looked up from a letter she was reading. "How lovely. When will we see them?"

"Hilary is busy assembling her household, but I asked Constance to Hoxton for supper this evening." He paused, as he had grown careful not to make assumptions on her time. "I should be very glad if you could join us, if you are able."

"Yes, I will look forward to it. However, I must look in on the works at Hammersmith this afternoon, and will not be back in London until evening. Don't wait for me. I will arrange to take a separate conveyance home."

The carriage rolled to a stop on Threadneedle Street. Archer handed Poppy down, his touch the faintest press of flesh on flesh. Mere courtesy. Polite.

"I'm off to a meeting at Parliament," he said.

She smiled. "I wish you well with it."

He watched her go inside, cursing himself for allowing it to get this way: so scrupulously, unremittingly *polite*.

It had begun the morning after that night that had shattered their marriage into two separate acts.

He'd awoken with an inchoate, sickened dread he used to suffer after nights of heavy drinking in his youth. It took one long, groggy moment for the memory of what had happened the night before to catch up with the feeling near his sternum that it had been unsavory. When it did, he was sharply, violently awake. He no longer had an appetite for breakfast.

He had dressed himself slowly that morning, taking care to put the Duke of Westmead back in order. He had lingered, dallying with his shaving water, gathering the courage to say what he'd resolved to say as he'd lain in bed the night before, shaking with the weight of what had happened.

He was going to be honest with his wife.

He was going to confess.

His only question was how to do it.

He must begin by apologizing for letting his temper boil over and bleed into his desires, and for insulting her. He *hated* that he'd done it. He *hated* what he'd said the night before. The acts that it had led to had been a mockery of what he really wanted.

What he wanted was not angry. It was as tender as it was unmerciful.

He would explain about his tastes, and what they meant to him. He would acknowledge they were considered odd and must be practiced with discretion. He would describe the pleasures that were possible between two lovers who understood each other's needs and limits.

He would apologize for hiding what he craved and for intending to go on with it without her knowledge. He would admit that he'd always taken comfort that the ritual was performed by a practitioner for a fee, kept strictly separate from his life, because he could not stand to be so vulnerable before anyone he cared about more deeply. He'd thought that to allow his wife such intimate knowledge of his soul would be beyond endurance.

But he'd been wrong.

Because when he looked at Poppy, he could not separate his body from his heart.

He wanted to trust her with his whole self, if she would have him.

And he wanted her whole self in return.

She did not have to give it to him. He would make that clear. She need not share his predilections. She owed him *nothing*. But if she gave him her heart, he would guard it like a treasure, whatever she decided.

He took Elena's key from around his neck and put it in his pocket. He would tell her what it was. And if she wanted this secret part of him, she could have that too.

He'd squared his shoulders, inhaled, and walked downstairs to the breakfast room, feeling like he might vomit from sheer nerves.

But Poppy had not been at her usual spot at the table.

Gibbs informed him she had risen early and gone out.

Queasily, he'd proceeded to the counting-house. He was relieved when he found her there, alone, deep in concentration at her desk.

As he had stood there, fingering the key, trying to think of how he might begin, she had looked up, her green eyes a glassy bay, and her face a picture of despair.

"Yesterday was a mistake," she said quietly. Politely. "I regret it very much. I hope you'll agree it's best forgotten."

He had stood there, stricken with a temporary speechlessness.

"You were right to suggest we keep our distance," she added. "I should not have challenged you on that matter. I won't intrude on your privacy again."

She had returned politely to her work, not bothering to look up when he finally murmured a foggy "of course" and walked away.

He'd returned the key to the cord around his neck. And if in that moment he felt cowardly, by afternoon he was grateful she had spoken before he had revealed the depth of his misreading. Before he'd irrevocably destroyed how she saw him.

They rode home together in a carriage many hours later and were polite. They took supper in the house and discussed her nursery: still polite. She retired early, to her own room, tediously, insufferably polite.

The days went politely on, and the night that had so shaken them was not spoken of again. But, damn it, it was *felt*. For as autumn gave its polite way to winter, and the air grew unseasonably cold, they still had not recovered from it.

Poppy was subdued and serious, no matter how he tried to mend the rift between them. She worked from sunup to late evening at the counting-house, gaining influence and respect among the architects and builders who worked at her direction. At night she wrote to gardeners and botanists around the world, detailing the premise of her subscription scheme. She said little to him of her work or her ideas, except when she wished to learn of a detail about finance. Covenants. Insurance. Risk. His knowledge of these concepts and his advice on how to execute them to her best advantage were all she asked of him.

And what he asked of her was, once or twice a week, permission to join her in her bed. The act was as brief and awkward as such an intimacy could be. A transfer of seed from him to her. Polite. It left him feeling sickened. And for all that, it didn't take.

He had gotten his marriage of convenience. Now he saw he was a fool for wanting it. He missed Poppy, the companionship they had shared.

He made attempts at recovering it, when he could pry her from her work. He took her to the opera, to the theater, to Vauxhall and Rotten Row. She was gracious but unmoved. He took her shopping, to the elegant arcades along Lombard Street and the vivid stalls of Cheapside. She brought home nothing more than plants.

His house—before her merely a place to work and sleep—bloomed with plants. Pots and jars and vases of cut flowers appeared just so, like weeds springing from the earth after a rain, making Dutch still lifes of every room. His study amassed piles of books on botany and bits of chalk where she did her garden sketches late at night and little bowls of citrus fruit that gave off a pleasant scent. He began to find pressed flowers between the pages of his books.

He was grateful for this invasion. Her presence in his home was like Persephone's in the underworld, a light amidst the darkness. Which made him her Hades, coaxing her here against her nature, plying her with pomegranate seeds. Tempting her to stay forever.

Because, by God, in that moment, in the counting-house, when she had looked up at him with empty eyes, he'd been certain—certain—that she'd leave him.

It was a mercy that instead she'd merely resolved to pretend it hadn't happened. He returned it by promising, with every word he said to her, to be better. To live as though that night was not suspended in their every polite word.

For one thing was very clear. If he slipped and showed her that part of himself again, it would destroy what little of them remained.

He would never show her.

He would rather have a bit of her than nothing.

He would rather be scrupulously, miserably polite.

Poppy arranged herself at her sunny desk on the top floor of the counting-house and sorted through her lists. She had begun to understand why her husband had such an intense drive for order. When one was responsible for complicated details with limited time and thousands of guineas on the line, one could not make a muck of one's papers.

She filed the latest missives in a tray for her secretary. She made notes in her ledger for requests for certain cuttings and seeds that would inform her decisions on what to grow and import and noted the coordinates along the overland distribution route.

That sorted, she unlocked the drawer of plans and found the draftsman's scroll with the latest designs for Hammersmith. She made a few notes on the irrigation system and jotted down questions she must go over with Mr. Partings this afternoon.

She paused and smiled. Sometimes it still shocked her, the precious thrill of her autonomy.

For all the ways her marriage was an exercise in loneliness, it was a triumph in this one dazzling way. Westmead had not dissembled. He had given her complete control over her affairs and the stature to enact them without brooking any quibbles. Duchesses did not have to prove their right to make decisions, in the way that other females did.

Without that constant struggle, she was building something marvelous. It felt fierce and good to have been *exactly* right about herself. But it did nothing to counteract the aching weight that pressed down on her chest whenever her thoughts turned to her husband.

She restored her papers to their various places and locked the drawers behind her. These cabinets contained the priceless fruits of months of work—the shipping routes, the greenhouse plans, the planting schedules—and she so feared them being lost or stolen she took them home with her at night. Now that her dream was so close within reach, the thought of losing even an inch of ground made her nauseous.

"Your Grace," her secretary said. "Mr. Van Dijk has arrived. He is having coffee in the lobby."

"I will join him presently. Please file the letters I left on the tray, and keep note of the size of the orders."

She smoothed her skirts and gathered her proposal for the European leg of her subscription network. Mr. Van Dijk, with a thriving botanical garden situated just outside Amsterdam, was the ideal person to serve as her partner on the Continent. Downstairs, she found that he was taller and younger than she'd expected. He rose to greet her with a smile.

"Your Grace. What an honor."

"The honor is mine, Mr. Van Dijk. I have always been so grateful for your correspondence. Not every botanist is willing to tutor an untrained girl. By post, no less."

"Well, it is rare to find an untrained girl as knowledgeable about plants as the young Miss Cavendish," he said in careful English. "It was clear from your first letter that you had a particular gift."

"You flatter me. Tell me, how was your journey?"

They passed a quarter hour exchanging pleasantries before she could no longer stand the suspense and pushed her proposal across the table. Mr. Van Dijk's eyes lit with interest as she explained the details.

"I will provide the capital to build a warehouse near the ports," she explained. "Your nursery would supply the list of plants you see on page four in the quantities indicated, which I expect will grow as the subscription pool expands."

His blue eyes locked on hers. He was a handsome man—golden in complexion from his work out of doors—and his eyes held frank admiration for her. It was like a cool rain on a hot day, after her months of staring at the blank chill in Archer's eyes.

"I will have my solicitors review the terms, Your Grace, as a formality. But what you propose is most acceptable. I regret only that I cannot claim I thought of it myself."

Poppy bade the man farewell and walked him toward the doors, warm with pleasure.

"Handsome devil," a thick voice said from behind her as she returned inside the inner sanctum of the lobby. "Can't imagine Westmead would like the way you flirted with him."

She whirled around.

Tom Raridan was sprawled in a deep-set leather armchair, lounging king-like before a silver coffee service left by other guests. Dressed in the nondescript clothes of a Cit, he did not immediately look out of place among the well-heeled gentlemen conducting business in the hushed mahogany room. But up close, she could see that his pale skin bore blossoms of angry pink around his cheeks and nose, and his broad form had given way to bloat. Spirits. Taking him just as they had taken his father.

"You are unannounced, Mr. Raridan. If you wish to call on me properly to apologize for your behavior, I suggest you write my secretary and request an appointment."

"Think I'll stay. S'quite comfortable." He gestured so expansively at the sumptuous room his hand knocked over a silver candlestick, which she lurched to catch discreetly before it clattered to the floor.

"What is it that you want?"

"Came to visit my girl. Have a look around. Keep an eye on ol' Westy."

The smell of ferment wafted toward her on his breath. He'd already been drinking, though it wasn't yet noon. A faint tremor danced down the back of her neck. Fear.

"You should go," she said firmly. "Excuse me."

He jumped up so quickly his knees knocked into the coffee service, causing it to rattle. A group of gentlemen looked up, annoyed at the disturbance. She flashed them a smile of apology and moved toward the door to the counting-house stairs, but Tom was quicker, inserting himself between her and escape. She was trapped in plain sight, and he knew it. If she shouted for help, she would make a scene that would be the talk of the City for weeks.

"You need to leave," she hissed.

"Fine establishment, this counting-house. Had a look around. He's even got you a desk like a gentleman. Bet you like it better here than that ugly house in Hoxton." He was so close she felt flecks of spittle landing on her ear. "Had to spread your legs awfully wide for that shabby setup."

She scanned the room for a means of discreet escape. Archer was walking through the door, just back from his meeting. Thank heavens. She waved.

Her husband started at the sight of Tom and strode toward them.

"You speak of the devil, you raise him from hell," Tom sneered into her ear. "Filthy mouthful they have to say about the likes of him in the bawdy parts of town. He should be careful, lest the wrong ears catch wind of what they say about him."

"How dare you," she hissed.

"If I'd known you were after a cully, I'd have been happy to oblige. My arse wouldn't mind a taste of the leathers from the likes of you." He touched her where her buttocks met her spine, above her dress.

She reared back, her entire body alight with disgust, and landed in the reassuring embrace of her husband. He placed a steadying hand on her back. She leaned into his touch, like it could clean her of Tom's. She'd never felt so grateful for his air of authority. His sheer bloody size.

"Mr. Raridan," Archer said with a deadly calm, his fingers laced through hers.

And then he reared back his fist.

A thwack broke out before she could so much as blink away her disgust. The entire room froze, thirty pairs of eyes fixed on the sight of Tom reeling back into a table stacked with porcelain.

China toppled and shattered. Tom stood dumb in a pile of broken glass and sodden tea leaves, reeling, but uninjured.

"That, Raridan," Archer said in a voice loud enough for every man in the room to hear, "is a very small taste of what you can look forward to if you come near my wife again.

"Go upstairs," he said quietly, ushering her a few paces to the service door.

And then he lunged back into the room.

CHAPTER 25

*I*gnoring the stares from the gentlemen around him, Archer jerked his jaw at a pair of burly footmen who'd come running at the noise.

"Sort him out." They knew what he meant.

"You best watch your pretty back, Your Grace," Raridan called as they picked him up and dragged him toward the doors. "I know what you're about, I do. And when I have proof, *oh*, I'll make sure your duchess sees it."

Archer willed himself not to turn and shove his fist into the man's jaw a second time.

He could feel the eyes of the entire room on him, no doubt aghast that the bloodless duke had just engaged in such a public, ugly scene. Speculating on the meaning of Raridan's threat.

For once, he didn't mind.

Let them wonder.

He needed to be with his wife.

She was waiting for him on the landing just through the double doors, her back pressed against the wall, her chest heaving.

"Oh, sweetheart," he murmured at the shaken sight of her. "Are you all right?"

She hugged herself and shook her head. Without thinking, he took her in his arms. She wound her arms around his waist and rested her head on his shoulder. Heaven, to have her back like this, even if only for a moment.

"Oh, Archer," she said, trembling.

He ran his hand along the back of her head, letting his fingers tug into her curls. "It's all right. He's gone. You're safe."

"I'm so glad you returned when you did."

"Me too," he breathed into her hair.

"I'm sorry for that."

He took her head in his two hands. "Do not apologize. My only regret is you didn't thrash him yourself."

"I didn't want to embarrass you with a scene."

What an utterly disquieting sentiment. "Poppy. You are so much more important to me than any scene. Make all the scenes you like."

She looked like she wanted to argue, but instead she brushed her fingers inside his coat to find the fob just above his hip where he kept his pocket watch. He froze, stunned at the familiarity of her gesture, at the light brush of her fingers against his clothing, warm and nimble as she tugged the gold chain to extricate the timepiece. If she noticed that he had stopped breathing, she did not let on, only winced at the hour.

"I'm late. I'm due at Hammersmith."

Just as delicately, she returned his timepiece to the fob. He had never before imagined such a gesture and now he knew he would recall it all his life.

She reached up and ran her finger along his jaw. "Thank you. Perhaps a judicious rescuing is not so bad from time to time. I see why maidens like it."

Oh God, her touch. How he had longed for it. For weeks his every confounded limb had been united in the purpose of finding ways to brush against her—a hand against her shoulder as they stepped onto the street, his fingers glancing upon hers as he passed her a sheaf of papers. And now, she was touching him. Willingly. Smiling up at him. Jesting with him.

And leaving.

He lowered his head and kissed her. He was not delicate or gentlemanly. He was not *polite*. He kissed her with all the longing that had built in him for months, months during which she was so rarely more than a few paces away—in his house, his carriage— yet remote.

When he finally tore himself away, her eyes were closed and her mouth was swollen.

"Oh, Poppy," he murmured. He braced himself against the wall on his forearms and placed a kiss on her forehead, limp and defeated. It was not rational, what he felt for her. It lived in his blood and his flesh, animating him against his own will, a feeling he hadn't known since he was a boy falling in love during stolen moments in the forest. A feeling he once thought he would give anything to avoid experiencing again.

He had fallen in love with her.

"I'll be home by eight," she said. She put a hand to his shoulder, a gentle cue to release her.

He stepped back. She turned. He watched her walk away.

What was he going to do?

When Poppy returned home that night, she was startled to hear the unfamiliar sound of laughter.

She followed it to the parlor, where her husband, looking unusually relaxed in a half-unbuttoned waistcoat and his shirt-sleeves, was sprawled on a sofa next to his sister, a carafe of wine on the table between them.

She smiled at the image of the two of them, happy to observe them for a moment before disturbing their twosome.

"Will you at last tell me how you are finding married life?"

Constance asked. "I find that the question has been most studiously ignored in all my letters."

Poppy stood quietly, straining to hear his answer.

A flash of desolation crossed his face, then disappeared just as quickly. "It's agreeable enough," she heard him say.

She sank back against the wall. She knew that look. It was the one that startled her when she looked up from her dressing table and caught an accidental glance at her own unschooled reflection in the looking glass.

A piercing, unbearable loneliness.

To see the same hurt writ across his features strengthened the regret she had felt this morning, standing in the stairwell in the sunlight, hearing his breath catch as she reached for his watch fob.

Maybe contracts could be renegotiated.

Maybe it was not too late.

A great, troubled sigh escaped from Constance. "Agreeable," she echoed skeptically. "I suppose you would say the same whether it was shockingly good or hell on earth, so I wonder why I persist in asking."

Poppy quickly entered the room before she overhead anything further.

"Duchess!" her sister-in-law sang, rushing up and nearly galloping her down with the force of her embrace.

Constance pulled back and squinted at her. "Darling, what in the name of Beelzebub is that atrocity you are wearing?"

She was wearing one of the new plain, sturdy gowns she had ordered to replace the fussy Valeria Parcs.

"My wife costumes herself as a working woman ought," Archer interjected. "We can't all live your life of leisure. Now come into the dining room and regale us with your tales of idle frippery and intellectual rot."

Poppy gave him a moment of silent thanks for sparing her an interrogation over gowns. It would not escape Constance that she had firmly shed the trappings of aristocratic womanhood, and to discuss why would only inch them toward a topic of conversation that was better left unspoken.

"So tell us of your time in Paris," Poppy said, as they arranged themselves around the dining table. Constance and Hilary enjoyed a rather more urbane circle abroad than was considered appropriate for ladies of their set in London.

"Oh, it was fabulous. The *on-dit* was delicious," Constance said. "One could not walk from the Tuileries to the modiste without hearing of the most remarkable tales."

"I trust they stayed safely tucked within your diary and were not ferried back to your friends at the *Peculiar*," Archer said. "I should hate to have to lock you in my cellar for the winter."

Constance rolled her eyes. "How many times must I tell you I was virtuous! I have conducted myself so spotlessly and above reproach these last months that I fear I may no longer be fit for company. Nevertheless, there are a few choice morsels I simply must tell *you*."

For the next hour Constance hardly ate, skipping from one masterfully recounted anecdote to the next. It was no small wonder to Poppy the girl was always covered in ink. Her eye for observation was quite remarkable. In fact, it made Poppy rather ill at ease. For surely, she and Archer would not escape the subtleties of his sister's notice.

"I suppose Paris will always outrival London when it comes to excitement," Archer said. "We are a steady, proper lot, the English."

Constance snorted at this pronouncement.

"Not all of us match you for dullness, my tedious brother. In fact, one of the most delectable tales I heard abroad concerned a bit of intrigue in our very own fair London."

She lowered her voice. "I'm told there is an establishment somewhere in Mary-le-Bone that is all the rage. It is so discreet it doesn't have a name, and the location is known only to initiates.

But it is said that an elite few go there religiously." She surveyed the table to make sure she had their full attention. "To be *whipped*."

Archer slammed his glass down with such force that claret sprayed across the white lace tablecloth.

Constance yelped. "Have a care! That is our mother's one-hundred-year-old Point de Neige."

"Constance," he barked, scraping back his chair. "A private word. Upstairs. Immediately."

It took only until they had passed the threshold of the door for the two of them to begin shouting at each other.

Poppy could hear the strains of it through the floorboards. She remained downstairs, leaving them to their disagreement. She felt rather bad for Constance. Archer's sudden fury seemed out of proportion to his sister's lapse in discretion. While the rumor was indelicate for mixed company, it was no great crime to tell an off-color tale among the privacy of family. It certainly did not warrant a fit of rage so voluble it thundered through a sturdy house.

Unless, of course, he was familiar with such a place.

Poppy sat there, at the deserted table, and scraped the tines of her fork through her blancmange as she thought about the marks along his back and the words that Tom had said about his reputation.

No. It was not possible.

Tom had surely said that to insult her. To think of Archer, so exacting and correct—Archer who wore his power like a cloak whether he stalked the halls of his counting-house or the Palace of Westminster—to think of him visiting such a place was unimaginable. And then there was the scornful way he spoke about the behavior of his father. She had never met a man less prone to indulging vices than her husband.

When the voices through the floorboards at last grew hushed, Poppy went upstairs. Assuming their silence was not an indication that her husband and his sister had killed each other, she would bid them good night and retire.

The door to the study was half-open. She knocked on it, then poked her head inside. Constance was crouched on the sofa with her entire torso hunched over her knees, her head nearly in her lap. She whispered something to Archer and her head moved blindly back and forth with the force of whatever she was saying, a pantomime of disbelief. Archer leaned over her and whispered back intently, his hand on her shoulder, his expression pained. His sister reared back, shaking her head violently at whatever he had said, and her hands fluttered up from her lap.

In them were two miniature portraits.

Poppy backed out of the room and shut the door.

CHAPTER 26

*I*t was several hours later by the time Poppy heard Constance leave.

As soon as she did, there was a knock at her own bedchamber door.

"May I come in?" Archer asked, from the hall.

She rose and peeked out at him. He stood there in his shirt-sleeves, his eyes red.

She moved aside, making way for him. "Of course."

He sat down at the edge of her bed. Two faint lines between his eyes stood out, making him appear years older. She wanted to reach out to him, but she held herself stiff, waiting for him to speak.

"Constance found the portraits. Of my … of Benjamin. And Bernadette. That's why we did not return." He glanced up at her. "I'm sorry. It was rude of us to leave you."

"I … gathered as much. The door was open. I didn't wish to disturb you."

"Ah." He leaned back on her bed until his head was flat with the mattress. He closed his eyes.

She could not but feel that his distress was partly of her own making. "Archer, I'm so sorry for leaving them out. I never thought to put you in that position—I simply wanted to put them in a place where you might see them, and remember—"

"I know," he said, opening his eyes and meeting hers. "I know that."

Helplessly, she sank down on the bed beside him, careful to keep herself at a distance from his person.

"Christ, Poppy, but she had the *oddest* reaction. She was horrified of course. But really she was just so, so … sodding *hurt* that I had never told her. She said her entire life she thought she had put me off marriage by burdening me." He screwed up his face in frustration. "God, am I *so* fucking awful as that?"

She plucked at her fingers to keep from doing what she wanted to do, which was draw him into her arms. "You are very far from awful."

"I didn't tell her because—Christ, you know how hideous it is."

"You wanted to shield her from it."

"Yes. But it seems I've done damage just the same—she scarcely knows how much I love her."

Poppy breathed in. She had never heard him say that word before, in reference to the living.

"Have you ever … *told* her?"

He blew out a long breath. "I did tonight."

She smiled. "Good."

"You know, I'm glad you left those portraits out. I would never have told her. But I'm glad I did it. I'm glad she knows."

"Secrets are a burden," Poppy agreed. She searched his face. "They weigh us down."

He reached up and touched her hair.

"You are a wise woman, Cavendish. Nearly as wise as you are beautiful."

He beckoned her down beside him. "Lie here with me?"

She hesitated.

She *really* shouldn't. For the past few months his attendance in her room had been brief and dutiful. They had remained dressed, aside from the necessary garments, and the entire process had taken no longer than five minutes.

But even that dispassionate attendance had ignited a most unwelcome response in her. She tried not to show it, but he must have known, for as he swived her, he reached down and used his clever fingers to ensure she reached a height, and never spilled until he'd heard her halfhearted little cry. This element of their coupling—the fact that she could not, despite herself, keep pleasure out of it—and that he knew her well enough to handle even this politely, made one thing very clear to her: she was not immune to him, no matter how hard she tried to be.

She never would be.

If she curled up beside him here, just because he was upset and wanted companionship, something far more vulnerable would be at risk than just her body.

She should say no and send him out the door.

Or she should say yes, and ask him for what she really wanted.

All of him.

She had thought, as a younger woman, that she was her best self alone. That she was meant to inhale solitude and turn it into energy, like a plant.

She had confused solitude with happiness.

She was not a plant.

She *missed* her husband. If she was not mistaken, he missed her too.

But between them there was the question of the truth. The one she'd hidden, and the one she suspected he had.

She searched for a way to transform this painful mess into a question and found only a quiet, beating panic at how he might answer it. It was so much safer to say nothing at all.

So she sank down beside him, a glutton for damnation until the bitter end. She left only an inch between them, their heads staring up at the ceiling as though they were watching stars instead of plaster.

He took her hand in his.

"I never asked you," he said, his voice carefully neutral. "How is work at Hammersmith progressing?"

Another freighted question. One easier to ask, no doubt, with both their eyes pinned upon the ceiling.

It was as good an opening as any, for the villa brought up that delicate subject of how they would go on. The house would be fit for habitation by the end of the week and she would move there, to oversee the progress of her nursery. The question was whether he would come with her.

Until this morning, she had been gathering her resolve to insist that they live separately, for good. So far, their efforts to conceive had not produced the desired effect. In a week's time she would know for sure whether the process must continue, but even if it must, he could visit once or twice a week until she was with child.

She could not live in this ragged, uncertain state indefinitely. It was a torture. Particularly when he was lying next to her, a condition that made her heart want to say and do all kinds of things that she shouldn't.

She braced herself, once again screwing up the courage to say the words.

"Poppy?" he whispered, quite helplessly. Just as he had said her name before he kissed her this morning in the stairwell.

She did a very foolish thing.

She said nothing.

Instead she leaned down and put her lips to his.

She did not *want* to kiss him, but she could not see how she could *help* it, when he was an inch away from her, whispering her name like some kind of incantation.

He ran his hands in her hair and pulled her down on top of him.

They were lost in it. She scarcely knew his limb from hers, his breath from hers. Their clothes fell to the ground. He was inside of her, her hands were on every plane of him, his teeth were scraping against her upturned wrist as he came and she went with him.

And then they were a tangle, panting.

She rested her head on his warm shoulder. Her lip brushed against the grooves there. And once again she knew—knew—they could no longer be both things at once.

Lovers or associates. Not both.

She would have to make him choose.

She put her finger to his largest, thickest scar.

"Archer?"

"Mmm?"

"Why would Tom Raridan have heard ill of you at a bawdy house?"

The foggy look disappeared from his face.

"Pardon?"

"Before you arrived this morning, Tom said something about you and bawds."

Her handsome, sated, naked husband, still dewy from the act of making love to her, transformed in an instant into the contours of the Duke of Westmead.

He rose up, away from her. "What *exactly* did he say?"

"I didn't fully understand it—something about cullies and whips. But his point was that you are spoken of in disreputable parts of town. And then when Constance mentioned that club, you seemed uncommonly upset. Almost as if ... you knew about the place." She drew a breath and rose up beside him and asked him the question that had been forming in her mind all evening.

"Do you?"

The look that crossed his face was all the answer that she needed. Even if this was not the exact truth, it was not so far away from it. It didn't matter, the nature of the details. What mattered was the decision she was asking him to make.

He was not required to answer her. They did, after all, have an agreement. But if he wanted this—her, him, this tangle, his custody of her whispered breathless name—the agreement had to change.

"Do you?" she repeated.

TELL HER. THE THOUGHT FLASHED THROUGH HIM LIKE AN ORDER from the heavens. *If you want her, you have to tell her.*

But how could he?

The last time she had seen a glimmer of the truth, it had nearly destroyed them. A taste of who he really was had been enough to sunder their relationship for months. How would she react if she knew the truth? What would he have left?

"You would *believe* Tom Raridan?" he asked.

The liquid expression in her eyes went cool.

"I merely asked you what he meant."

"No, you asked me if there's truth in it."

"And you," she volleyed back, "have not answered."

She put her hand back to his shoulders.

"Archer. Where did you get these marks?"

He shrugged her away, feeling ill.

"You can trust me." She rose and stood beside the bed, naked, her arms at her side. "You *really* can."

He really couldn't. She said that, but he had *seen* the way she looked at him that morning after the coupling in the study.

It was the way his mother had looked upon his father.

He could not bear to be looked upon that way.

Especially by her.

He made himself take a breath, relax his posture. "Tom Raridan is a drunken lout, and one to whom you have a long history of giving far too much credit. He wanted to provoke you and it's worked. You've let him."

"You," she said, "are plainly lying."

He didn't answer her. He could only look at her willowy, candlelit form and wish that it weren't true.

"Very well," Poppy said, bending down to find her shift. She paused and looked her husband directly in the eye. "You are well within your rights. But please understand this: when I agreed to marry you, all that you asked for was business. The deal you offered was fair. This—whatever *this* is—is not. I can only surrender so much of myself to a person who does not give as much as he wishes to take."

She waited for him to tell her she was not wrong. To express some understanding that she was admitting, in her way, what she felt about him.

To offer some admission that he felt the same.

To trust her, as she had trusted him.

He averted his eyes.

She watched him settle into his decision.

She felt that spark that had made her brave enough to speak the truth grow dull and flicker out.

"I think," she said, "it is time for you to return to your own room. And I think, at the end of this week, when construction on my house is finished, I will move to Hammersmith. Alone."

CHAPTER 27

*P*oppy opened her eyes to the sound of footsteps in the hall. Someone was moving through the house. Running.

Her room was still dark. Not yet dawn. The house should be silent and asleep.

"Archer?" she called out. Perhaps he had lingered late in the study and was only now going to bed. She herself had had trouble sleeping, her stomach in a bitter, queasy knot long after he'd left her room.

She peered out into the hall. "Archer?" His room was empty. Through his open door she saw his bedsheets were tossed aside, his nightshirt on the floor—a state of disorder at odds with his usual mania for neatness.

Gibbs rushed by, carrying a stack of linens. Enough to prepare for the onslaught of a flood. She dropped the poker to her side, relieved.

"What's happened?" she asked him. "Where is the duke?"

"There's been a fire on Threadneedle Street, Your Grace. He's gone to the counting-house. We've been ordered to prepare for any bodies that need tending, in case of burns."

Fire.

It was the menace of the city, making kindling of the ancient wooden buildings that jagged and jumbled along the close-packed streets. The threat of immolation was never absent from London's smoky air, a taste you breathed in with the coal smoke. Men like her husband paid exorbitant fees to fire brigades, investing in their powers with the desperate faith with which their forebears had bought indulgences to protect them from the flames of hell.

To live in London was to live in constant fear of fire. But Archer feared it more than most.

He was so careful. He kept ladders in the counting-house, ordered barrels of water stored on each landing of the service stairs, paid guards to watch his buildings overnight. At home, he insisted their rooms be on the parlor floor, despite the fashion to sleep upstairs.

"Have my carriage brought round," she called out to a footman.

She did not bother to dress. She put on her boots and stockings and donned her cloak over her nightdress and went running out the door.

Keep him safe, she whispered to herself as they clattered over the dark roads. *Don't let him do something foolish—trying to save lives, or things, or*—and then she remembered.

She'd forgotten to take her papers home with her. Her ledgers, files, correspondence, all her annotated plans—she'd overlooked them in the tumult, shaken from the scene with Tom. They would burn.

Years of careful research and months of breakneck work. The future for which she'd traded in her past.

All locked in the bloody cabinets behind her bloody desk.

Prayers could be changed midutterance.

Let me get there in time, she whispered. *Oh God, please don't let them burn.*

~

ARCHER STOOD ON THE STREET AND WATCHED THE BLAZE AND awaited the inevitable.

The fire had begun at a bakery downwind and slowly chewed its way westward, leaping from one rooftop to the next. The brigade's efforts to smolder it were valiant, but on it crept, engulfing buildings one by one until there was no doubt that the counting-house would burn. Now the flames were licking at the building two doors down. Within half an hour his life's work would be destroyed. His vault of files—the decade of carefully sorted information he'd treasured like a temple of priceless relics —would burn. Reduced to less than the paper they were printed on.

And yet he felt oddly calm.

He had been gutted by fire once in his life. He knew what could be lost. This one would take only objects with it. The building was empty. He had searched it himself. Counted every last man.

A carriage pulled up at the corner and a cloaked woman leapt out of it and elbowed her way through the crowd of onlookers toward the looming conflagration. She paused at the door of his building to glance at the approaching flames licking across the rooftops, and then dashed past the assembled watermen and inside the open doors of the counting-house. She was so fast she was inside before it dawned on him that the carriage bore his own crest and the woman bore the proportions of his wife.

What in the name of God was she thinking?

He sprinted after her, shouting her name. Closer to the blaze, the air was a wall of choking heat. He paused and ripped off his neckcloth, doused it in a tub of water. With this mask slung across his nose and mouth, he dashed inside.

The lobby was empty—she must have gone upstairs, toward the offices at the top. He thundered up the steps as fast as any man had ever climbed, taking them three by three. The higher floors were hotter, darker, occluded by smoke billowing in from the windows. He hacked into the cloth and wet his face and eyes against the burn of smoke.

He found her on the top floor, crouched over her desk. She'd unloaded the contents—her ledgers and reams of papers and ungainly draftsmen's scrolls—and was shucking them into her skirts like a child collecting blueberries in a pinafore. He could see flames licking up at the windows, creeping quickly from the chimney of the neighboring rooftop. They had minutes, if that.

He dashed toward her, his heart fit to explode. She was doubled over with coughing and yet still collecting papers in her dress—stubborn enough to burn alive. Without a word he scooped her off the ground, papers and all.

"Stop it," she rasped at him, knocking his arms away with her elbows as her hands scrambled to grab at the pages that fluttered from her cloak.

When he did not obey, she began to struggle to evade his grip. "My plans," she croaked at him, wrenching away. "I must save them. Put me down!" Tears streamed down her face, making trails in the soot that had collected on her skin.

He was stronger. He lurched as she fought him off, carrying her, flailing arms and papers and all, toward the stairs. She struggled harder, fighting him at every step. "Stop," she cried raggedly. "Let me go. There is time yet."

"There isn't," he bit out, clamping her against him as she struggled.

"Please," she cried, and lurched so violently he nearly lost his footing.

"You will die, Poppy," he shouted at her, barreling on toward the staircase doors. His voice sounded like some kind of animal. *"You will die."*

She stilled and allowed herself to be carried, limply, down the stairs, sobbing as though he had robbed her of her very soul.

Above them, he heard a crash. The first of the timber beams collapsed above them, filling the landing with burning ash. He took a mighty breath through his soaked cravat and lunged for the ground floor, careening into walls and rails in the darkness, his lungs searing, his breath a rattle in his chest.

At last, he reached the service door that let out to the alley. He kicked it open and rammed through it, taking the brunt of the force on his knuckles and forearms and shoulder to protect Poppy from the blow. Dazed, he carried her through the snowstorm of ash that floated down from above, gasping for air.

He dropped her and sank to his knees, heaving with his efforts. Sweat dripped from his hair into his eyes. He tore the cloth from his mouth and heaved in cold night air in painful gasps that seared his ragged throat.

He couldn't breathe. The roar and smoke and haze were inside of him, roasting him alive from inside out. He was back in Wiltshire, in the burning west wing, the baby's cries, the desperation, the crumbling incinerated staircase between him and his son.

"How could you?" a broken voice screamed at him. Bernadette. No, Poppy. He looked down, dazed, and he was not in Wiltshire but in London, staring at a woman crumpled in a pile of sooty papers.

"I wasn't finished," she sobbed. "I had time enough. It wasn't burning—all my work."

Rage cauterized his grief.

"Are you insane?" he screamed at her, taking a handful of her papers and smearing them into the wet ash until he felt them turn to pulp against the gravel. "Do you know what would have happened to you?"

"I don't care, I don't *care*," she sobbed. "It doesn't matter. Don't you understand?"

Behind them, the attic of the building collapsed in a great explosion.

"You could have died," he said, and this time he realized it was he who was sobbing. He held himself over her on his forearms, great tremors rocking through him, her body motionless beneath him, her eyes glinting with the reflection of the fire.

A member of the brigade came and pulled him off her. Someone wrapped a blanket around him. He heard urgent voices whispering his name. But mostly he heard his wife rasping the same words, over and over and over, like a woman who'd gone mad.

"I won't forgive you."

CHAPTER 28

*A*rcher opened his eyes to the filtered light of a wintry afternoon. He coughed, and felt the ragged burn of his lungs. Black phlegm came up in his throat.

Poppy stood over him and dabbed a kerchief to his mouth. If the fire had singed her nose and throat as it had his, she didn't show it. For hours she'd sat at his bedside, wiping his brow with cool linens and putting ice chips to his lips with nary a cough. For hours, he'd dodged and shrugged off her ministrations, wishing he hadn't married her, wishing she'd simply leave.

"Off me," he croaked at her. "Get out."

She pursed her lips. "You must rise. The solicitors are here."

"Send them away."

"They've come to discuss the damage."

"Sod the damage."

"Don't be insensible," she snapped. "Our work cannot move forward until the insurance assessments have been completed. Your financing covenants have been frozen. If you won't see the solicitors, I shall confer with them without you."

He closed his eyes and when he'd opened them, a trio of old

men had filed in against his wishes, all dressed in black like three crows come to examine a fresh corpse.

Mr. Tynedale, the oldest of their lot, bowed and began a crisp assessment of the fire. The contracts and currency were safe in Archer's vault at Hoare's, undamaged. The counting-house was irreparable, but handsomely insured. His Grace had been very perspicacious, prepared for the inevitabilities. He could easily rebuild. But there was the matter of assuaging creditors, lest the flow of capital to his portfolio be interrupted. It was critical to make a show of strength at his earliest convenience.

He didn't care.

Poppy peppered them with questions about operations, securing temporary quarters for the workers, the agreements with financiers.

She had learned quickly, his wife.

"Tynedale, leave us."

"Your Grace, there are several matters further to discuss," the solicitor objected.

"Out. Now."

The crows exchanged a look and trickled out. Poppy remained, wraithlike, aggrieved at him for sending them away.

"The least you could do is listen to what they have to say," she hissed. "If we do not secure our assets and reputation, we will be descended on like vultures by the creditors. They could cause delays for months."

"Enough, Poppy," he yelled, beating his head back against the wooden headboard. The pain of it centered him. He did it again.

"Stop that! You will injure yourself."

He opened his mouth and laughed, a nasty, mirthless snarl. "Will I? Rich words from the likes of a woman who *ran into a burning building.*"

"It was not yet burning," she said with a petulant toss of her head. For once, her determined jaw and tumbling hair did not move him. He wanted to shake her.

"Does your own life mean so little to you? And what if you are with child?"

She glared at him. "Yes. God forbid something happen to your broodmare. I was perfectly safe—"

"Enough," he shouted at her.

"No," she shouted back. "How could you reproach me for attempting to save my work? It is everything I have. I would have nothing if I lost it. Nothing."

He hated her, for those words. He knew exactly how much a fire could take, and sketches of plants did not begin to cover it.

"You have," he told her with excruciating slowness, "no idea what it means to lose everything. And God *help* you, Poppy, should you ever know."

She must have heard the note of disgust in his voice. She looked up at him, startled, as though it had only just dawned on her what he meant.

"I wasn't comparing— I didn't mean to imply—" she began.

But she *had*, damn her. She had never seemed younger. The very sight of her made him feel empty and exhausted.

"It's not the same," she said quietly, her eyes drifting to the floor. "You *loved* them, Archer. Be angry if you like, but please don't claim that it's the same. You've made it clear to me in every way that it is not."

He felt the blackness curling up from his chest into his esophagus. He felt it behind his eyes, in his shoulders, his calves, his feet, his toes.

He knew what was coming.

"Leave me," he said, rising out of bed.

"Archer, wait," she said, following him. "I insist I did not mean to—"

He waved her off.

She pounded on the wall with her fist and began to cry in furious sobs. "You know, you don't have a monopoly on grief. I had a family too, Archer. I did not spring from this earth *alone* and with *nothing*. It came about by *dribs*."

"Leave," he roared at her. "Did I not dismiss you?"

He bent over his knees, his head spinning, the blaze in his ears deafening once more.

"You're right, it was not sensible of me," she went on shouting. "It's only that these months I have felt so desperate, so bereft— because I am here, with you—with *you*—and yet I am *alone*."

She was unstrung, sobbing about their argument, his secrecy, his bloody scars. He heard the words but could scarcely make sense of them, blending as they were with the roaring in his ears. Sweat beaded on his brow and arms. He had to stop this. He had to seize control of himself before he well and truly let the rafters crumble.

He launched himself past his wife's devastated form and lurched out of the room. He stormed up the stairs to his study and slammed the door behind him, locking it with shaking fingers.

Poppy knocked at it and called his name through tears.

"I'm sorry. Please can we talk sensibly?"

"Do not disturb me," he bellowed at her through the door. His voice came out at half volume, his throat still caked in silt.

He sat at the desk and put his palms facedown on the top of it and simply breathed. The room smelled like ash. Because she had draped it with her *bloody half-burnt papers*.

They were everywhere, pinned up about the walls to dry. He rose up and tore them down. Nothing was supposed to make him feel this way. Was that not the reason he'd married her, so that there would be no occasion to ever feel this way again?

She was right. It *wasn't* supposed to be the same.

But it was.

He ran out of papers to cast down and knocked a stack of letters from the desk and watched them scatter on the floor. He opened drawers and tossed aside every possession of hers he could find: seed packets, grower's manuals, the effluvia of her intrusion into his life and space and heart.

He tipped over a shelf and sent her plants and porcelain smashing to the ground, making a mess of petals and pollen and sodden shattered glass. He took the drawers out from their nooks and emptied them on the floor.

Only when he had thoroughly upended every single nook and surface that bore traces of her incursion did he finally sink into a chair, distraught and shaking and disgusted with himself.

The room was shameful.

He was shameful.

He'd made a mess of her things, his things, the rug. The servants would think him a bloody monster. *She* would think him a bloody monster. He knelt and straightened the jumble he'd knocked from the cupboard. A glass jar of powdered leaves labeled *Pennyroyal Tea* rolled across the floorboards and landed near his knee.

He tossed it aside. He got halfway through the room before a creeping, dawning clarity overpowered the more blinding momentum of his sorrow.

Pennyroyal tea. It was used for—

He could not make himself finish the thought.

Of all the *monstrous* things.

She had laughed off his fears about the nursery. Scoffed, just now, at the possibility of pregnancy.

She knew very well she was not with child.

She had made sure of it.

He took the jar and threw it at the fireplace and watched it shatter.

And then he yanked the bellpull for a footman.

CHAPTER 29

*W*hat had she done?

She was weak with remorse. All day Poppy had seethed at her husband for pulling her out of the fire. Countermanding her—like she was a foolish child. Blocking her from saving the things that were dearest to her in the world. She'd been so focused on her anger that she had not given a thought to him, who had lost more.

She had known, and done it anyway.

Even if he did not love her, it was incalculably selfish. Cruel. The guilt of it made her body feel like a prison. It beat on her from within, unendurable.

"Archer, please," she whispered to the door.

The crashing behind it did not pause. She had pleaded with him to reveal himself to her, but she had never imagined him this way. Out of control.

She was responsible. She had provoked him until he exploded. She'd done it because she was furious that all she had to save was her papers. That her heart had not cooperated with their agreement. That she loved him, desperately, and he merely tolerated her.

She was going to tell him. It was unbearable to live with the words unsaid, swirling inside her, blackening her spirit. It was turning her into someone venal. Someone capable of the way she had treated him today. If he could not bear to confess to her the nature of his secrets, it no longer mattered. She would give him her love and take the penance she deserved.

The crashing behind the door, at last, stopped. She pressed herself against the wall as Gibbs came running.

Archer threw open the door and walked right past her, not sparing her a glance. He thundered down the stairs without a word.

The sound of the heavy front door slamming shut echoed up through the house before she could collect herself. Stunned, she edged her way into the wreckage of the study and peered out the window to the street. He was there, striding to his carriage. She hoisted the window open, prepared to plead with him to come back, never mind the public scene.

"Twenty-three Charlotte Street," she heard him tell the coachman.

Before she could get a word out, he was gone.

She looked down at the chaos he had made of the room. He had ripped down all her papers, broken vases, overturned the shelves. She bent down to pick up bits of broken glass and paused.

Oh dear heavens. *No.*

It was the pennyroyal tea. Packed away months ago by Mrs. Todd when she'd made the request in anger, and promptly forgotten. He must think—

He would never forgive her if he thought her capable of such a thing. But she wasn't capable. She hadn't done it, in the end. She hadn't even wanted to.

She had to find him.

She did not bother to order her carriage. She donned a cloak and slipped out her own front door.

The hackney driver she hailed gave her an odd look at the address.

"You're certain, madam? Not a part of town for proper ladies this time of night."

"Make haste," she ordered, not bothering to tell him that she was not a proper lady.

The street outside the address was quiet. The door marked twenty-three looked no different from the others, and no plate marked it as an establishment of business. Was it a private home? She rapped on the heavy iron knocker.

After a rather long pause, an unsmiling girl answered the door. She wore a dress of black, severely cut enough for a novice at a nunnery, but made from fine silk with the detailing of a lady's mourning garment. The girl said nothing, merely stared at Poppy expectantly. The room beyond her was hushed and dark, lit by only a few flickering wax candles. Poppy strained to see, but the girl blocked her line of sight.

"I need to speak to my husband," Poppy said. "The Duke of Westmead. It's urgent."

The girl looked at her appraisingly. "You have a key?"

"Pardon?"

"Do you have a key?"

"No."

"Then the establishment is closed."

"I am the Duchess of Westmead. My husband is here."

The girl stared at her dispassionately, unmoved by her title or her distress.

"Please, inform him I'm here," Poppy pleaded. "I beg you."

The girl shook her head. "Unless you have a key, you'll need to leave. Good night." Without malice, she closed the door in Poppy's face.

She heard a bolt slide into place behind the door. Unbelievable. What was this place? Not a gentlemen's club. Such an estab-

lishment would have a sign, a proper butler, some obeisance to
the basic laws of class and courtesy.

She thought back to Tom Raridan's vulgar words. But this
place did not bring to mind the brothels she'd seen in naughty
woodcuts—women with exposed bosoms and rouged cheeks
plying soused men with drink. The house had the silent air of a
cathedral.

Several men walked past her, their chatter stopping as they
paused to take in the unusual sight of a woman alone on the dark
street. Her hackney coach had left, and there were no others
idling.

Well, why should she cower here? Her husband was indoors—
ill and not himself and wrongly convinced of the worst of her.
Did that not give her the right to enter? If she found him with a
courtesan, so be it—she must speak to him. If she did not
unburden herself, she would not be able to bear the feel of her
own skin.

There was a narrow alley between the town house and the
larger edifice next door. She ducked inside it and felt her way
amidst the narrow moonlit channel until she edged upon a door.
Tom Raridan had once shown her how to pick a lock with a hair-
pin. She plucked one from her head and set to work. When she
tried the handle, the door opened with a creak.

She was in a servants' hallway, dim and unadorned but scrupulously clean. The house was still and silent.

She tiptoed through a door and into an austere reception
room. Dark curtains were drawn over the single window. A hard
schoolroom bench by the wall farthest from the fire was the only
seat. This was clearly not a home.

She paused to listen, but no sounds or voices echoed through
the halls. There was only the deep, velvet hush of enveloping
darkness.

She crept past an antechamber, and saw the maid bent over a
desk, oiling a row of keys that resembled the one she had seen

around Archer's neck. The girl turned at the sound of a bell and Poppy crept back into the shadows. She watched the girl gather a strange assortment of items onto a tray—a pitcher of water, a stack of clean linens, and a box whose scent she recognized immediately as peat moss. She used it to pack plants in crates to halt their deterioration. Surgeons used it to ward off rot.

Was it possible that Archer was more badly wounded than he let on? Had he hurt himself tearing apart the study?

The girl turned with the tray down a long corridor at the other side of the chamber. A faint knock. The swish of a well-oiled hinge. The murmur of female voices. "His wife was here," she heard the girl say, in a tone not meant to be overheard. "I sent her away." She could not make out the answer.

Poppy retreated to the servants' stairs as the door closed and the girl walked away. A faint, percussive thwack sounded from the chamber. An odd sound, like the swishing of a tree branch knocking at a window in a storm.

A moan. *His* moan.

He was in pain. She stepped into the hallway, not bothering to hide the sounds of her steps. If her husband was here, suffering, it was her duty to go to him.

She straightened her spine to her full height, took a deep breath, and opened the door, preparing to announce herself. But the sight within robbed her of her words.

She knew exactly where she was.

Of course.

An exclusive private whipping house.

Archer was bent over. Splayed on his forearms and knees on a black blanket, his head facing the wall. He was naked, save a linen shirt that was rent down the middle and falling off his shoulders, as though it had been cut from his neck. His head was thrown back in some agony or ecstasy, a scarf tied around his eyes to block his sight. He arched his back, his beautiful back, architecturally made, every tendon and ligament powerful and finely sculpted, beneath the web of scars. Scars, it was now clear, that had been made by the whips and birches that were organized along a shelf, as bald and neatly sorted as the tools in her own gardening shed.

The woman who stood over him was tall, with thick, dark hair pulled into a tight chignon. Not yet aware of Poppy's presence, she set down her handful of birches on a low sideboard and picked up a heavy whip, a leather braid with golden-corded fronds woven from something that looked fine and painful. She raised it in the air and with a flick of her wrist brought it down toward Archer's back.

"No," Poppy shouted. She raced forward, prepared to take the blow herself. The woman whirled around and the fringe cracked against the wall. Archer rose up on his knees and turned around, ripping at his blindfold.

The woman turned to look at Poppy. Her face bore not a spot of rouge or powder, and though she was not young, she was not old. Her dark hair was borne atop her head in a severe knot—no fringe, no ringlets, no ribbons. The planes of her cheeks were wide and the make of her jaw was firm and defined, her brows dark slashes above darker eyes. In another guise she would be considered a beauty, if a sober one.

A thin thread of bright red blood trickled from a cut on Archer's thigh and threaded down his leg, dripping along his ankle. His elegant, aristocratic ankle.

He stood, and as he spun to face her, she saw her confirmation that this torture, whatever it was, was not innocent. The shirt had dropped to his feet, and his arousal announced itself plainly, uncovered.

She backed from the room as he got the blindfold off. His face contorted at the sight of her, snapping from a glazed look of absence into a rictus of disbelief, then horror.

He said her name—croaked it, his voice still ravaged from the fire.

As his eyes met hers, her toes gripped the floor through her shoes and her ankles made them pivot toward the door. Her thighs propelled her legs, one step, then two. But even as her body turned and fled, and her eyes saw carpet become stairs, and stairs give way to alley—even as her arm shot out and flagged another hackney—even as she turned and saw him lurch into the street, coat covering his nudity, his bare feet digging into muck and gravel, that single bead of blood still threading down his ankle— even as she heard him shouting "Wait!" and *"Please"*—

Through it all, one thought filtered through the back of her mind.

Perfidious and fully formed and as urgent and insistent as the beating of her filthy, faithless heart.

She wanted him like that.

Abject.

Kneeling.

Hers.

"Go," she begged the coachman.

And as she watched the sight of him recede, it was as though she had two hearts, the way she had two legs, two hands, two feet.

Two hearts, and one was shattered.

One hated him for coming here, for betraying her, for baring to some other woman a truth that she, his *wife*, had begged him to reveal to her. A truth he had not trusted her with even on pain of losing her altogether.

But the other …

How it *wanted*.

CHAPTER 30

*A*rcher sat alone in Poppy's dressing room, where it smelled like her most strongly.

He fingered the message she had left behind. Broken shards of glass and tea leaves, carefully wrapped in a silk scarf with a brief note in her hand: *I never took this.* Along with it, her wedding ring. The small, simple plumeria of pearls.

He had not needed to find her ring to know that she would leave him. He'd seen it in her eyes as she had stared at him from the doorway at Elena's. The expression she had worn, just before she'd run, was not disgust.

It was far simpler: *hurt.*

He had feared the wrong thing. It was not the substance of his secret that had driven her away. It was the betrayal he'd made by keeping it.

It *was* a betrayal. He knew that now. He'd negotiated an agreement that allowed him to do what he'd been doing, yes. But had he not once explained to her that contracts based on fraud are null and void? And was he not, therefore, the guilty party—the one who'd misrepresented the terms on offer? For he had proposed a marriage of convenience when the fact was, even then, that he was hopelessly, irretrievably in love with her. Had been from the moment he saw her in a forest of her own devising wearing a crown of plumeria in her hair.

He'd pressed her to be his wife when he'd known full well what marriage to him would cost her. He could easily have found another way to help her. One need not marry the proprietor of a business to make a success of it. He'd seized the opportunity of her misfortune because he *wanted her*. And instead of offering her his real self—the one that was, yes, twisted and prone to moments of unhingedness, but *loved her*—he had offered her the fictional Duke of Westmead, with all his terms and limitations disguising an empty bargain.

He'd not just taken her independence. He'd duped her out of it.

He traced his fingers over the racks of expensive garments she had left behind. The thrifty, sensible dresses she wore in daily life she'd taken with her. What remained were embroidered damask gowns, fur-lined cloaks, paper-thin silk chemises cut along the bias. A rack of padded hoops and a shelf of dainty underthings, still wrapped in gold paper, never worn. The trappings of the Duke of Westmead's wife. A role that she had never asked for, and never wanted.

Had she not proved as much—throwing herself into that burning building with the desperation of a woman who had nothing outside of it to live for? He knew that she found his lectures on business tiresome and condescending, but if she thought that all she amounted to was plants and plans and papers, he had not adequately instructed her on the nature of value. For there was nothing, nothing in this world more precious or irreplaceable than her.

He closed the door on the abandoned, ghostly silks. Observing them would not change what he had done. If he was to fix it—and he was, by all that was holy, *going* to fix it—there was business to attend to.

He climbed the stairs to the study, still littered with the mess he'd made. He gathered up her filthy papers, strewn about the floor. He salvaged what seeds and flowers he could. He spent three hours smoothing them, arranging them into order, and packing them into tidy parcels to be sent on to her at Hammersmith.

When he had done his best to repair the damage to her things, he sat down at the desk and took a quill and drafted a note to his solicitor.

Tynedale: I need to confer at your earliest convenience on the matter of obtaining a divorce.

CHAPTER 31

Hammersmith, London
December 23, 1753

*P*oppy stood on the frosty lawn and watched a team of burly men use ropes and scaffolding to raise the last pane of glass to the framework of her conservatory.

"The tallest of her kind in England," Mr. Partings said with a grin. "And what a sight she is."

The structure was indeed beautiful, rising from the newly planted rows of trees to twinkle like a confection of spun sugar in the dying winter light. Beyond it, the walled gardens were freshly raked for the winter planting, and the force houses clattered with hired gardeners building beds for plants due to arrive next month from Virginia.

The scene was everything she'd ever dreamed of, and that it had been conjured in so short a time was nothing less than a miracle of modern industry and the powers of immoderate wealth. She should be weeping in joy and gratitude at the sight of it. Instead, she wanted only to weep.

"Is something amiss, Your Grace?" Partings asked.

"Not at all," she said, forcing her mouth into a smile. "It's only the chill in the air. Shall we have a cup of something hot by the fire to warm up?"

She led Partings inside the villa, made cozy now with woven rugs and jars of holly berries and the maelstrom of books and sketches that had descended in the past three weeks since she'd moved in, no matter the diligence of her housemaids.

"Ah, Alison," she called, seeing a male figure bent over a tea tray through the half-open library door. "Please see that a pot of chocolate is brought to us by the fire. And perhaps a bottle of brandy. I believe we have well earned a bit of winter cheer, have we not, Mr. Partings?"

The door opened, and the man stepped through, and her husband smiled at her.

She had to clutch Mr. Partings's arm to stay steady.

"I've been known to do the work of the gardener and the coachman," Archer said affably, "but I draw the line at butlering."

"Your Grace!" Partings said, folding himself into a low bow. "Have you come to see the conservatory? We've just installed the glass."

"Indeed, I saw it being raised as I drove up. A marvel. But then, when it comes to my duchess, I am never short of wonder."

Partings, bless him, went on chattering, neatly covering up the fact that her throat had seized and made it impossible for her to greet her husband.

"Indeed, the design is ingenious," the architect went on, unable to disguise his pride nor his excitement at this rare private audience with his employer. "The piping sits under the walls of the foundation, you see, such that the plants are not exposed to the furnace. Much better for regulating temperature. Perhaps you'd like a tour?"

Archer cocked his head at him, as if what he offered was at once thrilling and yet somehow not quite the idea at which they were meant to arrive. It was a look she had once found as much maddening as it was charming. The intended effect, no doubt, for she saw how easily it was working on Partings, who was scrambling to deduce whatever it was Archer had in mind for him.

"Your Grace, on second thought, I should depart," he said, pleased with himself for thinking of it, and more pleased still when her husband's smile confirmed he had achieved the correct answer. "I believe we are due for snow this evening, and it's best that I get home, lest Mrs. Partings worry."

"Ah, a pity," Archer said. "A spot of cheer another time, then. My duchess and I would love for you and Mrs. Partings to join us some evening for supper, to thank you for your work."

The absurdity of engaging in such a prosaic domestic scene with her husband, on whom she had not set eyes in nearly a month, helped restore Poppy's wits.

"I shall write to Mrs. Partings after the holidays with an invitation," she said.

"How kind," Partings enthused. "Good day, Your Graces. I shall see myself out."

She waited until he was gone to allow her gaze to fully fall upon her husband.

He was gallingly immaculate. After so long an absence, his handsomeness blazed out at her as it had when they'd first met, pristine and undiminished by the passage of time. She caught a glimpse of herself in the looking glass over the credenza and saw her hair was windswept into knots and her cheeks were chafed with cold. The same old score—him, breathtaking; her, disheveled.

"Cavendish," he said, locking eyes with her.

Her *traitorous* heart. It was pathetic in its simplicity, pounding away at the sound of his voice saying her abandoned girlhood name. It was a story so old and tired she wondered why anyone bothered to tell it: he had hurt her, and she had pined for him. Craved his presence these past weeks. Waited for him to come after her, to apologize, to explain himself, to let her rail at him until she could forgive him and set it all to rights. To assure her that she had not imagined they belonged together, however jaggedly they were cut.

But he hadn't.

The only word she'd had from him was a neatly ordered box of her fire-singed possessions. Such an eloquent rebuke she doubted his distaste for her could have been signaled more poetically by Alexander Pope himself. And that—his cold indifference—was worse than whatever scene she'd interrupted in the darkened town house. For all his secrets, his most hurtful crime was the one he wasn't guilty of.

He simply didn't love her.

And yet, here he was.

Today, of all the days he could have chosen. Which could mean only one thing: that ancient, doddering blackguard, Dr. Hinton, had betrayed her. Six hours was all it had taken for him to break his faith, despite his promise not to speak of her condition. She would have the old telltale's liver. But first, she must muddle her way through the inevitable confrontation with her husband. Standing in the corridor wringing her hands would not help her any more than pining had.

She turned on her heel and sailed past him to the library. "To what do I owe the honor of this visit?"

He followed her into the library and removed an envelope from his pocket and held it out to her. The packet was thick and sealed with crimson wax stamped with his ducal crest. Official peerage business.

"What's this?"

He cleared his throat. His voice came out low and nearly hoarse. "It's what you are owed."

She used her erasing knife to slice open the seal and looked inside.

Legal documents, just as she'd suspected.

She smiled tightly. "I see. More contracts."

No doubt they contained some coda to their marriage agreement demanding custody of her child, or her banishment to some far-flung country house in Scotland upon the birth. She walked behind her desk and took a seat. It would be safer to have the distance of solid furniture between them when she read his documents, lest she be tempted to slit his throat with the erasing knife.

"As you are aware," he said, lowering his voice further, "contracts based on misrepresentation are invalid."

"As I thought I made clear, Your Grace, I didn't take the pennyroyal. Surely you can't doubt that under the current circumstances."

He blinked. "You misunderstand me. I do believe you. But it wouldn't matter, legally speaking, if you had. *I* committed fraud and *you*, therefore, deserve to be released from our agreement."

She did not respond, because her mind was busy struggling with the words she was seeing on the page. She had thought many unhappy things about her husband in the weeks of their estrangement, but never had she considered that he might have gone insane.

She brushed her fingers to the edge of the desk, hoping that they would land on air, a signal she was having an especially vivid nightmare. But her skin touched down on solid oak. And upon it, a petition to the House of Lords for an Act of Parliament granting the Duke of Westmead a divorce on grounds of adultery and criminal perversion.

His own.

The pages fluttered in her hands. "Are you mad?" she whispered.

This would expose him. See him cast in the image of his father and made a public object of mockery.

He put his steady hand above her shaking one. "Please. Don't worry. I promise you. I'm only here to make it right."

He shuffled the papers and pointed to a clause on the second page.

"Here. Under the terms, you will be entitled to the dower settled on you at the time of our marriage. Your nursery, several properties, and the full equity in my investment holdings. Everything I have that's not entailed."

She gaped at him. Divorce was rare, and made women half creatures under law, dependent on their former spouses for every farthing. The settlement he suggested was unorthodox. It had no precedence in law or custom.

He cleared his throat. "You will worry for your reputation, I know. See page nine. It's an affidavit making clear that you knew nothing of my proclivities and were appalled to learn of them. That I betrayed your faith and my vows. Given my family's history, no one will blame you. There will still be a scandal, of course—that can't be avoided. But I'll do what I can to see you're spared the worst of it. I regret you must be implicated at all."

He stepped back. "I won't insist on this—the choice is yours. But if you would like your freedom, I want you to have whatever I can restore of it. And I'm sorry for taking it away under false pretenses."

He looked sincere. Repentant. Solemn.

He made not a bit of sense.

"You keep saying you have acted in bad faith. What is it that you mean?"

He moved around the desk and knelt beside her, meeting her gaze with a look so raw it was as though he had dropped his fine clothing to the floor.

"I asked you to give up your name and property in order to secure my own. I said that in return I would make no demands on your heart or independence. And I lied. I was in love with you. So I am in breach."

She felt dizzy.

Suddenly she understood.

These documents were not a rejection.

They were a testament of feeling.

Trust him to say it with a careful stack of papers.

He was saying he understood what she had given up by marrying him. Which meant he must also understand why she had done it anyway.

That whenever he was near her, her heart went to her throat. When he touched her, the boundaries of the world narrowed and reduced to only him and her and wanting. Because before him, she had never dared imagine there could be on earth a person so exactly tailored to suit the making of her character. Because long before she'd married him, she'd felt, somehow, he was her person, however unlikely and inconceivable that was. Her Archer. Her insufferable, impossible, unbearably lovely Duke of Westmead.

She worried the pages in her hands, too overcome to speak.

"What of your heir?" she asked, gathering time to come to a decision. "Lord Wetherby?"

"I signed over twenty thousand pounds to a trust preserving the welfare of the tenants of Westhaven. It will protect them long after the duchy leaves my hands. Even if Wetherby succeeds me."

"Ah." If her voice was faraway, it was only because she knew now what she was going to say, and she was searching for the words. But he looked up guiltily, like she had caught him in a lie.

"I know. I should have thought to do so before I met you. I should not have pressed you for your hand. But I can't say I regret it, Poppy. I can't say I regret a minute of my time with you."

Sorrow flashed through his eyes.

She found the words.

"I hate—" she began, but her voice faltered.

She could see him cringing, bearing himself up to withstand whatever dreadful thing he thought she was about to say to him.

She picked up the first page of the divorce petition and let her hands do what her voice could not. She ripped it. The torn pages falling to the floor shored her up.

"I hate that I have to destroy these," she said, shredding another fistful.

A tentative look crossed his face.

"I shall cherish them, Archer. Just as soon as I have destroyed them. They are the most romantic thing anyone has ever given me."

He winced. "If that is true, it is because I am an idiot, Cavendish. If I had done it properly, *this* would be the most romantic thing anyone had ever given you."

He took her wedding ring out of his pocket and slid it across the desk.

"I wish I had given it to you properly. I wish I had been honest."

She smiled, perhaps her first genuine smile in three weeks. "And what would you have said?"

"That I was looking to marry a fortune hunter and instead I met a woman who could make forests grow indoors."

"She sounds like a witch."

He smiled. "It's possible. It would explain why I stopped breathing every time she walked into a room and lost whole nights of sleep imagining her hair."

He looked so pained she reached out and took his hand.

"It was obvious she had no interest in marrying me. It was obvious I was unfit to be her husband. It was obvious that the things I wanted when I looked at her were the very ones I had promised myself I would never, *ever* want again. But I ignored all that because I was—I *am*—in love with her."

He picked up her hand and placed it on his shoulder, above his scars.

"Poppy, I was too afraid to admit that I love you. Even to myself. But I do. So much. Never mind that I'm a coward."

He was making an unseemly production of himself. He had not intended to deliver a soliloquy.

Poppy's fingers closed around his shoulder. He glanced up into her eyes, unsure what she would think of him, falling to pieces on his knees like this. In the dim light, the cool green of her irises had gone as soft and gray as the mist that rolled off the downs on Wiltshire mornings. He wanted to bury himself in what he saw in them.

She took his face in her hands.

"Archer," she whispered, her voice breaking. "What *coward?*"

"I asked you to trust me, and you did. You put everything dearest to you in my hands and took me at my word that I would treat them as if they were my own. But when you asked the same of me, I flinched. I couldn't bear to reveal myself."

He wound one of her curls around his finger and traced her cheek with his knuckle. "Cavendish, here is the truth. What you saw on Charlotte Street was not a chance occurrence. I'm an investor in the club and I have gone there for years. I enjoy being at another's mercy. So much that I sometimes feel I will buckle or go mad without it. I told myself that I was justified in hiding it— that if you knew how I longed to be on my knees in the dark, you might not see me the same way. That you'd think me weak. Or like my father."

She clenched his hand in hers. "Archer, you are not weak. And you are nothing like your father."

The sentiment was sweet. He wished he could believe her.

She squeezed his hand. "The man I see before me had his family ripped away and replaced with debt and responsibility and grief. And he rose to the occasion anyway. He took care of the people around him despite the damage that he shouldered. He tries so hard to be a good and decent man. And it is the trying *that makes him so.* It is the *effort* that is the mark of character. Not your parentage. And certainly not what you desire in the dark."

He did not know what to say.

Her eyes glowed. She picked up her wedding ring from the

desk and held it to the light. "Do you wish for me to wear this ring again?"

He could not hold back a ravaged sigh. "I love you. But I can't ask you to risk your reputation over tastes you do not share. Perhaps we could work out some arrangement—"

"Teach me," she said softly.

His thoughts went still and silent.

"Teach you?" he repeated.

"Yes. You see, I'm afraid I'm not done negotiating, Your Grace. If you want me back, you will have to show me exactly what it is that you enjoy on your knees."

She traced his thumb with her finger and smiled demurely, but with a glint of something avaricious in her eyes.

Every hair on his body suddenly stood at attention.

"You want—"

"Yes. Every day since I found you in that blasted town house, I have thought about the way you looked that night and *wanted* you that way. For myself. Every *single* day."

"*Fuck*, Cavendish." God help him, but those were the most arousing words he had ever heard.

He took the ring and slid it down over her finger. "Then you shall have me. Any way you wish."

He bent and kissed her. She was so soft. So feminine and sweet-smelling and gentle.

She bit his lower lip.

"Teach me how to leave you ravished."

CHAPTER 32

*P*oppy had grown nervous, waiting for her husband to settle his equipage in the stables for the night. In his absence she had belatedly recalled she was not, in fact, a fearsome broker of men's most intimate desires. She was a gardener from Wiltshire.

One who was very possibly going to humiliate herself.

"What's wrong?" Archer asked when at last he reappeared, his hair wet with snowflakes. He was carrying a length of rope and, dear God, a riding crop.

"Are those for me?"

He winked at her. The scoundrel *winked at her.*

She buried her face in her hands. "Archer, I feel so foolish. I haven't the slightest idea what to do."

He took her in his arms and pressed her against his body, smelling deliciously of blizzards. "You needn't do anything but stand here. I'm mad for you exactly as you are."

"What if I make myself absurd?"

He took her hand and ran it down to his breeches where, even through the thick wool of his coat, she could feel the distinct hardness of arousal. "You won't."

She took a deep breath and let her fingers linger. Right. She had always had this effect on him. All she needed to do was be the mistress of how she used it.

Had she not studied the final, curious plates in her stolen book, imagining just such an opportunity?

She picked up the riding crop. She liked the anticipation that flamed in his eyes when she held it in her hand and studied it. But she didn't wish to injure him.

"I want to please you. But I'm worried I will hurt you."

"You needn't. Pain is not precisely the point, at least not for me. But it heightens the pleasure of being overmastered. And I can take a lot of it."

The pleasure of being overmastered. The idea of giving that to him was enough to make her look at the crop with renewed interest.

"Will you show me what you like?"

He took the crop and gave a slight switch against the air. "A little flick. See? Just take care not to bruise my hands or face. And don't draw blood."

"How will I know if it's too much?"

"May I show you?" he asked, turning her hand palm up.

She gulped. "Yes."

He lightly switched the delicate inch of bare skin between her sleeve and her hand.

"Ye gods!" she yelped, snatching it away. His eyes were full of laughter as he put her smarting wrist to his lips.

"Do you see? It's not much worse than a bee sting. You won't kill me."

She hid her smile with her hand. This *was* rather funny. She was like a kitten being taught the gestures of the hunt by the very mouse she wished to eat for dinner.

"And what would you have me do with the rope?"

Her husband blushed. Actually *blushed.*

"Whatever you *want* to do, I hope," he said, laughing a bit at himself. "That's what I want. To be at your disposal. To surrender to your will."

"And what if I do too much?"

He smiled wolfishly. "Let's not get ahead of ourselves, Cavendish."

She rolled her eyes at him, though she had to admit, his mix of shyness and obvious excitement was putting her at ease.

He lifted up her chin. "I'm giving you permission to do what you like. You can be merciful or make me suffer. Withhold pleasures or give them in such abundance it's a torture. I want you to use me in any way you can imagine. But, Poppy—if you don't *want* to, then you needn't do anything at all. You can stop whenever you like. And if something is too much for me, I'll say the word …" He paused to think, then winked at her. "… *greenhouse*. And we'll stop."

It was strange to discuss such acts so frankly. And yet, she rather liked it. She liked the dreamy expression that cast about his eyes as he told her what he wanted. She wanted to give him exactly that.

"There's one more thing," he said. "Afterwards, I might be shaky. It can be quite intense. Be … tender with me. If you would." He coughed, and his cheeks went red again.

In that moment she loved him so much she thought she might drip like a puddle though the floorboards. She pulled him toward her and kissed his brow.

"I shall take excellent care of you."

He laughed, raggedly, and the expression in his eyes once again went lusty. "Not too excellent, I hope."

She leaned back against the sideboard and placed her finger to her lips, thinking. "Very well. Enough of your lessons, Westmead."

He watched her, a slight smile still playing on his lips. "You look adorable like that."

She glared at him. He was provoking her. He knew that condescension irritated her and he was using it to his advantage.

She crossed her arms. "Stop smiling or I shall have to abuse you."

He straightened out his face, gentle amusement still flickering in his eyes. "I hope so."

"Remove your cravat," she said sternly.

He shrugged off his overcoat and laid it over a chair, then unknotted his neckcloth, taking ample time to unwrap it from around his neck and fold it into a crisp rectangle. Ever fastidious, her husband. She picked up the riding crop and used it to upend the tidy bundle, smiling as it tumbled to the floor.

A flicker of annoyance crossed his face.

"Pick it up and bring it here."

He did as she instructed. That was better.

"Be still." She smoothed down his hair and wound the fabric over his eyes by several lengths, blindfolding him.

Yes, *much* better. He could not mock her fumbling attempts at mastery if he wasn't allowed to *see* them.

She took her time sliding his breeches from his legs, teasing at the soft skin between his thighs. Goose bumps rose where her hands traveled. He was not immune to her. Not even close.

She slid his shirt over his head and let it graze his hip bones as it fell to the floor.

She placed both of her hands on his chest and ran her nails lightly down his skin until she reached his navel. She breathed in warmth and sandalwood.

His mouth fell open a bit as her fingers swirled into the hair leading to his groin. So did hers. Her instinct was to kiss him, but instead she moved her hand to his male parts and closed her grip around his cock. He was aroused, but not urgently so. She ran her finger from his bollocks to the cleft between his arse. He widened his thighs in invitation. She dropped to her knees and took the head of his sex in her mouth. She wanted to make him very, very hard. He let out a groan as she took him deeper, and he ran his hands through her hair.

She waited until he was frantic, bucking to give her more of his length, then released him. "None of that. You are not to touch me unless I tell you to. Come."

She led him to the edge of her desk, knocking all the books and papers to the floor.

"Lie down."

She moved his arms over his head and tied them to the legs of the desk with the rope. He gasped at the chafing of the fibers along his wrists. He was fully, resplendently aroused now. She smiled at the sight.

"I hope the servants don't come in and find you like this," she said, her fingers landing on his nipples.

At this idea, he practically whimpered.

She twisted.

"Oh, you might *like* that? Wicked man." He hissed at the pain and the muscles of his abdomen contracted as his cock jumped in the air.

Intriguing.

She took the riding crop and ran it up and down the inside of his leg, allowing the ridge of it to dig into his skin. He sucked in his breath. She flicked it down on his inner thigh, where its imprint left a pink half-moon.

This produced an enthusiastic response from his loins. She teased his erection delicately with the end of her crop.

"What shall we do with this?"

He lifted his hips off the table.

"Naughty man."

She trailed the crop away from his groin and back up to his chest, pausing to flick several times over his shoulders. He gasped in pain, and for a moment she wondered if she had gone too far. But he was smiling.

So that was the alchemy. Pain increased his pleasure, just as he'd said. Mingling the two was the way to draw him to the dazed, erotic place she had witnessed in the town house.

God, how she wanted to see him in that place again. To take him there herself.

If he could still smile, it was time to raise the stakes.

"Enough rest for you." She untied his wrists and led him to stand before the armoire against the wall, leaning forward with his back to her. "Put your hands above you. Don't make a sound."

She ran the crop between his legs, letting it graze the cleft of his buttocks. He moaned. She flicked his arse painfully with the flat of her hand as punishment. "Silence."

He obeyed, but she felt him tense with arousal. She hit him again with her palm, harder, until his backside was bright red and his knees were shaking.

He let her. He no longer provoked her, only took what she meted out. He disappeared into her control, putting his most vulnerable self fully in her power.

The harder she hit him, the more he abandoned himself.

"Oh, my darling," she whispered, running her hand over the hot red marks on his skin. He leaned back into the pressure, wanting her affection as much as he wanted her aggression.

Trusting her.

He trusted her.

All at once she felt as if she held something very precious and very, very delicate in her hands. Like she controlled the universe, and she must be very, very gentle with it.

He leaned his head against the wardrobe limply, his shoulders trembling.

She felt his desire, and his powerlessness, like a caress of her own loins. She felt herself grow liquid, the room disappearing, nothing in it but him and her and the connection that ran between them.

She rested her cheek against his back. It was hot to the touch from her blows.

"What will I do with you?" she asked shakily.

His voice was like that of a man in a trance. "Hit me harder."

She moved her face to his neck and kissed him, tenderly, instead. When he leaned in to her mouth, she sank her teeth into the hollow between his neck and shoulder. He gasped. She placed her hands on his shoulders and urged him down, until he was kneeling.

He was crouched before the armoire, his knees spread, his powerful thighs flexed. The pose was at once servile and athletic. Gorgeous to behold. All hers.

She hit him as hard as she could square across the cheeks of his buttocks with her crop. He wrenched back in mingled pain and pleasure. She did it until her arm throbbed and he had fallen to his forearms. He looked just as he had the night she had discovered him in the darkened town house. All broken and bereft and aroused and strong and *wanting*.

"Turn around and show yourself to me," she ordered.

He was flushed and swollen with arousal. His cock pulsed in the air, wet at the tip, wanting attention.

"Touch yourself."

He put a hand around his erection and gripped it.

"Surely you want more than that," she said. "Surely you must be dying to stroke it. Would you like to?"

"Yes," he groaned, moving his hand up and down along the shaft.

She loved it, watching him in this private act. Seeing him aroused as he was only by himself. She wanted to see his face.

She untied the blindfold. His wrist paused.

She kissed his shoulder.

Panting, he looked down at her, with a gaze that spoke of ecstasy and torture all at once. He shuddered. His eyes met hers intently. And then she realized what he was waiting for.

Her permission.

She ran her hand to the tip of him and smeared his essence across the head of his cock with her thumb.

He let out a sob. She shivered.

"You want to come so badly, don't you?"

"Yes. Christ, yes. Please."

"Please what? What is it you want?"

He shuddered. "To spend. For you to watch me."

Her breath caught.

"Bring yourself to satisfaction."

He ran his tongue against his palm, then lowered it around himself, moistening his cock before he fucked his fist in long, intent strokes.

"Now. Spill for me," she ordered.

His eyes shot open and for a split second they met hers, and what she saw in them was naked, unguarded confession—a soul announcing itself. A cry came from deep inside of him. He yelled as a thick arc spurted from his loins. He kept his eyes open as he came. Staring right into hers.

She felt molten to her core, watching him watch her.

She fell to her knees and pressed her head to his hot, slickened skin.

"Oh, my darling," she whispered.

He buried his face in her skirts, tears falling from his eyes.

She held him as he recovered, stroking his hair, kissing each smarted mark left on his skin.

When his breath returned to normal, she retrieved a cloth and a pitcher of cool water from the table and dabbed away the mess he'd made.

"Thank you," he said, looking up at her. "It's never been quite so … I've never … thank you."

She bent down and kissed away the last traces of his tears.

"Was it all right?" he asked, looking up at her from below his lashes. "For you?"

In answer she took his hands and put them on her breasts. "Touch me."

He drew her to his lap and kissed her slowly, passionately. His hands were suddenly everywhere that she was. She put her own on top of his and led them down between her thighs.

What she had done to him had driven her half-mad. If he didn't touch her between her legs, she would faint.

His eyes lit with recognition. She was his now, the mantle of control returned. He gave her soothing little kisses on her neck and breasts as he tucked her against his side and lifted her skirts. She opened her legs for him and his fingers quickly found her most urgent, needy parts. He put a finger inside her as his thumb worked intently along the edges of her womanhood and his teeth gave her nipples dancing little licks and bites through her dress, like a physician who knew exactly how to tend her. Stars lit behind her eyes and she collapsed on him with a cry, shaking and boneless, her body like a fever dream.

He wrapped his arms around her and tucked her between his legs. They were silent as they held each other and minutes passed filled only with their panting. The very portrait of an utterly spent and wicked duke and his improper, debauched duchess.

ARCHER DRESSED SLOWLY, TAKING THE TIME TO FEEL THE SORENESS of his skin. To let himself savor it, the proof that it was real. Poppy had seen the part of him that desired to be commanded. And it had only made her want him more.

It had made her want him *more*.

"Thank you," he said to her, sitting back down beside her on the floor.

She looked unsteady, and so he smiled at her, and she smiled back. And then she burst into tears.

Oh, Christ. He had been so lust-addled he had not seen he had thoroughly horrified her, and now that she had had time to reflect, she had come to her senses. He'd been doddering with his waistcoat buttons and given her time to change her mind about him.

"What is it?" he made himself ask, despite knowing in his bones what the answer was.

"I love you," she sobbed.

He let out his breath in a ragged sigh.

That, he could handle.

He gently gathered her into his arms. "That's not a problem, Cavendish. I don't know if you heard my speech this afternoon, but I'm rather fond of you myself."

"Oh, Archer," she said into his neck. "I thought you weren't coming back. When you sent me that box of letters, I thought that this was over."

"No, sweetheart," he said. "I thought you would want them back."

"I only wanted you back," she choked out. "You're the only thing I wanted."

He took a breath to collect himself. "Walk outside with me."

She sniffled and shook her head. "It's snowing. We'll freeze."

He graced her with his finest leer. "Cavendish. I promise on my life that I'll find a way to keep you warm. Come."

He unlocked the double doors leading out into the garden.

A soft blanket of snow cloaked the trees and grounds. In the distance, the spires of the conservatory looked like a mountain of ice. Alone in this white canvas, it felt as if they were the last two people in the world.

He stood behind her and held her back against him, so she was cloaked in his warmth, as they gazed up at the house.

"When I first saw this house," he said into her ear, "I imagined kissing you out here, in this very spot, beneath the trees."

She squeezed his hand.

"It was so kind of you to find this place for me. I never really thanked you. It's perfect."

"It was selfish. I bought it because I could not stop imagining a family here."

She turned to him. There were snowflakes in her dark lashes. He used his thumbs to wipe them away.

"You're going to get your wish." She picked up his hand and placed it over her belly, leaving her fingers laced between his. "By August, I suspect."

"Oh my God," he whispered.

He had received an announcement such as this once before, and had felt pleased and even rather proud of himself. He had not known then the terror and love and joy and sorrow that now suffused him. And yet you would have to snuff out the moon to mask the smile that overtook him. He could feel that smile in his chest. In his ankles.

He closed his eyes and pressed his forehead to Poppy's lips. She kissed him lightly there, and he turned his chin up to her mouth. He found the rise of her breasts and marveled at the soft, lush curve of them—indeed, slightly fuller now—his hands could perceive what was not yet visible to the eye alone. He ran his fingers back down her waist to her stomach. It raised a fierce wave of possession in him, that nearly imperceptible swell between her hips, where a month before there had been a concavity. He heard himself growl as he kissed her more deeply.

"Not here," she laughed. "Inside."

They made it only to the threshold of the open door. He wanted to see the changes in her body without her heavy dress and the warm winter petticoats, and his fingers searched for the strings and began to unravel them, dexterity arising from sheer force of will. He unlaced her bodice and she wriggled out from under it, and he was so grateful, he heard himself say "good girl," and heard her laugh at the undisguised lust of his words.

He led her to a divan in the dimmest corner of the room—a corner that had a view of the snowy gardens. He settled her down and pulled her shift over her head and there she was, the same long limbs and milky skin.

He spent ten minutes reminding himself of the pleasures of that skin. He took his time with it, until she began to signal her impatience with her body. And as she lost herself, so he lost himself to her.

CHAPTER 33

*P*oppy lowered her veil over her eyes and stepped onto the street. It was early in the morning to visit an establishment such as this, but she'd known Archer would stop her if he knew where she intended to go, and so she'd left before he'd awoken. Such were the continued advantages of a constitution that rose with dawn.

She pulled her cloak around her and rapped the heavy iron knocker twice.

The unsmiling maid opened the door. "You again," she said.

"I've come for a word with your mistress."

The girl looked at her impassively. "Not unless you have a key."

Poppy had to concede grudging respect for the girl's particular brand of insolence. If she was apprenticing in the trade of her mistress, she was well on course to become an adept broker of pitiless contempt.

She smiled calmly at the maid. "Perhaps you would prefer I locate her myself. If you recall, I've done it before."

The girl betrayed no reaction, but after a moment she stepped aside.

"Wait on that bench," she said. "I'll ask if Mistress Brearley will see you, but I don't expect she'll say yes."

Mistress Brearley. So the woman had a name, like a mere mortal.

Poppy arranged herself stiffly on the ungiving wood, feeling like a naughty child, which she suspected was the intended effect.

After some time, footsteps broke the quiet.

Mistress Brearley was tall, dressed head to toe in the same severe black weeds of her house girl. Yet something about the dress she wore was alluring and familiar. *It was a Valeria Parc.* Dramatic in its sobriety, immaculate in its cut and the fine lacework that emerged from the long sleeves and rose up the neck. In a different color it would not be so unlike the dresses that hung in Poppy's wardrobe. This meant that Valeria had met the whipping governess, had fitted her and chided her posture and threatened to prick her with a needle if she fidgeted.

The knowledge made her feel more assured.

"Thank you for seeing me, Mistress Brearley," she said, rising from the bench. "I'm afraid we have not been properly introduced."

"I know who you are, Duchess," the governess said. Her accent was educated but clipped, with a hint of the northern counties. "What puzzles me is why you are here. Again."

"I came to ask a favor."

"If you wish me to bar your husband from my establishment, I don't consider such requests. But in this case, the matter is irrelevant, as Westmead has withdrawn his membership."

"You mistake the kind of assistance I require."

"Which is?"

"Instruction."

A flash of interest crossed Mistress Brearley's eyes. "He sent you here?"

"No. It was my idea to come. I find that his interests have awoken my own. I hoped I might hire you to teach me."

The governess crossed her arms, considering this. Then she turned and fiddled with a panel in the wall. It popped open, revealing a safe.

"If you wish to know what is practiced here, you must first engage a membership and sign an oath of discretion. We are closed to new members, but given you are Westmead's wife, and I am fond of him, I shall make an exception."

"You are fond of him?"

Mistress Brearley assessed her, then softened her expression. "I am no threat to your claim on his affections. I care for him only as an old friend for whom I want the best." The woman met her eye and for a moment, her face opened into a wry smile. "Particularly when such friends have the perverse habit of making themselves miserable."

"Ah." Poppy found herself laughing at this unexpected moment of understanding.

Mistress Brearley handed Poppy two sheets of paper and gestured at a desk.

I, Poppy wrote, *Poplar, Duchess of Westmead, hereby agree* ... She copied out the remaining script and signed her name.

"This will be the last time you use that title here. We don't observe the usual hierarchies. Each man or woman enters these walls with only the lowly power of their own humanity."

"Women are among the members of a whipping house?"

"All sorts are members of this club. And the pleasures they find here are by no means limited to whipping."

Oh.

Mistress Brearley locked the confession in her safe and handed her a heavy iron key.

"This looks like—"

"Your husband's? Yes. He returned it when he withdrew his membership. I have yet to put it back in circulation. Call me sentimental. Now it's yours. In the future, present it at the door to gain entry here. It will save you the impudence of my maid."

The mistress led her back downstairs and through one of the heavy doors that lined the corridor. The walls were lined with a plush layer of wool to absorb the sounds within and a rack of orderly shelves holding instruments of the profession. Whips in an array of different sizes and made from everything from hemp to leather to chains. Handcuffs, restraints, floggers, and carved cylindrical statues that resembled the male anatomy.

The next hour was an education in an exacting and physically demanding enterprise. The governess brooked no embarrassment and spoke as plainly as if she were describing farming improvements rather than erotic subjugation. She showed her how to snap a whip—a flick this way for a tease, a shocking snap for a crueler bite. How to tie a cilice, a blindfold, a restraint. How to measure out tenderness and torment in exquisite balance.

As she returned the items to the shelves, she looked over her shoulder and met Poppy's eye. "I would be remiss not to add that this is all merely *technique*. You must look within yourself for what you want from the assignation, and so must he. You understand?"

"May I ask, then, what you get from it? Why do you practice it?"

Mistress Brearley gave her that iron gaze.

"Because there is a heady power in being the one to bestow such intimacies. But then, you already know that, don't you, Poppy? The seduction of it. I could see it on your face the night you snuck inside my service door."

"Yes," she admitted.

"I hope you will come back and visit me. True expertise requires apprenticeship. In the meantime I believe I'll have a few items sent to your residence. Discreetly. A kind of wedding gift."

"I don't know how to thank you."

Again, the flash of a wry smile. "You needn't. You'll receive a bill."

"Thank you, Mistress Brearley."

"Be well," the woman said. She paused, and her face was kind.

"And be good to him. He must be quite attached to you to give this place up."

Poppy smiled. For today, since the first time since she'd met him, she'd awoken and known without question that he was.

Archer was not in the mood for wassail.

He was sore. And not languidly so. His skin stung from the icy damp of his carriage. His shirt abraded his back where he'd been struck with the riding crop. His head ached with tension.

And instead of going home to drown himself in a hot bath or a large decanter of brandy, he was on his way to his sister's damnable Christmas supper, his last hope for locating his wife, who had disappeared sometime before breakfast.

He had never felt less possessed of cheer.

He stepped out into the eerie quiet of the frozen square, emptied of residents who had long since left for the countryside for Christmastide. Inside, the house would be festively strung with greenery and lit with candles. The air would smell like cinnamon and frankincense and roasting goose. The long table would be lined with the orphans, bachelors, and widows his sister assembled every year on Christmas Eve, when the rest of the city retreated for the comforts of hearth and family. And every last one of them would be eager to learn what had become of his wife.

I haven't the faintest idea. Do let me know if you locate her. Happy Christmas.

He had no reason to suspect she had changed her mind and left him. She had made no grand pronouncements nor packed a trunk.

And yet he could not shake the feeling that the day before had been some fairy tale of his own invention. That he'd woken up to find it was a dream.

A grand, gilded carriage pulled up behind his, sloshing icy

muck onto his already freezing boots. He recognized the Rosecroft crest and groaned. His cousin would be keen to know where Poppy was, having not seen her since the wedding.

Rosecroft handed Hilary down, followed by a nurse bearing their velvet- and lace-bedecked son. Leading up the rear was the Earl of Apthorp. At least someone here would match him for humorlessness this evening.

"What are you doing in town?" he asked Rosecroft, after the civilities had been exchanged. "I'm told decent families depart the day Advent commences."

"We had planned to spend the holiday in the country, but we got caught up by the snow. Your sister prevailed on my wife to stay on to attend her supper."

"Lady Constance is planning a surprise—I take it she did not inform you of her plans?" Hilary asked.

Constance most assuredly had not. Last year it had been a living Nativity featuring a number of actresses in most unchristian raiments. The prior year, a trained monkey playing hymns on an organ.

"My sister long ago learned not to favor me with advance knowledge of her pageantry. She knows it only induces me to stay very far away. Especially after the incident with the opera dancers."

Apthorp's mouth fell open. "Opera dancers. On *Christmas?*"

Rosecroft clapped him on the back. "Steady on, lad. You shall survive to see Twelfth Night yet."

An elaborately coiffed blond head emerged from an upper window, followed by a frantically waving pair of arms in gold-embroidered gloves.

"Happy Christmas, my darlings!" Constance trilled down at them, dangling out the window. "Do come in, do come in—quickly now! You must see the surprise!"

"Lady Constance looks well, does she not?" Hilary remarked in a low voice to Apthorp. "Our time in Paris quite agreed with her. I suspect this will be her last season."

Oh, God help him. So this was why his cousin had thrown off her family's customary journey south: matchmaking. And with Apthorp, of all people. Was Hilary deranged? Apthorp was the steady sort, but stiffer than a frozen leg of mutton and every bit as humorless. Constance would spread the poor lad with her favorite rose-petal jam and devour him on toast, only to grow too bored to swallow halfway through the meal.

Apthorp glanced warily up at the joyous blond visage dangling from the window. "Lady Constance," he replied to Hilary, "is inches away from a broken neck. I suggest we go inside before she falls to her death."

"Where is the lovely duchess this evening?" Rosecroft asked as they went inside. "Not arriving separately?"

Here it was. The burning question. "My wife is indisposed," he muttered. She was due to join him here. If she did not turn up within the hour, he was going out to find her.

A pair of footmen opened the atrium doors, and his bleak thoughts were interrupted by the crisp, tart scent of evergreens. The exact scent of his wife's grove of English firs.

He paused in the doorway, inhaling.

And then he saw the surprise.

All around them, fronds of green. Thick, fragrant bowers were strung along the walls, spiraling up toward the ceiling and trailing down the sides of the room, such that to sit at the dining table was to sit within a winter forest. It was, indeed, remarkable. But he had eyes only for the woman who stood in green satin beneath it, fiddling with an errant piece of mistletoe.

"Cavendish," he said raggedly.

She flashed him a brilliant smile.

"You're late. The invitation was for six."

He did not care that he was surrounded by mixed company, including his sister and his godson. He strode over to his wife, picked her up against the column, and kissed her for all he was worth.

"Well, good evening," she said softly. "My fault for hanging so much mistletoe, I suppose."

"Damn you, I was worried you'd *left* me," he whispered, in between the kisses he placed on her forehead, her eyebrow, her cheekbone, her mouth.

"I only went to retrieve your Christmas gift. And when you discover what I've gotten you, I think you may find that my absence was well worth it."

"You could have left a *note*," he raged against her clavicle.

He put his head against her chest and hoped no one would see that he was subtly, very subtly, weeping with relief.

"My, my, these two," he heard Hilary say with a distinct note of amusement. "Such dramatics from the newlyweds. You wonder if they've had a moment's peace."

He didn't care to reply, as he was now kissing his wife's shoulder.

"Indeed. I had no idea marriage could involve such theatrics," Constance marveled. "I shall have to set about finding a husband immediately."

"Doubtless you shall," Hilary said, smiling meaningfully at Apthorp.

Archer finally set his wife on her feet, reassured that she did not, in fact, intend to flee the country to escape him.

"I love you," he told her, loud enough for all to hear.

"Did he just say," Rosecroft asked in a loud voice, "that he *loves* her?"

"Is that a tear I see in his eye?" Constance crowed.

"And to think prior to this day I've scarcely seen him laugh," Hilary mused. "Many said it wasn't possible."

He turned to them all, and blessed them with a serene smile.

"I do love my wife. Most fervently. Now I kindly invite you to leave us so that I may demonstrate to her exactly how much."

WHEN ARCHER LOOKED BACK ON HIS LIFE, HE WOULD REMEMBER that those first mornings in the house in Hammersmith, the house that would become their family home, the air had smelled like roses and fresh rosemary.

Her room—*their* room, he corrected himself when he awoke on Christmas morning, for he did not intend to let her sleep alone ever again—was still warm and redolent of her scent, but she was not in it.

This time, out of deference for his newly tender sensibilities, she had left a note beside him on her pillow.

Your Christmas gift is in the library.

He wrapped himself in a dressing gown, yawned, and padded down the stairs.

"You shall run me ragged with your zest for bloody wakefulness," he called out as he entered the room. But she wasn't there. The room was empty. A small wrapped box sat on her desk. His name was on the little tag.

Inside, another note: *You will find your gift in the cupboard below the bookcase.*

The hairs pricked along the back of his neck. He opened the cupboard and peered inside. On the shelf was a small leather whip, with short, soft fronds and a filigreed silver handle—rather feminine and delicately made and nothing like Elena's. Four twined bundles of sturdy velvet ribbon, the kind used for binding hands and limbs without abrasion. A switch of fresh green birches, soaking in water in an enameled tub he recognized from Poppy's workshop. And beside them, a thin, leather-bound book embossed with the words *Les Interdits.*

He opened it to the first page, where he found an inscription.

Archer,

I'd like to propose a cordial agreement. I will look forward to a happy

lifetime of re-creating whatever images please you. And you will keep me
up late at night exploring the ones that please me.

   All my love,
   Poppy

IT WAS ONLY LATER THAT MORNING, AS SHE DROWSED LAZILY IN HER husband's arms, that Poppy realized why she felt so happy.

It was after she found Archer in her library wearing nothing more than his dressing gown and a gratified expression, paging through a book of erotic engravings so shocking they could only have arrived from a particular address on Charlotte Street. After she'd taken the book and confessed to him her very great interest in plates IX and XIV. After he'd suggested that before they undertake them, she make him *earn* the privilege of her favors. After she'd whispered that a man who was planning to do such unspeakable things with her no doubt deserved to get on his knees. After he moaned under the snap of a lovely green birch twig from her garden and lost himself deliciously. After he carried her to bed and she allowed him to return the favor.

It didn't have to be a struggle, she realized. It could simply be a gift.

Her husband pulled her to him tighter and took down the pins that held her hair and let it fall into a tangle around her shoulders.

"Aren't you the picture of innocence," he said, his voice a tired, approving rumble.

And she was. Save for a black leather cord around her neck, and an iron key that fell between her breasts.

He dragged her against him. "I love you, Cavendish."

"Show me, Your Grace," she whispered.

And he did.

EPILOGUE

onstance stepped down from her carriage and onto the lawn of her brother and sister-in-law's home in Hammersmith. The lawn was riotous with the blooms of early August, and the insufferable insects they attracted. She yelped and fended off a bee with her fan. A group of Poppy's hired lady gardeners giggled at the sight of her as they passed by with a cart bearing a haul of fuzzy purple flowers.

How perfectly typical. One would think that given the momentous event that had taken place here just this morning, these grounds would be quiet and peaceful in honor of the blessed occasion. But leave it to Archer and Poppy to celebrate the birth of their first child with more of their favorite pastime: work.

Alison met her at the door, looking positively misty-eyed. At least someone here knew a miracle when he encountered one. And her brother, ensconced in a house teeming with color and disorder, with a wife with whom he was besotted and a healthy baby in the cot, was a miracle indeed.

She threw herself into Alison's arms.

"Is my niece amazing?"

"Amazing," he confirmed, politely disentangling himself from her grip as butlers were wont to do when overly emotional young ladies assailed them. "They are in Her Grace's bedchamber expecting you."

"I will show myself in."

The house smelled like growing things and trickled with light and moving air. At Poppy's door, she stopped.

What a sight.

In all her years, Constance had never imagined her brother in a scene of such domestic tranquility. And yet, there he was, sitting in a chair beneath the window, nestling a tiny baby in his arm. So natural you'd have thought he'd been born to cradle infants.

She had meant to say something arch, but instead, damn her and her sentimental heartstrings, she started crying.

"Oh my," she sniffled. "Oh my, let me see her."

Archer met her eye with a smile and beckoned her forward with a nod.

She bent down to make eyes at the sleepy creature in his arms. She had a smashed little nose and a tuft of riotous dark hair—clearly her mother's daughter. The baby opened her eyes just a glimmer, and they were brown, the picture of Archer's.

She put her lips along the child's tiny, downy head.

"She's perfection," she warbled.

Poppy and Archer laughed, but she could not help it—she continued crying. Archer handed the baby to Poppy and draped an arm around her shoulders.

"What, distressed you are no longer the baby of the family?"

She must be forgiven just this once for speaking with no artfulness. "It's just that it feels like we're a family now. I'm so happy."

He pulled her toward him in one of the rough hugs he had taken to giving her so frequently of late. "Constance. We were always a family."

She wrapped her arms around him and cried into his shoulder.

Perhaps he was right. But before the arrival of Poppy Cavendish, they had not been a happy one.

When she finally collected herself, her brother put her in his chair, covered her with a blanket, and allowed her to hold his daughter, breathing down her neck all the while in case she proved unequal to the task. Fair enough, as prior to this day she had never touched a baby so new and small, and certainly never wanted to.

"What will you call her?"

"Plumeria," Poppy said.

"What a glorious name. I should not have expected my brother to allow you to call her something so whimsical. In my day he was a very stern and joyless figure."

"Archer chose her name," Poppy said with a mysterious smile.

Constance whirled around and looked at him, properly shocked. He merely shrugged.

"A pleasure to make your acquaintance, Lady Plumeria," she said to the baby's impossibly perfect rosebud lips. "You and I are going to get into *ever* so much trouble together. In fact, I shall start planning for your christening. We will dazzle them, won't we?" She sighed, thinking of all the parties that must be arranged before she left for Paris. "It is going to be a very busy autumn. I'm in an agony with all my planning."

"It's August," Archer said. "The season's months away."

"I know! There's barely any time at all. I have a little project in mind, you see, and one must arrange these things delicately."

"Dare I ask her what that means?" Archer asked Poppy.

"You remember my friend Miss Bastian?"

"Indeed," he said. He got a funny look in his eye, no doubt recalling he had once had the tortoise-headed plan to marry her himself, until his gallant sister had had the good sense to rescue him.

She grinned at him over the baby's head. "I have decided to wed her to Apthorp."

"Wed her to Apthorp!" Poppy laughed. "You speak as though the two in question have no choice in the matter."

Archer, who knew her powers, clearly did not find the idea so amusing or far-fetched.

"Whatever conspiracy you are plotting," he said, "please give me your word you will not get that poor girl into trouble."

"Of course not!" she objected, as though she had not done that very thing to Poppy. But had it not led to this shocking display of happiness? She wished her brother would accept that she had a genius for seeing people to their fate, and leave off questioning her. She worked in the service, ultimately, of love. One had to place divots in the path to give the seeds of romance a place to blossom. She could not be blamed if unsuspecting people sometimes bruised themselves falling into them.

"I shall only use the power of suggestion," she assured him, not entirely prevaricating. "But you must agree that something must be done about your Apthorp. Thanks to your precious waterway bill, he is always about, perfectly dull and in the way. And since you are busy, it is *me* who is left to entertain his opinions on hounds and waistcoats. Given his affection for bland conversation, Gillian's prattle will no doubt delight him. Plus, it would be an exquisite coup for her to snag an earl. And you know how I love to stage a coup."

"May I offer a suggestion?" Archer asked.

"Certainly."

"Don't do it. Apthorp isn't as harmless as he looks."

"I agree, he is perfectly deadly." She tapped the baby's nose. "That is," she told the infant, "his *attempts at conversation*."

"You," her brother said, "suffer from too much time on your hands. I should put you to work in my counting-house."

"No, let me have her for the nursery," Poppy said. "She can use her gift for letters to deal with all my dreadful correspondence."

They exchanged a look of perfect understanding. You would

think they shared a single brain, the way they finished each other's sentences.

Constance rolled her eyes at both of them. The downside of bringing couples together and making them fall hopelessly in love was that they could then unite to plague her.

"Mock me if you wish, but I should have far less time at my disposal had you not forbidden me to gossip. It is only because I have been so very obedient and virtuous that I find myself adrift."

"Surely we can put your talents to good use. Why don't you write something?" Poppy suggested. "Like poetry. Or a play."

Constance tapped a finger to her lip.

"You know, little Plum," she mused to the baby, "I do think I should be frightfully good at it."

THE END

THANK YOU!

Thank you so very much for reading *The Duke I Tempted*. If you enjoyed Poppy and Archer's story consider leaving a review on **your retailer of choice** or just talking about it in real life to your cleverest romance-loving friends. (This is my first book, so every peep of word of mouth is greatly appreciated!)

WANT MORE?

If you want to be the very first to know about absolutely everything the best way to stay in touch is to **sign up for my newsletter**. It is rare but delightful and comes with perks like glimpses of scenes from the cutting room floor, opportunities for free excerpts, and photos of my cat in cute outfits.

And if you want to spend more time in the world of Charlotte Street, Lady Constance Stonewell—to absolutely no one's surprise—is about to get into a whole world of trouble:

When a rebellious young lady accidentally ruins the life of the most boring peer in London with a single salacious rumor, she does what any honorable woman would do: proposes a whirlwind sham engagement to save his reputation. But when her bland-as-stale-toast faux intended proves he is decidedly less dull than meets the eye—not to mention shockingly adept at unexpected forms of wickedness—she finds herself falling for him.

There's only one problem: he can't forgive her for breaking his heart.

EXCERPT: THE EARL I RUINED

"Heavens, Apthorp, what *is* this place?" Lady Contstance Stonewell asked, wrinkling her nose at the damp. "Tremont said you'd taken up residence at Apthorp Hall, but he didn't mention it was abandoned."

Julian Haywood, the Earl of Apthorp, could only stare at her in horror.

Above them the old floorboards settled with a sickly creak and a large false widow spider lowered itself from a rusted iron chandelier and dropped onto Constance's gloved hand.

She raised a pale, wry eyebrow and flicked it off. "Tell me, is it the ghosts that drew you here, or the spiders?"

He finally found his voice. "You *mustn't* be here. We must get you out of here. I'm going to find a litter to take you home."

She waved this off. "No need, my coachman is waiting in the mews. I told him I'd be an hour. I need to speak to you. Have you somewhere more...tidy...where we might have a little chat?"

"Constance!" he said more forcefully than was polite, hoping his improper use of her Christian name would shock her into listening to him. "You *must* leave. Right now."

In answer she craned her head quizzically, leaned toward him and sniffed. Her eyes lit up with that glow of mischief that made her such a divisive presence in the nation's most aristocratic drawing rooms.

"Apthorp," she said, with a sly smile. "Have you been *drinking?*"

"Not nearly as much as I'd like to," he muttered. "Please, you have to leave."

She chuckled as if he had made a splendid joke and remained planted where she stood.

It physically hurt to look at her, standing in this filthy kitchen with her laughing eyes in her beautiful yellow dress, her pale hair frizzing in the damp.

He had to *save* her.

"Come with me upstairs," he said urgently. "If you take a sedan chair and keep the drapes pulled no one will know you were here."

"Very well, if you insist. But first, I must speak with you."

He drew a shaky breath. There was only one explanation for her resistance: she must not have seen the papers. Which, in keeping with his luck, would make today the *only time in history* Lady Constance Stonewell was not the first to know every scrap of gossip on two continents.

He had to do the honorable thing.

The miserable, *humiliating*, but honorable thing.

He had to tell her what was being said about him.

He drew up his last shred of dignity. "Lady Constance, I hope you will forgive me for speaking of improper matters, but you see, there has been a scandal. If anyone were to learn you were here you'd be—"

"As ruined as you are?" she cut in cheerfully.

He sank back against the door. "So you know. Of course you do. Everyone knows."

The amusement in her eyes faded and she let out a shaky breath. "Not exactly. I know because I wrote the poem. *Saints & Satyrs* is my circular."

She gave a weak nod and stood stiffly with her teeth bared in a guilty grimace, blinking, as though she couldn't quite believe it herself.

His frantic desire to get her out of his house by any means necessary was suddenly replaced by a very still kind of quiet. A quiet that began in his bones and rose up through his blood. The kind of quiet the body undertook when the mind needed all the energy one possessed to make sense of what one had just heard.

A statement that could not—*must not*—be true.

He had never begged for anything in his life. He was far too proud.

But today, in this moment, he could only whisper a plea: "Tell me that I misheard you."

Constance looked up into his eyes, then quickly looked away. "I suspect you must be very cross with me," she said in a small voice.

Cross was not the word for it.

He gripped the dusty table to keep from retching.

She walked around the table to come closer, the butter-yellow hem of her dress collecting grey strands of dust as it dragged across the dirty floorboards.

She was saying things as she came closer, speaking in a rapid, high-pitched clip that he barely understood.

"I really didn't mean you any harm! I thought I was averting a disaster. But then, what is disastrous for Miss Bastian and what is disastrous for *you* are not quite the same, and in any case, it was an accident. I regret it now, but you see all is not lost because—"

She was rambling, but her incoherence hardly mattered. His heart was so cracked that had she said his own name he would have struggled to understand her.

"Why are you here?" he croaked out.

He could hear the misery in his voice and didn't care if she could hear it too, because for the first time in his life he did not care what she thought of him.

She turned, and looked at him, and her big blue eyes were soft and plaintive.

"To fix it," she whispered.

And then, as if by magic, the light in her eyes hardened into the bright cobalt glint he had admired so many times: a look of fierce, glittering resolve.

"Lord Apthorp, I am here to do what integrity demands when one's actions have, however inadvertently, ruined the reputation of another person. I have come to offer you my hand in marriage."

ACKNOWLEDGMENTS

Thank you to my delightful, kind and clever agent Sarah Younger and the Nancy Yost Literary Agency for helping put this book into the world. Thank you to my editor Peter Sentfleben for understanding my vision and also insisting I remove that clichéd sub-plot about the evil one-dimensional villain. (RIP.) Thank you to my copy editor Michele Alpern for the delicate yet precise hand with tracked changes and to Kerry Hynds for the gorgeous cover and forebearance in the face of my particularlity about fonts. Thank you to DoyDoy and Emily for pep talks and early reads. Thank you to RWA for the Golden Heart; please don't kill it it is so rad. Thank you to the Rebelles for your camaraderie and advice and to all the friends and writers who helped make this book better—I owe each and every one of you wine. Thank you to my editorial assistant Nonie, who is a cat. Thank you London. I miss you already.

And thank you to my husband. Hey we're still married. That's pretty cool.

ABOUT SCARLETT

Scarlett Peckham is a four-time Golden Heart® finalist in Historical Romance who writes steamy stories about alpha heroines. Her *Secrets of Charlotte Street* series follows the members of Georgian London's most discreet—and illicit—private club. She splits her time between London and Los Angeles. When not reading, writing, or thinking about romance novels she enjoys drinking wine, watching The Real Housewives, and admiring her cat.

She loves chatting about books on **Twitter**, turning them into pretty pictures on **Instagram**, and doddering around haphazardly on **Facebook**.

Website: https://www.scarlettpeckham.com/

Newsletter Signup: http://eepurl.com/cRBukb